D1155973

OTHER PEOPLE'S DREAMS

Also by Tessa Barclay and available from Headline

A Professional Woman
Gleam of Gold
A Hidden Beauty
Her Father's Child
The Millionaire's Woman
The Saturday Girl
The Precious Gift

The Corvill Weaving series

A Web of Dreams
Broken Threads
The Final Pattern

The Wine Widow Trilogy

The Wine Widow
The Champagne Girls
The Last Heiress

The Craigallan series

The Sower Went Forth
The Stony Places
Harvest of Thorns
The Good Ground

OTHER PEOPLE'S DREAMS

Tessa Barclay

HEADLINE

First published in 1998 by
HEADLINE BOOK PUBLISHING

10 9 8 7 6 5 4 3 2 1

British Library Cataloguing in Publication Data

Barclay, Tessa
Other people's dreams
I. Title
823.9'14[F]

ISBN 0 7472 1851 X

Typeset by Avon Dataset Ltd, Bidford-on-Avon, Warks

Printed and bound in Great Britain by
Mackays of Chatham plc, Chatham, Kent

HEADLINE BOOK PUBLISHING
A division of Hodder Headline PLC
338 Euston Road
London NW1 3BH

OTHER PEOPLE'S DREAMS

Chapter One

Any man embarking on a discussion with Lindsay Dunforth soon began to feel that she was at least twice as clever as he was. By the end of the conversation he was usually sure of it.

William Tadiecski, being interviewed for the post of Research Analyst, had the feeling at its strongest. All the more so because he'd thought it was going to be a pushover.

The City grapevine had informed him that the post was vacant. The headhunting firm whose advice he'd sought had told him the Personnel Officer, Cyril Bartram, was a pussycat. With a successful record in Wall Street behind him, he thought they'd jump at him. But no. The Personnel Officer was at the dentist having root canal treatment, so his place had been taken by a guy from the Bond Trading room, Naismith. What did Naismith care about the hiring and firing in the Investment Division? He left it mostly to Lindsay Dunforth. And Lindsay Dunforth was certainly no pussycat.

In the first place, Lindsay Dunforth was a woman. He'd only uncovered that fact a few days ago. Naturally he'd thought the head of the Investment Portfolio Department would be a man. It was a law of nature that the heads of important departments had to be men. Well, not quite such a firm law as it used to be. On Wall Street there were a few women glittering up there in the firmament along with the stars – but then they looked the way you expected them to look.

It was another law of nature that financial females wore tailored suits and silk blouses with neatly tied bows. Their skirts were as short as fashion allowed, to show off shapely legs in sleek nylon tights. The magazines called this, so he was told, the Feminine Frame-up – all business-like so far as you could analyse the clothes, but not above using sex appeal when it would do them some good.

So William Tadiecski had come to his interview prepared to be impressed by a feminine version of an Armani suit and to show his approval of the pretty legs.

Wrong.

'So what made you decide to give up this successful career on Wall Street?' Lindsay Dunforth was asking.

'I wanted to come to London.' He smiled at her. He'd always found his smile had a good effect.

Not on Ms Dunforth, who leaned back in her chair as a signal to Naismith to take up the point.

While Mr Tadiecski explained the superior appeal of London, she studied him. He was thin and wiry, as so many mid-thirties Americans were these days. She thought he might be a marathon runner in his spare time. He had a long narrow face with very watchful brown eyes. His hair was perfectly barbered in a short cut which showed off the glints of auburn. He wore a dark grey suit of the kind she had nicknamed Harvard-Business-School, and a sparkling white shirt with a dark red rep silk tie.

In a word, he was a perfect example of successful New Yorker. So what was he doing in London?

About the urge to try a different city, interviewer and interviewee chatted easily. An interview at Oistrav's Bank was never a gruelling event. No, no, we're perfectly civilized while we try to turn you inside out, she told herself, and smiled a little.

That's better, thought the interviewee. When she smiles she's really quite something.

She'd been a total surprise. No tailored suit. Instead, a dress of soft dark silk with a tiny flower pattern, cut somehow so that it clung in the right places without being in the least come-hitherish. Above the dress, an oval face, olive-skinned. Lips rather thin, so that you thought she was severe – until she smiled. Her eyes lit up too, showing blue glints among the gun-metal grey of the irises. Dark hair pulled back to reveal pretty little ears with little grey pearls in them. On the whole she looked like someone's sister, come up to town for an afternoon at the Royal Academy or some such.

William Tadiecski had no way of knowing that Lindsay Dunforth had worked hard at achieving just this effect. Not for her the masculine-feminine charade of most City women. She had long ago decided it didn't suit her. Moreover, she knew it was an asset to be different.

She *was* different. She was that rare thing, a woman who at just turned thirty was head of a department in an influential merchant bank. And it was her duty to hire the right man for the post of Research Analyst. This man had all the right qualifications – a degree in Business Studies, a career with some of the best firms on Wall Street, letters of commendation from his former bosses.

Why then did she instinctively distrust him?

Her colleague Naismith had run out of polite inquiries about the comparative pleasures of America versus Europe. It was her turn to take it up. 'That's something that intrigues me,' she said. 'Why London? If you wanted a change of city, you could have gone to the West Coast – lots of action there these days. Or Frankfurt. Germany's the financial leader of Europe, I'd have thought you'd have preferred Frankfurt.'

'Yeah, well, I don't speak German too well. And you can say what you like about Frankfurt but London is where it's at, in my opinion. But another factor was a personal thing. I wanted to be able to get at my dad.'

'Your dad?' she echoed, her voice rising in disbelief.

'Well, it's a bit embarrassing,' Tadiecski said, looking down. 'My dad just got married again. He made his pile in real estate – I don't know whether you ever heard of him, Mainstream Property Development? No? Well, it was an American operation, of course, he practically concreted over the Everglades in his day. But he retired a couple of years ago and took up his weekend hobby full time – that's to say, he became a painter.' This was said with a roll of the eyes and an impressive deepening of the voice. 'And he – well, he fell in love with one of his models, and got married, and she's taken him to Provence to make like Van Gogh, you know?'

Naismith gave a faint chuckle and Lindsay smiled again. 'My goodness, what a drama,' she said. 'But why do you feel you have to uproot yourself and come to London?'

He shrugged. 'He's sixty and rich. She's eighteen and an airhead. I give it eighteen months, two years at most. I want to be around to pick up the pieces.'

'You're a very dutiful son, Mr Tadiecski.'

'That's pronounced Tadjeshki,' he said. 'But call me Tad.'

Not while I can still add two and two and make it come out four, she said to herself.

'It's easy to get to Arles from London,' he went on. 'I can hop over from time to time just to keep an eye on things, do it in a weekend easy.'

'That's true,' agreed Naismith. 'A little touch of French food and wine . . . Does you good.'

It was clear that Naismith was in favour of Mr Tadiecski. Naismith was a wine buff, known to the junior staff as Noovie Naismith from his devotion to *le Beaujolais nouveau*. Anyone who had a reason to go to France and drink the wine must be a good chap, in the opinion of Naismith.

But Lindsay had no such illusion.

'Besides making a geographical move, you're changing your line of work,' she remarked. 'From your CV it's clear your ability is in trading. What makes you want to go over to research, Mr Tadiecski?'

She saw by the flicker of his glance that her use of his full name had been noted. But he let it pass. 'Well, you know what they say about the trading floor,' he said. 'It burns you out by thirty. I've had an asbestos suit on for the last four years, I guess, because I've survived a bit longer. But it's time to change. And I'm good at research. It's one of the things that made me a good trader.' He picked up the leather document case he'd set on the table before him. 'I've got some examples of things I did in my spare time at Hurley Gounett. Perhaps you'd like to have a look.'

They were in the boardroom of the bank, sitting at one end of the long rectangular table of shining maple. Peter Gruman, retired Chairman of Oistrav's, had suggested it would be less formal there than in the office either of the absent Personnel Manager or of the two department heads. Coffee was available in an elegant vacuum jug, Worcester china on a silver tray gleamed in the weak March sunlight. Outside the elderly acacia tree that lorded it over the courtyard spread dark boughs against blue-grey sky. The sound of City traffic was muted both by the double glazing of the big windows and by the fact that Oistrav's was in a little paved quadrangle of its own.

The papers were produced. Naismith took up the top two or three, Lindsay leafed through some of the rest. She found she had some spreadsheets, a fold of computer print-out, and a transparent file containing a stapled report. She chose to read that. It was an able piece of work, a statistical analysis of mineral production in South Africa before and after the coming of the Mandela regime. From the analysis, the author had made recommendations about trading possibilities. It was an analysis she herself agreed with.

'Now then,' said Naismith, 'this is very impressive, Tad.' He waved the print-out he was holding. 'This is last year's manufacturing output for the Pacific Rim countries, Lindsay. You'll recall, the bank lent a goodly sum to one of the companies Tad approves of.'

'Gee, that's lucky,' Tad said with an irreverent grin.

'You enjoy analytical work?' Lindsay asked.

'Sure, you can't do well on Wall Street if you don't pay attention to the trends. Although,' he added, nodding at his own thought, 'sometimes you pull something off just by instinct. Nobody can deny that working in the market, you have to have a gambler's instincts. Sometimes you get a hunch out of nowhere, and you know you have to go with it.'

'And what if it doesn't come off?'

'Ooh . . . then it's rough. Nobody loves you.'

'That hasn't happened too often in your career,' Naismith mused, 'judging by what your employers say. You're a winner, by all accounts.'

'That's the name of the game, isn't it? To have the nerve to back your play, whether it's based on intellectual know-how or gut instinct. And you can always comfort yourself by remembering that it's not your own money, you're gambling with opium.' He laughed and shrugged.

Lindsay flinched at the financial slang. Opium – OPM – other people's money. 'You think that eases the responsibility?' she asked.

'I'm sorry?' he rejoined.

'You think it makes things easier because you're gambling with other people's money?'

'Well, doesn't it? Few traders take that kind of risk with their own dough. When a buddy comes to you with a tip for private investment, it's always a "sure thing", now isn't it? Otherwise he wouldn't recommend it.'

'I like to think that any investment my department makes is as near as possible to a "sure thing",' she said. 'It's true we're putting other people's money to work, but it's not just money – it's other people's dreams.'

'I beg your pardon?' He was puzzled.

'Their dreams – to retire and have a little place in the country, to see a son or a daughter through university, to go to Provence and be a Van Gogh. It's not just money, Mr Tadiecski.'

He gave her an odd look, as if he was thinking she had strange notions for a hardheaded business woman.

'Well, of course, we at Oistrav's are known for our prudence,' Naismith said, spreading oil on the waters. 'And with the help of analyses such as these, Tad, we can hope for sound investment to continue. Now, then, Lindsay, is there anything further you want to ask Tad?'

There was a great deal she'd have liked to ask him, but whether she would get straight answers she rather doubted. She gave her faint smile and shook her head. Naismith stood up, extending his hand to the other man.

'You'll hear from us by and by, Tad,' he said. 'You understand that of course there are other applicants.'

'Sure, that was up front when I let my name go forward.'

'So we'll call it a day now, and thank you for coming to see us.'

'Yes, thank you,' Lindsay added, always careful about good manners.

'On the contrary, thank *you*.' He had gathered up his papers and was putting them in the document case.

'May I ask you one last question?' Lindsay inquired. 'I've asked all the others.'

'Go ahead.'

'Have you any objection to working under a woman?'

He met her inquiring glance, and she could tell he was debating whether to say something complimentary: 'Not if it's a woman like you,' or something of the kind. But instead, after a momentary hesitation, he said, 'Ability is the criterion, Ms Dunforth, not gender.'

A good reply. But she wasn't sure he really meant it.

'Well, he struck me as being the best of the bunch so far,' Naismith murmured as the secretary ushered the applicant away to the lift.

'Did you think so?'

'Didn't you?'

'He struck me as a bit devious.'

'Devious? In what way?'

She found it hard to explain. 'He was thinking awfully hard before he answered questions.'

'Good lord, everybody's always on tenterhooks in an interview.

And you have to admit you got a straight answer when you wanted to know why he'd chosen London.'

'Ye-es. A straight answer – and a long one.'

'What's that mean?' Naismith grunted. 'You say he's thinking up his answers and when he gives you chapter and verse you criticize that. You're hard to please, Lindsay.'

'Well, he's going to work in my department.'

'Yes, yes, I understand you want to make the right choice. And in my opinion Tadiecski's the one. That fellow from Gowry Yeld was reliable but a bit dull, and the girl from Manchester was too bright for her own good. I read Bartram's report on the others, he didn't seem too impressed. No, I think if we tell him Tadiecski came over well, he'll recommend him to the Chairman.'

The Chairman's decision would be the important one, but Lindsay knew she could influence Henry Wishaw against the Personnel Officer's decision if she wanted to. The point was, did she want to? Just because something about William Tadiecski irked her, did that give her the right to queer his pitch?

She had to banish the problem from her mind, for other matters needed attention. She'd instructed her team to buy in U.S. Lennox Chemicals, with a view to portioning out the purchase among her investors. Her job was to look after a large group of clients, some individuals, some big organizations, and many pension funds. It was her responsibility to buy and sell for them, to look for lucrative new issues, to move quickly out of an area where financial trouble was brewing. Her department was always busy, but particularly this spring, in the aftermath of a general election and with a little tide of new companies being floated abroad. She'd marked out U.S. Lennox weeks ago when she first caught a hint that they were going public.

Her secretary, Millicent, had messages for her. She listened while she consulted her computer screen. It showed her what had been achieved in the dealing room: the acquisition target for U.S. Lennox hadn't yet been reached but they were getting there, well before the rest of the market woke up and competed. One of her team had taken a dive into utilities: she made a note to ask him what had prompted that.

She set about returning her phone calls. Some numbers she tapped in with a sigh – it was only going to be Geoff or Sam trying to sell her shares she didn't want. But it was essential to keep up contacts, for even the most aggressive salesman of dragging shares (known as dogs) occasionally turned up with a gem.

She was too busy to go out to lunch. Instead she put her name on the sandwich list and was rewarded in half an hour with the delivery of a smoked turkey sandwich on granary and a salad in a cardboard container. Coffee never needed to be ordered: it flowed like a dark brown stream around the offices of Oistrav's Bank from gleaming coffee-makers in every department. Lindsay sometimes thought that the City ran on coffee and was fuelled by sandwiches delivered at one o'clock by faithful vendors from back-alley shops.

Around three o'clock the activity on the trading floor began to die down. There was the usual flurry of small transactions on the screens as traders caught up with last-minute instructions from clients, but few of them were of any interest to Oistrav's. There was the sense of winding-down, and Lindsay Dunforth began to check off the items on her list of 'must-do' for the day. Nan Compton came in to report that the desks were clearing.

'Everybody happy?' asked Lindsay.

'You might say we're feeling smug – we got almost all the U.S. Lennox before the rest of the market caught on. But we'll be paying more for it tomorrow if you want to go on to your target.'

'Umm . . . I'll think about that. Might be a good idea to back off.'

'But if you do that and the price keeps rising we'll have to go a lot higher than you estimated –'

'On the other hand if we duck out, the rest of them might stop and say, "Why did we jump on this bandwagon?" And then the price will come back to par.'

'Well, that's true, I suppose.' Nan gave a lazy grin. 'That's why you get paid a great big salary – to try to work out problems like that.'

Nan Compton was the senior dealer on Lindsay's team. The two women had come into the City at more or less the same time, their careers bringing them together and parting them as they fought their way up. Lindsay had chosen Nan out of a group of applicants when she first set up her own team. It was done partly out of friendship and partly out of a sense that Nan was good, solid, reliable . . . Never brilliant, never likely to reach the very top but then she never seemed to want to. A good friend, a good team-player, that was Nan.

'Packing up now?' Nan asked. 'How about a glass of wine at Dandy's?'

'I can't today, Nan. I've got a couple of things to do on the way home.' The fact was, she'd just decided to consult Peter Gruman.

Peter Gruman was the recently retired Chairman of Oistrav's Bank. During his later years there he had made a protégée of Lindsay, and to everyone's amazement and in some cases dismay, he had promoted her to the post of head of the Investment Portfolio Department.

'He's going senile,' a few angry male voices had muttered. 'Or her car's parked overnight in his garage.'

'She's not the type,' others would argue. 'He genuinely thinks she's clever.'

'Well, she is, to land a job like that! But just wait – she'll come a cropper in the first six months.'

Six months went by, and then six more, and Lindsay Dunforth was not only still head of the department, she was making a lot of money for her clients. She was attracting new ones who heard of her success. Now, almost two years into the job, the doubters had decided to stop doubting.

Yet from time to time the clever and successful Lindsay Dunforth felt the need to ask advice from her mentor and friend. As Nan Compton sauntered out to meet colleagues at Dandy's, Lindsay picked up her mobile phone to call Peter.

'Of course, my dear, any time,' Peter said when he at last replied. It took him a long time these days to walk to the phone; arthritis was slowly immobilizing him but he wouldn't have a mobile phone because, so he said, it was beneath his dignity.

'Could I drop in now? On my way home?'

'Why not. I'll put the kettle on for some Earl Grey.'

Lindsay, who secretly hated Earl Grey tea, said, 'Great!' She picked up her handbag, loaded it with her phone and her note-pad and her organizer, and made for the door. 'This day's gone on long enough, Millicent,' she told her secretary. 'Go home when you're ready.'

'Thank you, Lindsay. I'll just finish these dockets and get them off and then I'll go. Anything special for tomorrow?'

'Mr Bartram will probably want to talk about the applicants – leave a space for him in the diary, will you? And there's a possible Treasury announcement – make sure to find out when and have a messenger ready to get the document.'

'Right. 'Bye now.'

''Bye.' They never said 'goodnight' at the end of the day as normal people might. Their day usually ended when trading died away, sometimes as early as three in the afternoon. But then they started at seven-thirty in the morning, and the senior members of the firm were usually at their desks even earlier. There were many occasions when they stayed late at night, sometimes to watch a crisis developing in the markets, sometimes to plan a strategy for the bank's well-being.

The hours were very antisocial, the strain was enormous, yet Lindsay loved it. When she walked out of her office with her capacious handbag over her shoulder, she always felt a sense of achievement, of satisfaction.

Today that satisfaction was tempered a little by the need to make a decision about her new Research Analyst. And why he should bother her so much, she didn't know.

Chapter Two

Peter Gruman lived in a penthouse in the Barbican. People sometimes wondered aloud why an arthritis sufferer should choose such an unhandy spot, but Lindsay understood it very well. From among the geraniums on his balcony he could look out over his beloved City, the world in which he had been a warrior and a victor for so many years.

When the lift bore her up to his corridor he was waiting with his door open. He left it for her to close and latch as he made his painful way to his kitchen. The kettle was steaming, and the dreaded Earl Grey was already in the teapot. When she joined him there he gave her a kiss and a pat on the cheek with a deformed hand.

'Well, my sweet, what's the hot gossip today? I see on my screens you've been after U.S. Lennox.'

'Yes, got most of what we need.' At his nod she picked up the tea-tray to take it into the living room.

Three armchairs were arranged to allow visitors a perfect view out of the plate glass windows. The towers of the financial district soared into the grey sky, catching the light from the west as the day declined. Black tile, coppery windows, grey brick, constructs of metal tubing painted blue and green, marble of muted white and creamy beige – the patchwork colours were mingled into a soft medley by the spring evening. Among the severe rectangles of modern architecture, the spires of City churches still pointed skywards, crowded among the new buildings but still undaunted in their message that the things of the earth were less important than the things of the spirit.

'Shall I pour, Peter?' One must always ask. Sometimes his hands pained him less and he could handle the pot and the cups. Sometimes the mere lifting of a spoon made him wince.

'Yes, please, my dear, and no cheating on the sugar –'

'But you know you're supposed to cut down –'

'Oh, poof, so I can't burn it off by exercise, but if I can't have sweet tea, what's the use of going on living?'

Laughing, she poured for him and put in the obligatory three lumps. In her opinion that was what made his Earl Grey drinkable. She, who never put sugar in tea or coffee, always felt she was drinking scented hot water. But she never said so to Peter, who was her dearest friend.

He sat now in his favourite armchair, facing towards the world he'd been so loath to leave. He had a patrician profile – long straight nose, firm full lips and aggressive chin. His hair was thick and full, though silvery now. His bushy eyebrows shaded watchful dark eyes, brown so deep as to seem black. There were lines in his face – laugh lines at the mouth, frown lines on his brow. Handsome still, and to be reckoned with even though he spent most of his time now in a penthouse flat.

They caught up with the news: Peter's grandchildren were off in various parts of the world, so that there were always tales to be told of ski trips or surfing or cook-outs. Lindsay's family, by comparison, seemed dull. Her daughter Alice was at a nursery school close to Putney Heath and her mother, Celia, worked from their home there.

Celia often rang Peter to chat with him about computer topics. She was a writer of specialist computer programs for which Peter could sometimes give pointers, for he kept his eye on the financial world by means of his own machines.

At length, after his second cup of tea and his third chocolate biscuit, Peter wrinkled his nose and sighed. 'Well, Lindsay, what's the problem?'

'How did you know I have a problem?'

'Because when you're worried there's a little tiny groove between the top of your nose and your left eyebrow, that's how. Is it the U.S. Lennox? That seems a very sound opportunity –'

'No, it's something quite different. You know we've been interviewing candidates for the post of Research Analyst?'

He nodded. He still knew almost everything that went on at Oistrav's.

'Well, I've struck a bit of a snag.'

'In what way?'

'Most of the applicants haven't been all that marvellous. One today had excellent qualifications but . . .'

'But?'

'I don't know. He worries me.'

Peter looked intrigued. 'And who is this gentleman who has the power to disturb the unflappable Lindsay Dunforth?'

'His name's William Tadiecski. Pronounced Tadjeshki but call me Tad.'

'Oh,' said Peter, with the faintest hint of putting up a protective arm. 'He not only worries you, you don't like him.'

'I don't like him *because* he worries me.'

'You said his qualifications are good?'

'Better than good. Noovie Naismith quite fell for him, partly because he's got an errant father in Provence he's going to visit at weekends. You know how Noovie loves anyone or anything to do with France.'

'How is Noovie?' Peter asked with fondness in his tone. 'One of the few advantages of retirement is that I don't have to listen to his discourse on the wine regions of the Rhone.'

'Noovie is fine, bonds are doing well, the bonuses for his team were tremendous so of course he's got a lot of pull at the moment. And he says he's going to tell Cyril that Tadiecski is the man for the research post.'

'And he's not?'

Lindsay shrugged. 'I know I'm being stupid about it. But there's something . . .'

'Can you give me an example?'

'Well, in the first place, why is he applying for a job with Oistrav's when he could get something much higher up the ladder in New York?'

'But you asked him that.'

'And got this long tale about keeping an eye on his father and a new wife in Provence.'

'It sounds reasonable. And Wall Street people do get the urge to try a different culture. You see, Wall Street is very narrow – both geographically and mentally. And there's a brutality there that can sometimes become repulsive so that . . . quite a lot of people decide to move to a quieter situation.'

Peter had worked on Wall Street in his time, so his view carried weight. Lindsay nodded at his words. He regarded her questioningly. 'You're not convinced?'

'Well, it's just that it's important not to make a mistake. My team will depend on his research. If he's not the right man, it can be like having a stone in your shoe – you can get along but it's not easy going.'

He turned his eyes from her to the view. Lights in office windows were beginning to show up against a sky of deepening grey, chequerboard yellow in the frame of the tall buildings. He loved that moment, when the City became a Mondrian of rectangles within rectangles.

'You brought a copy of his CV?'

She smiled. He knew her so well. She never went anywhere on business without the requisite documents. Out of her capacious shoulderbag she produced the folder containing the information about William Tadiecski. Opening it, she laid it on Peter's knees. He picked up the first paper. While he read it she rose and quietly cleared away the tea things. His manservant, Darrow, would be back soon to prepare an evening meal and tidy up, which consisted mainly of stacking financial journals and brushing biscuit crumbs off the carpet.

When she returned from the kitchen, Peter was halfway through the documentation. He closed the folder, looking up. 'Can't see anything wrong with him, my love.'

She hesitated. She could have said, Feminine intuition is against him. And she knew Peter wouldn't disregard that. Intuition was important in the City.

'He's got a personal recommendation from John Blebel, head of Hurley Gounett,' Peter went on, pointing. 'Johnnie used to work under me twenty years ago. Would you like me to ring him and put out a few feelers?'

She glanced at her watch. It was early afternoon in New York. 'Would you, Peter?'

'Of course. I'll have to go into my office – his address and phone number are in my desk.' He levered himself up, and she knew better than to offer help. She took up the folder he had set down to leaf through it while he contacted his former colleague.

After a few moments she heard his hearty tenor from the study. 'Yes, it's me, Gruman . . . Yes . . . Of course, put out to pasture now . . . Well, why don't you drop in next time you're in London? Of course, love to see you . . . How's Julia? Give her my love . . . And Bess? No! When was this? If I'd known I'd have sent a christening mug . . . How old? Ten months, that's a lovely age . . .' The catching up went on for some minutes, then there was a slight change in tone.

'You're right, I didn't call to exchange family news . . . No, nothing desperate, just looking for a hint or two about a man who's new here in London . . . Yes, that's him, you're quick to guess it . . . Well, I've got Oistrav's head of Investment Portfolios here, wondering whether he's what you'd call an okay guy . . . Yes . . . Yes . . . Really? *Very* impressive . . . No, she's just in a hesitating frame of mind . . . Right, I'll pass that on . . . Thank you, Johnnie, that's a great help. Yes . . . Yes . . . Bye-bye for now.'

Lindsay was packing up the papers into her bag when he emerged from the study.

'You heard all that?'

'I gather he's an okay guy.'

'So Johnnie Blebel says. And I've never known him to be wrong.'

She couldn't help giving him an arch smile at that. Not a single dealer in stocks and shares could say he'd never been wrong. But she accepted his meaning, that Blebel's opinion was to be relied upon.

'So you think I should stop being silly and tell Cyril Bartram to hire Tadiecski?'

'You're never silly, dear. But I think you should stop seeing problems where they don't exist.'

Two little taps on the doorbell told them Darrow was back from his afternoon off. It was time for Lindsay to go. She kissed Peter on the cheek in farewell. He murmured, 'Don't worry about it, he'll be all right.' She nodded assent.

Darrow was taking off his coat as she reached the little hall. 'Everything all right, miss?' he inquired.

'Fine thanks, Darrow.'

But it wasn't. As the lift swooped down to the ground floor she found herself thinking that though she was going to take Peter's advice, she was still uneasy. And that was a first: usually she and Peter were in complete accord after a discussion on policy.

Still, in the past it had been different. Then their discussions were about forward planning, or market forecasting. Personalities had never come into it before. This William Tadiecski still bothered her but she was beginning to think it was just a personal foible on her part. Certainly his former boss in New York had given him the all clear. So that was the end of it.

She went home, as she generally did, by Tube to Putney Bridge and then by bus up the long hill to the Heath. Generally it was a peaceful journey because she stopped work before the rest of the office-going world. But because she'd dropped in at Peter Gruman's, she was caught up in rush hour travel.

Tired and irritated, she went up the tree-lined side road to the house. As she put her key in the door, it opened and Alice erupted through the doorway.

'Mummy, you're ever so late and I've been waiting ages and ages!'

She swept up the little girl into her arms, to kiss her in greeting. 'I'm sorry, Alice, I had business to attend to.'

'Well, can we go for our swim at once? 'Cos Tracy says it's time for my tea and if we don't hurry I'll have to eat it and you know you say I mustn't swim on a full tummy –'

'All right, all right, let's go straight to the pool.' Lindsay threw her shoulderbag and her coat on the hall settle.

Together they went through the house and out to the back. There a door opened on to a tiled patio roofed by a pergola bearing, at the moment, bare wisteria boughs. On the other side of the patio was the pool – old-fashioned, rectangular, and made of stone – covered by a modern glass cantilever shell.

It was for the pool that Lindsay had bought the house. When the estate agent first brought her to see the place, he'd been very apologetic about the pool. 'Totally neglected since the fire, I'm afraid, and as you can see, pretty much a mess. But I think if you had it filled in it would make a lovely sunken garden.'

Lindsay hadn't contradicted him. The more he thought the pool was a drawback, the less she'd have to pay for the house. The ruin, it might have been fairer to call it, for a fire had reduced it to a very bad state some years before. Most of the roof was gone, the window frames had burned and fallen out, the interior had suffered water damage from the firemen's hoses and the rain. The garden was a wilderness in which Lindsay espied fine old rosebushes struggling to survive.

The pool was nothing but a gaping rectangular hole among the weeds, with ragwort growing among the puddles of rainwater at the bottom. She had bought it for a song. Or at least, as Peter Gruman had said, for an operatic aria. Nobody else had wanted it much and yet the plot of land on which the house stood was valuable in that, should planning regulations ever change, it was a fine place for a block of exclusive flats.

But planning regulations were unlikely to be relaxed in the near future so the owner of the property thankfully accepted

Lindsay's offer. That was four years ago, when Alice was still a baby. Ever since Lindsay, her mother, and their live-in home-helps Tracy and Eddie Taylor, had been working at making the place livable.

Eddie Taylor was the kind of man who, given two pieces of wood and a nail, could produce a dining suite. Short and stocky, he had been a member of the crew who scrambled about putting on a new roof. This had been a lengthy operation so that Lindsay discovered two things about him. The first was that he and his wife were desperate to find somewhere to live. The second was that Eddie couldn't read or write, so that his ability to earn a living was precarious.

Lindsay offered them the basement flat on condition that Tracy looked after the house and Eddie helped to repair it. They leapt at the chance and neither Lindsay nor her mother had ever regretted it. True, Tracy's cooking left a lot to be desired. If the ingredients couldn't be decanted from a tin or taken out of a microwave, she was at a loss. But Lindsay's daughter Alice was a great admirer. She thought her beans on toast were perfection and her fish fingers masterly.

But if she couldn't cook, Tracy made up for it in polishing ability. Everything in the house that was capable of shining, shone. The moment anyone dropped anything, there was Tracy's plump figure bending down to pick it up and tidy it away.

The first job Eddie had been asked to undertake once the roof was secure was the pool. 'No problem,' he said, quite unsurprised that the family thought the pool more important than papering the walls of the living room. Thanks to his Herculean labours, the pool was not only swimmable within four months but two months later had glass walls and roof.

Here every evening, on her return from the City, Lindsay and her daughter swam for at least half an hour and in full summer, even longer. Lindsay had been swimming champion of her school and a member of her college swimming team. It was through her swimming that she had met Bob, her husband and father of Alice. That meeting had its good point and its bad. The good point was that she had Alice: the bad that she had a permanently absent husband.

As she swam lazily back and forth along the length of the pool, her thoughts were far from memories of Bob Dunforth. Nor was she thinking about the troublesome William Tadiecski, or the events of the day at Oistrav's. The caress of the water as she cleaved her way through it always washed away any vexations. She loved to swim. It was balm to her body and her spirit.

The same was true of Alice, who dived and splashed and cavorted like a little tadpole. Lindsay had taken her into the water when she was scarcely a year old. From that moment water had been a second home to the little girl. The great moment of her day was when Mummy arrived home. Almost at once they would go together into the poolhouse and plunge in.

They'd been perhaps longer than usual when Tracy, in floral nylon apron and flip-flops, appeared at the door. 'Come on now, Lady Alice, if you think I'm hanging about doing pasta hoops for you at the same time I'm getting Granny's dinner, you've another think coming.'

'Ooh, pasta hoops!' crowed Alice, and made for the side at full speed. 'And extra tomato sauce?'

'Only if you're dressed and in the kitchen in ten minutes, miss!' said Tracy over her shoulder, departing.

'How long's ten minutes?' The little girl scrambled out and grabbed up a towel from the pile that always lay on the poolside bench. Her skinny little arms flailed at her equally skinny body with the towel.

'Ten minutes is six hundred seconds,' Lindsay said. 'If you count up to six hundred slowly, that's ten minutes.' She knew that Alice couldn't count past twenty with any certainty and smiled to herself as her daughter began loudly, 'One and two and three,' as she scrubbed herself dry.

Lindsay herself emerged from the pool later in a much more leisurely fashion, taking time to shower the pool chemicals off her skin and hair before she left. She wouldn't be eating dinner at home tonight. She had a date with Barry for eight-thirty in a Japanese restaurant in Upper Richmond Road.

Clad in a thick red towelling robe and with her wet hair hanging down her back, she padded into the house and upstairs. As she passed her mother's workroom she called, 'I'm home, Cecie.' Among various little peeps and chirrups from a computer she heard her mother reply, 'Have a nice day, dear?'

'Average . . .' She went into her bedroom leaving the door open. In her bathroom she towelled her hair almost dry then combed it through. She never did anything much in the way of hairdressing. She would either pull it back and tether it with antique combs bought in Camden Passage or wind it on top and fasten it with a clasp. Most people at Oistrav's couldn't make up their minds whether the little brown tendrils that escaped to frame her cheeks were accidental or planned: either way, it looked good.

Her mother came in as she was taking a dress out of her wardrobe. 'How average is average?' she inquired.

'What? Oh, that – well, it's nothing much. I stopped off to talk to Peter about it so it's dealt with. How about you?'

'Well, I've translated the statistics into a graph and done it up in four colours and three dimensions for him but he'll have to tell me whether the time-scale is right before I finalize.'

'Mm,' agreed Lindsay with her dress over her head. She only half-listened to her mother when she got into computer-speak. In her own work she used computers extensively, but the strange business of translating other people's information into a database was beyond her.

Almost every few weeks Celia Claydell would begin on some new project, for which she would apply herself to facts supplied by her client and hitherto unknown to her. From this Celia would build a program to fit requirements: how selective breeding would alter a herd of sheep and in what time scale, or a dictionary of Roman Law during the period of the Late Empire with its effects on European legislature.

Celia was good at her work and in demand. She earned good fees. But more important to both women was the fact that she could pursue this career from home. Celia had been the constant childcare factor in their household since Alice was born: she had nursed her through measles, taught her to eat first with a spoon and then with fork and knife, and now took her to nursery school in the morning and collected her at midday.

'. . . think we should plant chrysanthemums this year,' Lindsay heard as she emerged from her dress.

'Should we? Where?'

'In front of those dark evergreens, to take over when the cosmos die down.'

'Just as you like, Cecie, you're the boss.'

'Oh, am I? You wouldn't think so from the way Tracy treats me. I asked for an omelette to eat after I'd seen Alice to bed but now she tells me I'm getting Peking duck with orange sauce. On a tinfoil plate, no doubt.'

Lindsay smiled to herself. It was a familiar tale. Her mother would ask for something simple such as an omelette or a ham sandwich. Tracy would go to the freezer and extract something more elaborate. But if Celia asked for Linda McCartney's vegetarian curry, Tracy would tut-tut and make a thick corned beef sandwich. In Tracy's opinion, she knew best.

'It's all right for you,' Celia complained as she saw her daughter's smile. 'You're off out with Barry to some good restaurant –'

'Come with us –'

'Good lord no! What would Barry say?'

'He wouldn't mind, he likes you.'

'Daughter dear, I haven't reached the ripe old age of fifty-four without realizing that, no matter how much he seems to like me, my daughter's boyfriend would rather have my back view.'

Celia was very hopeful that Lindsay and Barry would marry. Ever since Robert Dunforth walked out on his pregnant wife five years ago, Celia had been on the lookout for the right man for her daughter.

She'd thought Thomas Barnwell was the one. He'd appeared on the scene soon after the birth of Alice, and from the speed and passion with which Lindsay had thrown herself into his arms her mother had thought it must be very serious. After the relationship had lasted three months, she'd begun thinking about how Lindsay should set about divorcing the absent Bob.

But almost as suddenly as it had begun, it was over. 'What went wrong?' she asked Lindsay in perplexity. 'I thought you were absolutely gone on him?'

'A bit too far gone,' her daughter said ruefully. 'It began to dawn on me about two weeks ago that we were having the same conversation over and over again – we really had very little to say to each other, it was all to do with going to bed –'

'Lindsay!'

'Well, you asked, and I'm telling you,' she said, with the honesty that could sometimes be so frightening. 'We had nothing in common except sex, and I suddenly found myself thinking, Will it still be so important when he begins losing his hair?'

'Oh, *darling* –' She shook her head. 'When you're in love you don't think about things like that.'

'Exactly. So I wasn't in love, was I?'

'But then why . . . ?'

Lindsay sighed. 'To prove that Bob didn't ditch me because I was unattractive, I think.'

'I could have told you that! Bob left because he didn't want to settle down to being a father and head of a family, that's all.'

'Maybe. I don't know. Anyhow, I found myself asking if it was a good idea to make another mistake on top of the first one.'

Falling in love with Bob Dunforth hadn't seemed like a mistake at the time. He was one of the group of friends she made at Cambridge. They were drawn together by their love of water-sports. Lindsay loved to swim and Bob was a scuba diver.

Every summer they would go off on some diving expedition. With Bob she explored the Red Sea, the Mediterranean, the Greek islands. They would travel with other students, back-packing, living on next to nothing, spending hours each day in the underworld of the sea, looking at coral polyps, at barnacles and tube worms, collecting specimens for study in the university labs. Bob was hoping to be a marine biologist, Lindsay was studying mathematics but hadn't yet settled on a career.

As soon as they'd obtained their degrees they married. Looking back, Lindsay sometimes felt that she might have forced the pace. Unhappy at home because of her father's uncertain temper, she'd longed to be gone for good, to have a home of her own.

And the fact that she'd been headhunted from university straight into a Stock Exchange job made marriage possible from the financial point of view. Her salary, and her instinctive know-how when it came to investing her own money, provided them with a more than average income.

For two or three years it had been wonderful. With nothing to tie them down and Lindsay's earnings as a basis, they'd gone abroad as much as they wished, on diving expeditions as far afield as South America.

But then Lindsay became pregnant. And within one month of being told about the expected baby, Bob was gone. She got a letter from him, from Brisbane. He'd joined a team of divers who were trying to help save the coral on the Great Barrier Reef. He didn't expect to be back in England in the foreseeable future. No address to write to, no contact telephone number. He couldn't have said 'Goodbye for ever' more forcefully if he'd spelt it out in fireworks.

So Celia, recently widowed, moved in with her daughter.

Lindsay bought the fire-damaged house. Together they set about repairing the house and at the same time their own damaged lives. Celia slowly recovered from the twenty-five years of an unhappy marriage. She began to spend time on her appearance, had her black hair properly styled, put some flesh on her bones so that she looked less gaunt. Lindsay threw herself into her work, built up an image that made her unique, made money for the bank on a large scale.

It was still something they were working at but Celia thought they hadn't made a bad job of it so far. If only she could see her daughter divorced from that renegade husband and married to the right man, everything would be marvellous.

Lindsay knew how her mother felt but she wasn't so sure. As she went downstairs to ring for a taxi to take her to her meeting with Barry, she was wondering as she often did if she wanted the great upheaval of going through a divorce and setting out on a life with a new man. She liked Barry, she liked him a lot. But was he worth giving up her freedom for?

She had a house that kept her poor because of the work still to do on it – but it was her own house, to do with as she pleased. She had a happy household where everyone got along together. She had a mother who was independent, with a career of her own. She had a bright little daughter about to start school in the autumn. She had a job she loved, which took up most of her waking hours and a lot of her energy. Everything was perfect as it was.

Wasn't it?

Chapter Three

Barry Wivelstone was already at the restaurant when she was shown in. You could always depend on Barry for good manners and attention. If they were meeting at a rendezvous he was always there first, at a theatre waiting to give Lindsay the programme and take her coat to the cloakroom, at a conference ensuring she had the information package and a good seat, before he rushed off on an antique hunt on his own.

He rose now to beam a welcome at her, towering over the little Japanese girl who had led her to the table, six foot of well-groomed masculinity, clearly successful, alert, happy in his life and his career. He'd decided this morning that the grey weather demanded a brighter tie than usual. Its coppery shot-silk echoed the auburn of his hair. He had light brown eyes, very shrewd and observant. For a big man his hands were unexpectedly delicate, as they needed to be, for Barry was a fine arts auctioneer.

'I'm not late, am I?' Lindsay asked as she took her place.

'Not at all, not at all. You'd like a drink?'

The waitress took their order. Another diminutive creature arrived with a beautifully decorated menu. Barry conferred with her in Japanese about the food: his work involved him in dealing with Japanese artefacts so that in his travels he had learned the language. Lindsay never intervened when he did this although she herself had had to learn some Japanese for business purposes and sometimes thought Barry made mistakes. She often wondered what the Japanese thought of Western efforts to speak their language – but of course they were too polite ever to correct anybody.

When they'd settled on chicken teriyaki for the main course they sipped their drinks and tried a few of the nibbles that always appeared looking like bouquets of blossoms. 'Had a good day?' Lindsay asked.

'We're preparing for next week's sale, remember I told you, Persian miniatures?'

'Oh yes. Big money, I think you said.'

'Oh, absolutely. People who collect them will pay anything. I've been rereading F. R. Martin to brush up a bit – when prospective buyers come in on viewing days some of them go on about the minor painters so you have to know who they're talking about.' He crunched little snippets of Oriental radish and chatted for a time about the profits from selling early Persian art. It was quite a while before he remembered to ask Lindsay about her day.

She shrugged and told him it had been much as usual. Barry chose not to understand the workings of the City. She'd learned some months ago that if she really tried to talk to him about some problem of hers, his light brown eyes would glaze over although his voice would continue to say encouragingly, 'Oh yes?'

They had met almost a year ago and had been lovers for about half that time. He was a handsome man, strong, well built and, despite his outer look of control, capable of a very earthy passion. His eager desire had rekindled in Lindsay a physical longing which surprised her. After the marital disaster with Bob and then her mistake with Thomas, she'd tended to be very wary, sublimating her physical needs in her work and her family. Generally she avoided anything more than business friendships with men. But Barry had caught her at a vulnerable moment.

Feeling bereft and lonely after Peter Gruman's recent retirement, Lindsay had rather quickly accepted Barry's suggestion of a drink at the Star and Garter. They first happened on each other at Meneman's, where Barry worked. One of the portfolio clients on whom her colleagues felt she spent an unprofitable amount of time had asked her to go with her to an auction of decorative silver, to choose something as an investment. Barry Wivelstone was strolling through the showroom, just to keep himself informed although it wasn't his department. He made polite conversation for a while, thus learning that Lindsay lived in the same part of London. He rang a few days later.

Now they were what the gossips of the trading floor called 'an item'. All the dealers at Oistrav's were intrigued to think that the nun-like Mrs Dunforth had fallen for a man at last. How hard she had fallen was a matter of much discussion and wagering. Some of the men said she'd be married in a year, some even went so far as to prophesy she'd leave the City to start a family in far-flung Putney. Most of the women scoffed at this. 'Don't be so old-fashioned! Lindsay could handle a job and a family of ten if she wanted to!' And some added, 'And anyhow, this romance will find itself running second to a trading desk some day soon – it can't last.'

Lindsay knew only too well that Stock Exchange types are inveterate gossips. She tried to keep her private life very separate from her office life. But her business friends met Barry at occasional official functions. Some of the girls said he was 'dreamy', others remarked that he seemed to talk only about antiques. One of Lindsay's male colleagues made a scathing remark which she overheard: 'He'd never make a trader – traders have to *listen* as well as talk.'

Lindsay was beginning to think it would be nice if she could find a way to interest Barry in her job. She enjoyed hearing about the discovery of some long-lost carving or the record price for a jade bowl, but sometimes she too had interesting things to tell. But some people simply can't come to grips with a balance sheet and Barry seemed to be one of them. Trying to instruct him made her sound schoolmarmy.

But the physical side of their relationship more than made up for the lack of shared interests elsewhere. She was grateful to Barry, and gratitude bound her to him. Moreover he was approved of by her mother and, more important, Alice.

Alice suffered from a shortage of menfolk. She followed Eddie Taylor around like a puppy, getting under his feet when he was trying to climb up and down ladders. She fell into an adoration of Barry from the first moment she saw him, all the more so since he brought her presents – brightly coloured comics which Granny disapproved of, chewy sweets from the Pick'n'Mix, a heart-shaped red velvet pincushion on St Valentine's Day.

That these were bought for him by the postboy at his office never entered Alice's head. And though Lindsay guessed it, she kept it to herself. Alice needed men in her life, being brought up as she was by her grandmother, her mother, Tracy Taylor, and the teachers at nursery school.

Lindsay's mother seemed to hope that there would be a wedding. Lindsay herself didn't know whether she hoped for it or not. From little hints in conversation she gathered that to be a satisfactory wife to Barry Wivelstone meant being the hostess type, a 'little woman' who would entertain overseas collectors brilliantly without ever intervening with inappropriate remarks about the Stock Market.

So marriage was an idea she shied away from. For the moment it was enough she'd found someone who wanted her, and in return gave her the reward of the pleasures of love.

When Lindsay and Barry left the restaurant, they walked through the crisp March night to Barry's flat. He lived in a block whose windows overlooked the bridge and St Mary's Church, a poetic view. It was still only a little after ten yet since Lindsay had to be up ferociously early they were soon in each other's arms under the antique canopy of Barry's bed.

Later, languorous from lovemaking and unwilling to go, she dragged herself from his sleeping embrace. As she dressed real life began to flood back again. It was almost always the same: an interlude of physical intensity, a slow emergence, and then this feeling of loss, of things being spoiled by having to creep away.

Barry would say, 'Why don't you stay? You could go to the office from here just as easily.'

But that wasn't so. The morning regime in her own house was important to her. Her alarm would wake her at ten minutes to six. She would rise quietly so as not to disturb the household, although sometimes Alice would tumble out of bed to come into her room while she showered and dressed. Coffee meanwhile made itself in the machine and Alice would beg a faint tint of it in her glass of milk. When Sudin came for her in the car at six-thirty she would open the door before he had to ring. If Alice was up, she would wave from the doorstep in her dressing-gown as they drove off.

Sudin Goswami had come to Lindsay almost accidentally. She used a firm of hire cars to take her from Putney across the sleeping city to Oistrav's, and after a while it so happened that the same plump, brown-skinned Asian driver kept turning up. He would take Lindsay to Pewter Lane, as the last trip of his night-shift. It soon became clear that he was taking pains to be the driver who was called for her journey.

A friendship grew up between them. She gave him tips about investment, he told her about his family, she responded with news about her daughter Alice, he found her a dressmaker to make the soft silk dresses she'd adopted as her style, she sent him customers for the produce of the smallholding his uncle managed. During the last five years Lindsay had become almost as bound up in Sudin's affairs as she was in her own.

As he took her across Putney Bridge in the still-dark morning, he was discussing the weekend ahead. No one in the Goswami household ever seemed to take a weekend off. Quite the contrary. He was ferrying his wife and children, his sister and brother-in-law and *their* children, in a minibus to visit the greenhouses in Essex. There Sudin's father and uncle grew pak choi, sweet dumpling gourd, okra and other tender vegetables now so much in demand for Oriental cooking.

'There's a family party coming up, my eldest son is getting engaged –'

'What, Ram? But Sudin, he's only sixteen –'

'Well, it's been a settled thing for years, of course. And he's getting a bit restive, wants to start a pop group – my father and I thought it would settle him down to serious things if he got engaged.'

She shook her head. The entwining arms of the Asian family still seemed to her a little oppressive even after five years of friendship with Sudin.

He said unexpectedly, 'You ought to get married again, Mrs Dunforth.'

'Good gracious! What brought that on?'

'Well, Alice is growing up, yes? It's time she had a brother or sister – it's not good for a child to grow up on her own, you know. It results in all sorts of complexes and inhibitions.'

This was said with great seriousness. Lindsay studied the kind, earnest face at her side. She didn't allow herself to smile at the idea of Sudin knowing anything about the problems of growing up without brothers or sisters. In his family there seemed to be plenty of each.

'Before you can get married, you have to find the right person,' she pointed out.

'Ah, that's where you Westerners make the big mistake! In our family, all that kind of thing is taken care of. I could find you the right man in a minute, Mrs Dunforth!'

'And what would he be like, Sudin?'

'Oh, rich, of course, and intelligent, because you couldn't settle down with anyone who was less intelligent than yourself, and kind, because you want a good father for Alice –'

'Stop, stop! He doesn't exist,' she laughed.

For the rest of the trip he sketched for her the man she should be looking for as a second husband. She didn't tell him about Barry, nor that she already had a husband living – he thought of her as a widow. She was amused, helping with hints about what this imaginary husband would have to do: take kindly to Alice, not mind having a live-in mother-in-law, understand about computers, help finish the house renovations. Most importantly, he mustn't mind being awakened at six in the morning as she left for work.

Still smiling to herself, she got out of the car in Pewter Court outside Oistrav's. She nodded good morning to Studley, the doorman. She ran her magnetic card through the checking device and went up in the lift to her floor. There once again she used the card to open the door of the trading room. Security was tight at Oistrav's, as at every other City institution with secrets to guard.

Only when she checked the day's appointments in her diary did the smile fade. One of the items was a session with Bartram and Naismith, to settle who was to get the post of Research Analyst.

She knew she was going to agree to giving the job to William Tadiecski. It would be illogical to hold out against him. But she didn't like it today any better than she had yesterday.

While they were all still in Bartram's office concluding the matter, he rang Tadiecski. 'Good morning, Mr Tadiecski, I wonder if it would be convenient for you to drop in some time today? Yes, news about the researcher's post . . . Well, it isn't *bad* news . . . Shall we say two-thirty? Fine, fine, see you then.' He turned to the others, approval in his eye. 'Seems a nice chap.'

'I thought him very agreeable,' said Naismith. 'And by the way, we don't have to struggle with that terrible surname, he asked us to call him Tad.'

'It's Polish, is it?' Bartram asked, nursing a jaw still sore from yesterday's dental visit.

'I suppose so but as you no doubt could tell, he's a hundred per cent American. Seems to me he'll be a great asset.' He glanced at Lindsay. 'I'm sure you think so too, Lindsay.'

'Of course. And now if you'll excuse me, I've got a deal going through that needs a bit of attention.'

That wasn't strictly true for the buying of U.S. Lennox was going smoothly. By midday her target would have been reached, well within the price limits she'd set. But she found she didn't want to sit discussing the recent addition to Oistrav's staff. Silly, no doubt.

At about a quarter to three that afternoon, when she was sitting with the remains of a lunchtime sandwich next to her computer screen, Cyril Bartram came in with the new Research Analyst.

'Lindsay, I want you to meet Tad. Tad, this is Lindsay, head of Investment Portfolios – oh, I'm forgetting, you met yesterday!'

'We did indeed. How're you, Lindsay?'

'Welcome aboard,' she said, shaking hands.

He thought she looked less distant today. But then it would be hard to look distant with a half-chewed salad sandwich on a paper plate at your elbow. She was wearing a different frock: dark grey silk sprinkled with pinkish daisy-heads, and pinkish-pearl studs in her ears. On the third finger of her left hand there was no wedding ring although he'd heard that she was married and preferred to be addressed as Mrs, not Ms.

During his introductory tour with Bartram he met most of his future colleagues. But it was Lindsay Dunforth he remembered as he left the building an hour later. Lindsay Dunforth, probably the cleverest of the whole collection, and though not perhaps absolutely the prettiest (because there was a stunning blonde in Venture Capital) certainly a looker.

He knew very well she hadn't taken to him. If he'd been asked yesterday, he'd have said she'd try to get someone else for the post he was taking. It was nice to know that she didn't allow her judgement to be swayed by personal feelings. And in the course of a week or two he hoped to have won her over. As a rule he found it easy to get people to like him.

And in the ensuing weeks, it might be true to say that he gained some ground. He had a gift for anecdotes, so that in slack moments on the trading floor he would entertain his co-workers. From time to time from his perch on the edge of someone else's desk he'd glance up, to see Lindsay Dunforth looking through the glass walls of her office with something like envy.

'. . . So the liftman said, "We've been up to the fiftieth floor and down four times now, sir, what floor did you want?" And Harold said, "The doc just told me a vacation at high altitude would do my sinuses good and I wanted to find out if it was true before I spent the money." '

His listeners groaned 'Oh, Tad', chuckled, or hit him playfully on the arm. He saw Lindsay turn back to her work, and he thought again how tough it must be to cut yourself off from your colleagues behind a wall of glass.

'Oh, that comes with the territory,' said Nan Compton when he mentioned it over a drink one evening. 'Don't department heads have their own offices on Wall Street?'

'Some. But there are others who like to prove they're still one of the boys.'

'Oh, well, Lindsay was never one of the boys,' Nan said. 'There's always been something different about her.'

'Yeah,' agreed Tad. 'I thought at first maybe she was weird – that sort of country-lady look and she gave me a lecture about not being careless with other people's money –'

'Yes, that's one of her things, always has been. I think it's 'cos her father frittered away all their money – she and her mum had a hard time, I think, until Lindsay began to run a sixth form stock market club and actually made money.'

'Started at school, did she?'

'And went on with it at university. She never cost her family a penny – which was just as well because I think the last farthing in the family bank account went on paying lawyers.'

'Lawyers? They were being sued, or something?'

'Quite the opposite. It's really rather tragic, Tad. I think it's scarred Lindsay in a way. You see, her dad was a nutcase – oh, I don't mean certifiable, or anything like that,' she interpolated, seeing his surprise. 'Look, never let Lindsay know I told you this. I only know because I was her friend all through Cambridge, when Mr Claydell – that's Lindsay's maiden name, Claydell – her father was pouring the last of the money down the drain. You see, Lindsay had a little brother – Roy, I think his name was – who died when he was three. An accident of some kind. Mr Claydell blamed the charwoman –'

'The what?'

'The cleaning lady. She'd made up some special cleaning mixture in a lemonade bottle and the kid drank it and died. The verdict at the inquest was death by misadventure but Lindsay's father brought a case against the cleaner –'

'This is a really sad story, Nan.'

'Yes, isn't it? You wouldn't think to look at Lindsay that she'd got this kind of thing behind her. In full control, you'd say, wouldn't you?'

'Well, she certainly seems to have a lot of cool . . . So what happened about the court case?'

'It was thrown out. So Mr Claydell tried bringing a case under a different heading and that took ages but in the end it got heard and he lost again. So he tried something else, and the charwoman emigrated to get away from him.'

'And that was an end of it –'

'Not a bit of it! He tried to bring a case under the laws of New South Wales or Victoria or something. And that proved so expensive that he ran out of money. And then he just withered away, living on his wife's earnings – she was a mathematics teacher at first but she went into computer stuff because she could do that at home, because Claydell couldn't be left, you see, he was so unpredictable.'

'My God, Nan.' Tad picked up his red wine for a big swallow. 'That's really awful. I'm sorry now I thought snide things about her. I thought she was a bit – you know, cracked – when she gave me this lecture about other people's dreams. Or putting on an act, maybe.'

'No, she's quite sincere. She knows how important money is, and how it's used. She saw its misuse keep her mother tied like a prisoner to a man who was slowly poisoning his life, and of course if Lindsay herself hadn't shown this early talent for investment, things would have been a lot worse.'

'Mmm,' he agreed. 'She must be doing tremendously well these days – salary and bonuses and all. D'you think she still plays the market for herself?'

'Of course, we all do –' She broke off. 'You're not suggesting insider dealing?'

'No, no, of course not. Strictly *verboten*. But she must get some great boardroom tips. It must be quite a temptation to make easy money.'

'You know, you're cynical, Tad,' she said, and thinking they'd spent quite long enough on Lindsay Dunforth, turned the conversation to other topics.

Nan was beginning to feel more than a little attracted to William Tadiecski. She didn't want competition from Lindsay Dunforth, whom she'd known for years and to whom she owed a lot but who was undeniably cleverer and prettier.

Nan was attractive, but with the pared-down look of a woman athlete, tanned, lithe and sleek. She'd had a succession of live-in lovers, some of them from the world of finance and some of them surprisingly diverse – an advertising executive, a TV actor, a Harley Street dentist. To her colleagues at Oistrav's it was a sign that Nan was in love again when she tried a new hair style. They were all interested to note that since Tad appeared, she'd had her neat cap of straight brown hair lightly curled and tinted.

There were five traders on Lindsay's investment team, two of them women. Nan was there because Lindsay had chosen her. The other girl, Ellaline Maitland, was very shrewd where finance was concerned but Nan felt she was no competition in the romance stakes; she was plump, giggly, and recently married. Ellaline's husband, Tony, took up all the attention not devoted to work. The two women had been on their desks for several years now.

There were also three men, seldom the same for long. Staff in dealing rooms were always on their way to somewhere better. At the moment the three men were Alec Joyce, a stocky young man who played computer games on his screens when business was slack; Milo Makionis, of indeterminate nationality but a demon when it came to scenting out good opportunities: and McCormick Lockhart, known as Mac, the highest earner on the team and the one with the biggest ambitions.

This team occupied five desks in the trading room. There were about two hundred desks in all, each with its stack of computer screens, telephones, calculators, piles of brochures and annual reports. Despite the fact that telephones were rigged so as to flash several times before audibly ringing, the room was always noisy. It was also short of daylight, which came in through windows giving on to Pewter Court. Specially installed daylight lamps were supposed to compensate, but still it seemed a rather twilight world.

Nan Compton was the senior trader, with whom Lindsay conferred most often. Once a week there would be a general meeting in her office to review results and make plans for the future. Sometimes Tad was asked to join the group so that they could have the benefit of his forecasts, but his services were used by all the departments. After a month or so it dawned on Lindsay that if she wanted to have a quiet word with him, the time to catch him was lunch time.

It seemed he almost never left the office at lunch time. There was nothing absolutely unusual in that because, since stock markets exist in all the world's time zones, a crisis was just as likely to blow up at Britain's lunch hour as at any other.

Yet there were spells when everything was set fair. Generally traders and bank officials would go out, simply to get away from the low light levels and the chatter, from the constant hum of air conditioning needed to keep the machines functioning, from the static electricity that built up so that clothes caught on chair edges and hair crackled when you combed it.

Tad almost never went out. Lindsay became aware of it when, chatting casually with the sandwich delivery boy, she heard that Tad had a standing order for each day of the week.

'Every day?' she said in surprise.

' 'Sright,' agreed Micky. 'Corned beef and tomato on Monday, roast beef and salad on Tuesday, tuna on –'

'Right, right, I believe you,' Lindsay laughed, and only later thought it odd.

She herself was often at her desk all through the lunch hour, simply because it was a quiet time when she could get boring jobs done. Shortly after her conversation with the sandwich boy, she had occasion to want to talk to Tad – nothing important, just to check a fact. She rang his office, a tiny corner off the main floor surrounded with reference books. No reply. A little later she tried again. Still no reply. She shrugged and forgot it for the present.

A few days later she took the trouble to walk down the corridor to the Research Analyst's office in search of him at lunch time. On his desk was a cellophane-packaged sandwich on a paper plate with a paper napkin alongside. The whole lunch-pack was untouched. And it seemed to her that it had never been intended to be opened. The purchaser had never really wanted it in the first place.

Well, that was possible. Sometimes one didn't want to eat at one o'clock, the hour at which Micky was allowed in with his tray of food.

But when later in the afternoon she went to speak to Tad in his office, she couldn't help noticing the unopened sandwich packet in his wastepaper basket. And the next day – because she looked, on purpose – she saw another unopened packet.

How odd. To order food every day and apparently never eat it as most people did, at the desk while engaged on some task . . .

In fact, Tad was never at his desk at lunch time, as far as she could gather. So where was he?

Brought up short by this question, Lindsay rebuked herself. The man had a perfect right to order sandwiches and then not eat them. It might be odd but it wasn't a crime. Still, the purpose of having food sent in was to save you the trouble of going out to eat. You stayed in because you intended to do some piece of work.

Tad wasn't at his desk, so perhaps he left the building after all. Casually she asked Studley, the hall porter, if Mr Tadiecski had gone out. It was perfectly easy to check, because each staff member had a magnetic card which recorded exits and entrances, the daily record being kept on computer.

But Studley had no need to check the computer screen. His memory served him well. 'No, miss, Mr Tadiecski almost never goes out at lunch time.'

Almost never went out at lunch time. Was presumed to be at his desk but was never there. Where did he go? What was he doing?

Snooping?

Chapter Four

City firms are more or less paranoid about security. They have so many secrets that could be valuable to the unscrupulous. There had been so many scandals in the recent past, causing the loss of millions in money and an even greater loss of public confidence.

The moment that Lindsay thought the word 'snooping' she went cold. Then commonsense reasserted itself. Tad Tadiecski wasn't at his desk when she thought he might be. He hadn't gone out so he was presumably somewhere about in the building.

That didn't necessarily mean anything nefarious. He was probably learning his way around Oistrav's. She herself had done the same when she first joined the bank, looking for the reference library, the quickest way to the Chairman's office, the door to the inner courtyard with its benches for summer lazing.

But then, she thought, that was only in the first week or ten days. Tad had been at Oistrav's over a month now. Surely by now he knew his way about?

There were other reasons why people might put up a little smokescreen. An affair, perhaps. Tad could be meeting a girl. Yet from what she'd been told, Tad almost never went out at lunch time. Surely even the most passionate affair didn't entail secret meetings every midday? And of course the girl would have to be an Oistrav employee – otherwise why meet inside the building?

The quickest way to make a secret love affair noticeable was for someone to change her habits all of a sudden. By now if any girl had taken to staying in the building every lunch hour, avoiding her usual lunch companions every day, those same companions would have pried and peeked until they found out why. And of course if the affair was secret there were lots of better places to meet, secluded little spots all over the City.

And then lastly, why should it be so terribly secret? Unless the girl was married, like Ellaline Maitland? But Ellaline was unusual, part of a young marriage that obviously meant a lot to her and would be endangered by a casual affair. Most of the other girls at the bank were more sophisticated, in what were sometimes called 'open marriages' where a little fun with someone else was allowable.

So it probably wasn't a love affair. What then? Gambling?

Some City men – and a few of the women – were inveterate gamblers. It was very much frowned upon except for an occasional flutter on a horse or the Lottery. Those who got in deep at casinos kept it very quiet. And you had to go out of the building to play lunch time faro or roulette.

There had been one or two poker games in the past but these were conducted after business hours, in each other's flats. It was inconceivable to Lindsay that there was a lunch time poker game in the building. The messengers and porters would be sure to spot it and gossip about it, and thus let the cat out of the bag.

Moreover, security was tight. To move from one department to another you had to use your magnetic card. If the screens showed a number of people – say six or seven – gathering in one department at lunch time, the internal security department would have moved in on them.

What was left?

Snooping.

Lindsay scolded herself. Just because she'd had a sense of unease about Tad Tadiecski, that was no reason to suspect him of snooping. And yet, it had happened in the past. An incomer from another firm had proved to be what MI5 might have called a 'mole', sent to find out what Oistrav's planning department had in mind for the coming year. At the moment there were big changes in the air – the 'windfall tax' was going to make forecasting for the shares of utilities such as gas, water and electricity very tricky. Heads of departments at Oistrav's were in continual discussion about its effects.

But then who would send a New Yorker to snoop about such a very British problem?

Yet why not? Tad was a research analyst. He could look at balance sheets for firms in Britain, in Europe, on the Pacific Rim, anywhere in the world, and make sensible inferences from what he read. These days finance was global.

Tax manoeuvres used in one country might very well be picked up and used in another. And of course the windfall tax was only one new aspect of British finance – there must be a dozen others that were causing concern abroad.

Telephone calls took her mind away from the puzzle. There was a busy afternoon ahead. She gave the matter no more thought that day.

Next day at one o'clock she went to Tad's cramped office. It was empty. On the desk lay the wrapped sandwich on its paper plate. Tuna, she noticed and gave a half-smile at the idea of a spy who planned his sandwiches ahead.

She stood in the little room, hesitating. Then, impelled by anxiety and curiosity in equal amounts, she pushed the office door closed. She opened the top drawer of the desk. Inside lay pads of paper, pencils, felt tip pens, a pocket calculator of a very expensive type, a stapler, and all the other necessities of office life. She tried a side drawer. A rolled up tie which showed a stain, perhaps red wine. A packet of man-sized tissues. Disposable razors.

She shut the drawer quickly. What was she doing? She was *snooping*. She shuddered in distaste and walked to the door.

Yet at the door she paused and looked back. In for a penny, in for a pound. She'd looked in the shallow top drawer and one of the two side drawers. Might as well look in the other. Hating herself, she went back and pulled at the second drawer. It was locked.

Well, why not? People had private things – diaries, address books, family photos.

Lindsay herself had such belongings in a drawer in her desk. But it wasn't locked. Anything she didn't want known to the world was safely filed under a password on her personal computer, and such was the case, she was almost sure, with everybody else in the firm. City people are always very gadget-minded, the first to have the latest and tiniest pocket organizer, the quickest to try a new CD-ROM. Lindsay would have taken a bet that few of her colleagues kept anything important in a locked drawer.

She went back to her own office. This time she was determined to follow up her suspicions about Tad's activities. She waited until close to two o'clock, when he might be expected to return from 'lunch'. Then she went back along the corridor to his room and hovered there.

Ten minutes later he appeared from across the trading floor. Through the glass wall of the corridor he espied her and hastened his step.

'Looking for me?' he inquired.

'Yes, you know that outline of Canadian fuels you did for the Bond Division – have you got a spare copy?'

'Sure. Come on in.' He ushered her in then went straight to a shelf from which he plucked a folder. From it he produced a copy of the document she asked for.

'You haven't eaten your lunch,' she said, nodding at the sandwich on his desk.

'What?' He followed her glance. 'Ah . . . no . . . London sandwiches leave a lot to be desired, I find.'

'In what way?'

'Well, you know, in New York, if you order a sandwich you get something ten inches thick with dill pickles and potato salad on the side. I can't get used to these itty-bitty things.' He was smiling at her as if to invite sympathy for this nationalistic sentiment.

'I hope wherever you went for lunch you got something more to your liking?'

'Oh . . . yeah . . . good old British steak and kidney pie in a pub. Not bad, but I don't take to warm beer.'

'Well, thanks for this,' she said, waving the sheets of paper as she left.

Steak and kidney pie and warm beer. *But he hadn't gone out.* She'd already checked the security screen and it showed him as having never left the building.

Now she was really worried.

The last thing that the bank needed was any kind of scandal, any kind of fuss. If Tad Tadiecski was up to no good then he must be asked to leave, as quickly and quietly as possible.

Of course before you could dismiss a man, you had to have a reason. Lindsay had no evidence that Tad was doing anything wrong. If she challenged him openly – 'Where do you go inside the building during the lunch hour?' – he'd invent something. He'd say he went to the loggia, an open area like a conservatory on one side of the building, to spend a quiet half hour doing the *Financial Times* crossword. Or to one of the men's restrooms for a smoke, since there was a no-smoking rule throughout the main body of the building. But he didn't smoke, and the day's papers had been in his wastepaper basket. Still, there were other lies he could tell.

She decided not to make an issue of his walkabouts. Besides, she was almost certain he would discontinue them. She was right.

Next day Tad was to be seen going with three other members of the trading floor, laughing and joking on their way out. Just out of interest, Lindsay checked. There was no unused sandwich packet on his desk: the 'standing order' had been cancelled.

Still, she couldn't leave it there. She wanted to know what he'd been doing and she was almost certain he might have been checking up on the trades. Business was of course conducted by telephone and computer, but a written docket had to be completed for every trade. These were collected up periodically by a 'messenger', a male or female member of the bank staff who wore a brightly coloured armband bearing the Oistrav's Bank logo – a set of old-fashioned initials, OB in dark blue on a buff background.

Only the senior staff were allowed to examine the dockets. This was for fear that a dealer might alter one. The chance of benefiting through an alteration in that way was slim because all calls made on Oistrav's phones were tape-recorded, so that everything could be checked if there was a query. Nevertheless, a lot could be learned by an inquisitive mind looking through the dockets.

The messengers made collections at frequent but irregular intervals. But not during the lunch hour. The messengers were down in the canteen at that time. The first afternoon collection from the docket trays was at a quarter past two. So anyone drifting through the trading room between one and two might learn a lot.

The main collection of dockets was kept in the Controller's office. There they sat, waiting to be checked against subsequent money transactions when trades were completed. The Controller's office was accessible by the same magnetic key-card which opened the other security doors. Even easier than strolling among the desks of the trading floor would be to go into that office and spend half an hour browsing.

In the next few days Lindsay drifted about casually, keeping an eye on the Controller's office, strolling among the trading desks, 'sipping' information by glancing through dockets, looking over a trader's shoulder at his screens. If anyone glanced up at her, she would lay a hand momentarily on a shoulder in token of friendly interest.

It wasn't unusual. She did this from time to time to get the feel of the markets, particularly when she was considering a change of tack for some important investment portfolio.

So as not to seem too particular, she extended her strolls into the Venture Capital room and the Accounts Department. Once again, nothing unusual in it. It was part of her job to know what was going on.

She was struck by a thought as she stood chatting to Loring, assistant manager in Venture Capital. Huge sums were being considered for loan every day. A spy need only come in during the lunch hour, switch on a screen, call up a heading that interested him, and information of enormous value to an insider-dealer could be gained.

Of course he would need a password. Some passwords were easy to guess. One of the traders on the floor was known to use the names of his two girlfriends: if you used the first and didn't gain access, you could try the second and be almost sure to get into his files. Lindsay had once been told, by a young man who came to clean out a virus from one of her mother's computers at home, that supposedly secret passwords were the easiest way into almost any database.

She could at the next conference of heads of departments call for another tightening up of security. But these were always being issued. They had effect for a few weeks and then slackness crept in again.

Besides, if Tad really was up to something, a message demanding tighter security would only alert him. And she still wasn't even sure that he was up to anything.

On a Thursday afternoon in late April she went home by Tube and bus as usual. Her head was full of problems. The Chancellor would be giving a budget in mid-summer: before then she had to try to guess its effects and guard her clients from any losses.

She had in her care trade union pension funds, two or three educational trusts, investments from some very big insurance firms. These were more important than vague suspicions of a man whom she might be suspecting quite unjustly.

The truth was, she'd found nothing to justify her suspicions. She ought to forget the whole thing and concentrate on real business.

Alice was waiting for her on the doorstep. 'Come on, come on, look, the sun's shining, it'll be lovely in the pool.' Alice loved to swim into a patch of sunlight coming through the glass roof, and then to lie on her back with the warmth streaming down upon her.

'Just let me let them know I'm home.' She went to the kitchen door to put her head in. 'I'm back, Tracy.'

'If you're off to the pool, take the clean towels, they're by the back door.'

'Right.'

She and her daughter dived into the water together. They raced each other to the far end, Lindsay taking care not to outstrip Alice by too much. Then she watched while the little girl showed off the latest fancy dive she'd invented, a sort of curl-cum-swan dive that resulted in a great deal of splashing.

Revived and restored, they went back into the house. Alice departed at once for the hot drink that Tracy insisted she have except in high summer. Their housekeeper was convinced that cavorting around in cold water must result in a chill unless you took precautions.

Lindsay went up to dress and do her hair. Her mother called out a hello as she went by. 'Come and look. I'm replanning the garden.'

Celia in moments of leisure between paid projects would embark on grandiose plans for improvement. She would put up splendid computer graphics, list the cost of everything including landscaping, drainage, paving and plants. The house was costing a fortune to restore so, having rescued the old roses and cut down the weeds, Lindsay felt she'd done the best she could for the time being. But she agreed to look at the print-out over the evening meal.

'What's for dinner?' she inquired with some apprehension. Who knew what Tracy might dish up?

'Aha, I've taken over tonight's preparations,' Celia said. 'Have no fear, it won't be the dreaded turkey roll with frozen chips.'

Celia wasn't really interested in cooking. But when she had spare time and got the urge to cook, she would plan a menu and follow the cookery book meticulously. Tracy would sniff in disdain as Celia mused over the instructions. 'Fuss and fandango,' she would mutter. But she always seemed to pounce on any leftovers to serve to her husband Eddie.

Lindsay put on old Levi's, a loose shirt and leather moccasins. When she came downstairs it was getting on for six o'clock. Interesting aromas were drifting out of the kitchen. Alice came to greet her in the hall, to beg to be allowed to stay up and share the meal.

'No, darling, you know eight o'clock is too late for you to be eating.'

'But I *want* some,' mourned the little girl. 'I never get to eat what Cecie cooks.'

'I'll tell you what, we'll ask her to make something special for you now.'

'Really, Mummy?'

'Yes, of course, why not? She's a great chef, she can do anything.'

They went into the kitchen. Celia was stirring something in a saucepan. Tracy was standing by looking impatient.

'What's that, Cecie?' Alice demanded, darting to her side and dragging at the tea-towel Celia was using as an apron.

'Pineapple béarnaise sauce. Don't tug at me, love, I'll tip the pot over.'

'Can I have some? I want some!'

'Pineapple béarnaise?' said Lindsay, with raised eyebrows.

'It's an Australian recipe. This is International Night – corn chowder, Sussex chicken à la pineapple béarnaise, poached mangoes for dessert.'

'I want some poached mangles,' begged Alice.

'I said you'd make something special for her,' Lindsay explained, 'since she can't stay up to share all this splendid stuff.'

'I'll tell you what,' said Celia. 'How about my special corn chowdered eggs? On toast?'

'Ooh, *lovely*!'

The hastily invented speciality turned out to be scrambled eggs with a little of the thick corn chowder spooned over them. Perfectly content, Alice ate it up, played a game with her mother, and went upstairs to her bath. After ten minutes of being read to from Christine Pullein-Thompson, she was fast asleep.

A tranquil household. As Lindsay came downstairs from tucking Alice in, she remarked to herself that it was a complete contrast to the tension and the noise of the bank's trading department.

Tracy Taylor, having set the table for two in the dining room, had retired to her own sitting room to watch television. Celia was pouring wine to go with the meal. Lindsay went into the hall to collect her mail. She left in the morning long before it was delivered so it sat on the settle waiting for her to remember.

There was a handful of envelopes. She went into the dining room, sat down, picked up the wine her mother had poured, and took a sip or two. It was a docile Niersteiner. 'Is this what we get when we eat international?' she inquired.

'Well,' said Celia, 'that béarnaise has turned out a bit odd, I didn't know what else to drink with it. I'll get some Chablis if you like.'

'No, no,' Lindsay said absently, reading. 'Here's the estimate for the wood for the banisters. Eleven hundred pounds.'

'What? For a handrail?'

'Well, cherrywood . . .'

'Ridiculous,' said Celia, and went out to fetch the soup.

When she returned her daughter was sitting white-faced, staring at something she had taken out of a cheap buff envelope.

'What's the matter, Lindsay?' she cried, dropping the soup tureen on the table and running to her.

'Look,' said Lindsay.

Celia took what she was holding. It was a polaroid photograph of Celia and Alice coming out of nursery school, hurrying across the rainy pavement to the car.

'What –?' she asked.

'Look on the back.'

She turned it over.

Written in thick black capitals were the words: 'BACK OFF!'

Chapter Five

Celia's hand shook. A mixture of horror and fear struck her. She dropped the photograph.

'Who sent that?' she gasped.

'I've no idea.'

'Someone . . . someone took a picture of Alice and me . . . What for?'

'It's a threat.'

'A threat?'

' "Back off or else . . ." '

Celia leaned against the table for support. 'Or else what?'

Lindsay said nothing. The words wouldn't come. Some unspecified cruelty was implied, something she dared not say because that made it more real.

'Back off from what?' Celia asked.

'I don't know.'

'But Lindsay! You must know why someone . . . someone . . .'

'I don't know, Mother. I . . . really don't know.'

She sat staring at the photograph, which had landed on the table near her. The small faces gleamed up at her from the shining surface. Her daughter and her mother, the two people dearest to her in all the world.

A wave of nausea rushed over her.

She stumbled up, ran to the downstairs cloakroom, and was sick. Her whole body was riven with revulsion. After a few minutes, recovering, she splashed cold water on her face and washed out her mouth. She went shakily back to the dining room.

Her mother was sitting at the table, eyes closed and lips pressed together, trying for composure. She looked up at Lindsay. 'All right?'

'Yes.'

'We ought to have some brandy. Brandy's good for shock.'

Lindsay found the brandy decanter in the sideboard. Pouring

two large measures, she brought the snifters to the table. She placed one at her mother's elbow, lowered herself into her chair, and sipped the drink.

'Is it some lunatic?' Celia suggested.

'I don't think a lunatic would put that message on the back.' She picked up the print, turned it over, and studied the big capitals.

It is said that handwriting is recognizable, even capitals. If so, this was not a handwriting that she knew well enough to identify. She shook her head.

'But it's someone who knows you.' Celia drew a breath to get the courage to say the next words. 'Someone at Oistrav's?'

A colleague? A working companion? Could someone she worked with be capable of this crude threat? She was shaking her head even while her brain was telling her it had to be someone at Oistrav's. There was nowhere else where she was engaged in anything from which she could 'back off'.

'If it's someone there –' She broke off. Tad Tadiecski's features swam momentarily before her mental vision. But then, Tadiecski was at the bank from seven-thirty in the morning until about four in the afternoon. This picture must have been taken around midday, when Celia picked up Alice from nursery school. At that time Tad was at work, visible to her if she cared to come out of her office and walk along the glass-walled passage.

An accomplice?

Now wait, she told herself. First you suspect him of unspecified misdemeanours inside the building, and now you're proposing he has an accomplice.

An accomplice in what? What was Tad supposed to be doing or have done?

And back off from *what*? Lindsay had been doing nothing unusual. She had walked about the building to get some hint of what Tad might be up to, but she had done nothing unusual. Nothing threatening.

Yet someone had taken the trouble to take a picture and write a warning on it. She ran the names of her colleagues over in her mind. Someone high up the ladder? Or a dealer who was engaged in something illegal? Or merely a messenger or a porter, stealing stationery and petty cash?

No, nothing small, nothing petty. A wrongdoer worried over some minor theft wouldn't make a threat so heavy, so terrifying.

This man, whoever he was, had gone straight for the jugular – her family. He wasn't worried she'd find out he'd taken ten packets of manila envelopes: he was worried she'd catch him out with a briefcase full of money, big money. And had taken proportionate measures.

Celia said, putting down her glass, 'I think it's sweet tea that's good for shock. That brandy's made me feel quite woozy.' She ran a hand through her hair, making it stand on end. 'Shouldn't drink on an empty stomach. We'd better eat something.'

'I couldn't, Cecie.'

'Yes, we'd better. Not all this' – her sweeping gesture took in the table with its soup tureen, and the food in the kitchen – 'something simple, bread and butter, crackers and cheese. C'mon.'

She pulled herself to her feet. Lindsay rose also. They went into the big friendly kitchen, where the chicken à la some kind of béarnaise was still waiting to be served. Celia wavered towards the cooker, turned off all the heat, switched on the coffee-maker and after two or three attempts got the breadbin open. She looked around vaguely for the bread knife. Before she could find it and do any damage with it, Lindsay put it in a drawer.

'Let's just have biscuits and coffee.'

'Yes.' With a sigh her mother subsided on to a hard kitchen chair. 'Sorry about this, chickie. I'm not used to spirits, you know.'

'A cup of coffee will clear your head.' She busied herself getting mugs ready, set cream and sugar out, and when the coffee hissed she poured it at once. Biscuits were in a replica Jacobs Cream Crackers tin.

They sat in silence for a few moments, letting the coffee balance out the effects of the brandy. After a moment or two Celia picked up a biscuit and began to nibble.

Lindsay was struck with the feeling of déjà-vu.

Often, all through her girlhood, they had sat like this together, taking comfort from one another after a hurtful scene with Lindsay's father. Emlyn Claydell would visit his disappointments on his wife and daughter. It was *their* fault his son had died, they should never have hired such a woman to clean the house, they should have supervised her, prevented her from bringing her lethal mixture in a lemonade bottle, they should have been watching over Roy, they should support him in his pursuit of justice, how dared they be composed and untouched when the law failed him yet again . . .

And the planning about how to pay the bills, the decisions to do without heating in the upstairs rooms, the scrimping to keep the old car serviced and roadworthy. And the house becoming dingier and dingier from lack of paint, the towels and sheets becoming threadbare, Celia desperate for some kind of work she could do from home, tutoring children for examinations, logging statistics for market research . . .

With the death of her father Lindsay had thought those days were behind them forever. Now they had a house in which they felt secure, money enough to repair and restore it, Celia again had a career she enjoyed, a grand-daughter she adored, freedom to do as she chose, to live, to enjoy life at last.

And now this . . .

'When we've sobered up we'd better call the police,' Celia said.

'No!'

'What?'

'We're not going to call the police.'

'But, darling! We must! We must get some sort of protection if that snap means what I think it means.'

'No! I can't bring in the police.'

'Lindsay, talk sense. What else can we do? We can't let Alice be endangered!'

'No, of course not, but what could the police do? They couldn't put a guard on the pair of you –'

'But surely –'

'Oh, they might for a day or two, but they haven't the manpower –'

'But we must have protection, Lindsay! We can't cower indoors for the rest of our lives –'

'No, no, of course not, Mother. No, let me think.'

'Lindsay, there's nothing to think about. Somebody's threatening our baby and we've got to –'

'Listen, Mother, just let me think it through.' She took a big swallow of coffee to clear her constricted throat. 'Somebody – I don't know who – thinks I'm doing something to endanger him and wants me to stop. I don't *know* what I'm doing so how am I to stop doing it?'

'But you must know, Lindsay –'

'I don't, I truly don't. Oh, there's a man at Oistrav's that I've been giving a glance at, but I haven't done anything out of the usual, there's no way I can change my actions to show I'm obeying that warning. I mean it, Cecie, I'm baffled.'

Her mother studied her. 'That's scary,' she muttered. 'But the police –'

'If I call the local police they'll do what they can. But I feel – and I think you must feel the same – that this is something to do with Oistrav's. If I call in the City police all kinds of trouble could ensue. You know what it's like in the City these days – the merest breath of scandal causes a panic. If I let it be known that someone within the firm is threatening me, the follow-on could be tremendous –'

'I don't care about the repercussions on Oistrav's,' Celia cried. 'I only care about keeping Alice safe.'

'Don't you think I want that? Of course I do. But I think there's a better way of doing it.'

'How? How could we do it?'

'Well,' said Lindsay slowly, 'if you and Alice aren't here, you can't be endangered, can you?'

'Not here? Leave the house?'

'Yes.'

'And go where?'

'Let me think about it.'

Celia knew her daughter well enough to respect the plea. When Lindsay thought about a problem she generally came up with a solution. Celia drank her coffee and ate some biscuits and then, her head cleared of the brandy fumes, she put the meal she had prepared into the larder to cool and cleared the dining table. These domestic tasks took about half an hour.

That done, she went into the living room. She sat in her favourite armchair and with what patience she could muster, she waited.

About half past nine Lindsay joined her.

'Tomorrow,' she said, 'take Alice to nursery school as usual –'

'*What?*'

'Don't worry, it'll be all right. When you get to the school take her right through to that door that opens on Standerton Lane –'

'At the back?'

'Yes, go straight through to the back and out to the road. There'll be a car there. Get in with Alice and you'll be driven away to a safe place.'

'But where are we going?'

'I don't want to tell you, because you might let it slip to Alice and you know how she chatters. If she were to say anything as you walked into the school and that photographer was watching, that would wreck the whole thing.'

'So I'm to do just as I'm told, like a schoolchild?'

'It's best, Mother. The minute you see the car, you'll know it's all right.'

'And my own car – what's going to happen to that?'

'Eddie will fetch it back here later in the day.'

'Um.' Celia was dissatisfied. She was used to planning, to reducing things to digital signals so that they were clear and organized. To have to take so much on trust went against her nature.

'How long are we going to be away?' she said in the end.

'As long as it takes me to find out who's at the back of this.'

'You're going to take that on? Yourself?'

'Yes.'

'And how long might that take, may I ask?'

'It can't be long, Mother. My guess is someone's got some big scam going, and if I don't find out what and nip it in the bud, Oistrav's could be in very big trouble.'

'Oistrav's! What do I care about Oistrav's! Call in the Fraud Squad and let them handle it!'

'No, the minute the Serious Fraud Office is called in all the fraudsters start scuttling for cover. They clear away the evidence. It isn't hard these days, Mother, you know yourself – you can clear things out of a computer like lightning so that only the brainiest expert can pick up any clues. No, I'm going to go after whoever-it-is on my own until I've got something definite to hand to the police.'

'But –'

'I'm in a far better position to find things out than any incomer from the Serious Fraud Office –'

'But you'll be in danger!' Her mother threw out both her hands, as if to grab at her daughter and drag her clear.

Lindsay moved out of her reach. It was symbolic, a reminder that she was beyond the grasp of motherly concern these days. She was angry, angry at herself for the fear she'd felt at first. 'Whoever sent that picture to me is in danger. Does he think he can threaten my family and get away with it?'

'Darling, he's prepared to do something bad – you'd be no match for him –'

'You think not?' she flashed back. 'He's not clever, is he? The minute he feels he's in trouble, he does something rash like sending threats through the post. That's not a planned action. He doesn't think ahead. I think I've got more brains than he has –'

'Brains – of course you've got brains – but perhaps brains won't be enough with someone who –'

'Yes, who what? Think about it, Mother. There's no specific threat. It's scare tactics. I refuse to be scared. Once I'm sure you and Alice are safe, we'll see who's best at this sort of game – I can be scary too, you know, on my own terrain.'

'Once Alice and I are safe . . . That means hidden away somewhere. So are you going to ring this person who's taking us away?'

'No. I'll arrange that tomorrow –'

'Tomorrow? Why not now?'

'It's not necessary. Tomorrow I'm going to the office as usual. I'll leave the house as I always do at six-thirty. If anyone's watching there'll be nothing different. You'll leave in your car as you always do in time for nursery school. When you get there –'

'I take Alice right through to the back and we're driven away to Never-Never Land.' Celia sighed and made for the door. 'I'd better go up and pack a few things –'

'No! No luggage! If anyone's watching you're just taking Alice to school.'

'But we'll need clothes, toothbrushes –'

'You can stop once you're well on the way and buy things. Take your credit card.'

'And what's Alice going to say to all this?'

'Tell her it's an adventure.'

'Well, by heaven, it is,' Celia said grimly. 'And what about Tracy and Eddie?'

'I'll ring Eddie from the office at about nine-thirty to go and fetch the car. I'll tell him that I'll explain when I see him.'

Neither of the two women slept much that night. When Lindsay dragged herself out of bed in the morning she was thankful that Alice slept on peacefully and so did Celia, lulled at last into an hour of uneasy sleep.

She opened the front door to find Sudin in his big Ford rolling to a stop outside. She got in beside him. He gave her his usual smiling 'Good morning'.

She let them travel the length of the Heath and down Putney Hill before she spoke. 'Sudin, I need your help.'

'My help? Of course, Mrs Dunforth.'

'My family has been threatened –'

'Threatened?' Shocked, he turned towards her, momentarily distracted from his driving. 'Who by?'

'We don't know, it's anonymous –'

'What do the police –'

'I'm not calling the police, Sudin. I'm handling this myself. But what I need is to get my mother and my daughter out of the house and away where they can't be found.'

'Yes?' he said, waiting. He respected Mrs Dunforth's judgement. She would make this understandable to him if he waited for her explanation.

'Will you arrange for someone to pick them up at the back door of the church hall where the nursery school is held? It's in Standerton Lane, off Standerton Road –'

'I know it.'

'Have a car there, inconspicuously because someone seems to be watching –'

'This is very shocking, Mrs Dunforth. Of course I will send someone. I will send my brother Chandra.'

'Thank you.' They arranged the details, Sudin nodding and beginning to smile as she explained.

He deposited her as usual in Pewter Lane. As she left the car he said, 'All will be as you have requested. And tomorrow? Tomorrow is Saturday, I shall not see you again until Monday. What shall we do?'

'I'll be in touch by telephone. Thank you, Sudin.'

'It is my pleasure.'

That morning she looked about her with more than normal interest. As usual she was first on the trading floor, but others soon appeared. Friday – there were always deals to finalize before the weekend, loose ends to tie up and tidy away.

She found herself scrutinizing each face. Is it you? Or you? A criminal, a coward threatening my family from the shadows?

But everyone seemed as usual. Ellaline Maitland was wearing a new dress for a Paris weekend ahead. Tad Tadiecski came in with a container of coffee and a bag of *pains au chocolat* which he offered around. Alec Joyce had a computer game he'd bought the day before and was longing to try at his desk.

It was all so *ordinary*. Yet it had a dreamlike quality, as if she were seeing them all through a pane of tinted glass. Any one of these people could be an enemy. How could it be real when she knew them to be goodnatured, hardworking, and dependable?

Yet in City people there could be a shaft of steel. They took tremendous gambles, they tested themselves every day by risks that would terrify the man in the street. She knew very well that a man who could stand up to the pressure of the dealing room had enough strength of mind to threaten her. And perhaps intend to carry out his threat.

At nine-thirty she rang home on her mobile phone. Tracy Taylor answered. 'Oh, morning, Mrs Dunforth.'

'Tracy, will you ask Eddie to go to the nursery school and pick up Mrs Claydell's car?'

'Broke down, has she?'

'No, she's had to go away on family business, she took a taxi to the station and left the car there for Eddie to collect –'

'Gone away?'

'Yes, she and Alice – something came up – ask Eddie to look at the gears, Cecie says she has difficulty getting into reverse.'

'Righto,' Tracy said, accepting whatever Lindsay said. Tracy had very little curiosity. Her world revolved around Eddie who, she knew, would enjoy tinkering with the old Deux Chevaux. Although unable to read and write, he was a good driver and a great mechanic. How he had ever passed the driving test, Lindsay couldn't imagine.

At one o'clock Lindsay had a business lunch. She endured it stoically, making what she hoped was sensible conversation until at last she could with good manners withdraw. Once out of the restaurant she sought out a quiet nook with a paved yard and a sundial. Here she got out her mobile phone. She dialled the number Sudin had given her. When the phone was picked up at the other end she asked for Mrs Claydell.

'One moment, please,' said a polite Indian voice.

And one moment later she heard both her mother and Alice. It was Alice who seized the handset. 'Mummy, Mummy, what do you think! They've got lots and lots of houses like our swimming pool only they've got *plants* instead of water!'

Alice and her grandmother were safely lost on the

smallholding in Essex where Sudin Goswami's many relatives grew exotic vegetables. No one would ever think of looking for them there.

Chapter Six

Lindsay's day was longer than she'd hoped. While she was out at the Malmaison, phone calls had come in, some of them from overseas. There were e-mail messages on her computer. Just as she was clearing up to go home, Barry rang to remind her of a date for Saturday evening, an important banquet honouring some European fine arts guru.

'Oh –'

'Don't say you'd forgotten?'

'No, of course not.' There it was on her personal organizer, staring up at her. But she had forgotten, all the same. Her mind had been elsewhere all day.

'So I'll pick you up at seven-thirty –'

'No need, Barry. I can get a minicab –'

'Why on earth should you? I'll be there at seven-thirty.'

Perhaps it was just as well she had a date. She'd been half-inclined to go straight from the bank to Burnham, to see how her mother and Alice were settling in on the nursery farm. But perhaps it was better not to depart so much from her usual routine. She had no idea whether she was being continually watched but she felt that whoever had sent the photograph could be on the lookout to see her reaction. Better not to go rushing off to the Goswami smallholding.

Besides, she was tired. She hadn't slept, and after the shocks of yesterday, today had had its ups and downs. She would go home, and tell some yarn about her mother's absence to Tracy and Eddie, and have a meal, and get a long night's rest, and laze about as she usually did on Saturday – so that the watcher, if there was one, would never suspect that part of the household had gone to ground elsewhere.

Tracy welcomed her with the information that since Mrs Claydell and Alice were away, she was taking the opportunity to give their rooms a good turnout.

'Don't touch Cecie's computers!' Lindsay gasped in alarm.

Tracy sniffed. 'As if I would.' She'd had enough stick the first time she decided to disconnect them all, the better to dust them.

'Any calls?'

'The phone rang. Was busy, wasn't I, so I let the answering machine take it.'

Eddie appeared as she went to the poolhouse. 'Had a look at the Cit-rone, can't find much wrong 'cept old age.'

'Oh? Well, Cecie must just have got into a kink with the gears, you know how she does sometimes.'

Eddie's round face creased up in amusement. 'Worst driver I ever saw, your ma. Doesn't help having that old tin can. Why can't she get something new?'

Lindsay didn't attempt to explain to him that Celia was bound by ties of affection to the Citroën. It had been the one thing she'd managed to salvage from her marriage to the obsessive Emlyn Claydell.

A long swim soothed away the day's tensions. She sat down to an early meal prepared by Tracy – frozen salmon in a cream sauce, frozen peas, tinned new potatoes. Coffee she always insisted on making for herself otherwise she'd have been given freeze-dried granules from the large jar of supermarket own-brand that Tracy preferred.

While the coffee machine did its work, she went to investigate the answering machine. There was a call from the provider of fine woodwork whose estimate for the cherrywood banister she'd received, a call from a friend in Spain who was coming over in June and asking her to get tickets for the opera, and then a voice that didn't introduce itself.

'Mrs Dunforth? Did you get my artwork? Take notice of the message on the back – it's no joke.'

The phone at the other end was put down rather roughly. After that, silence.

She ran the tape back to replay it. She heard the voice again, cold, rather coarse. She played it three more times and learnt these facts: first of all, the voice was English so it couldn't be Tad Tadiecski; second, there was some slight attempt at disguise by roughening the accent but the man was basically well educated; and lastly, it was no one she knew.

But that meant nothing. She'd already considered the possibility of an accomplice.

She recorded the message on to another cassette. She thought she ought to keep it as evidence. When she caught this man, whoever he was, she could hand him and the tape over to the police for prosecution for that at least, although if he was engaged in a financial fraud he might well find the matter dropped. Banks had no love for court cases.

She spent the rest of the evening thinking. She always gave a lot of thought to whatever she did, rarely acting without trying to consider all the consequences. It was what made her so effective as an investment counsellor: she tried to see four or five moves head, like a chess-player.

Her conclusion was that on Saturday she would act as she always did – go shopping in the High Street, eat lunch at one of the pubs on the Heath, have her hair done for the banquet in the evening. On Sunday she would go to Essex. If there was a watcher, she was fairly sure she could elude him. Plotting and planning, she lay awake till nearly three.

The banquet at the Dorchester on Saturday evening was as tiring as she had expected. She had dressed to do Barry credit in a gown by Caroline Charles, a long clinging sheath of knitted silk in dark blue and cream stripes. She'd had her hair dressed up on top of her head in a cluster of loose curls, and wore small sapphire earrings. She was sweet to all Barry's colleagues, especially the women who were as well dressed as she was and were trying to guess where she bought her clothes. She made polite conversation in French with the guru, who kissed her hand with dry old lips.

The food was good, the wine was excellent, but by ten-thirty she was beginning to fall asleep. Her lifestyle had been established a long time now: up before six, bed by ten if possible and if not, no later than eleven. It made her a woeful companion at the theatre or a disco.

She was half-asleep in the car by the time Barry delivered her to her door. When collecting her earlier he'd produced a present for Alice, a set of absolutely hideous hairclasps in blue plastic, just the kind of thing the little girl loved.

'Oh, I'm sorry, Alice is away –'

'Away?' It had never happened before in the twelve months he'd known her.

'Yes, it's a . . . a neighbour, she's staying over with a school friend. It's good for her, to be away from home for a night or two.'

'Oh, well, I'll leave it on the hall table for her.'

But of course the absence of her little girl started a train of thought in Barry. One of the reasons Lindsay always came to him and never the other way round was that she didn't want to have to explain to Alice why Mummy was sharing her room with a man. Here was the ideal opportunity – Alice was gone for the moment, he could have Lindsay all to himself tonight and tomorrow morning too, because it was Sunday tomorrow and she didn't have to rush off to that awful bank of hers.

So when he drove up to her house, he switched off the motor and got out with her. Sleepy, Lindsay said, 'You're coming in for a nightcap?'

'I'm coming in for the night,' Barry replied, and with his arm around her guided her indoors.

She knew there were reasons why she should say no to this, but she was half-asleep and couldn't get her mind to function. Besides, this was Barry, dear old reliable Barry. Whatever he did was always right.

They went upstairs through the silent house, Barry urging her forward but allowing her to guide him to her room. Once there, he enveloped her in his strong embrace. She yielded to him at once, comforted by his force, warmed by his desire. Dreamily she responded to his moves, sank into bed in his arms, let him take her with his usual earthy roughness. Barry scarcely noticed that she reached no summit of passion. Or if he noticed, he told himself that there would be another opportunity in the morning, for a long, enjoyable session together.

He was wrong there. At ten minutes to six Lindsay's alarm gave its apologetic little buzz. Automatically she switched it off at once. Last night, sleepy, she'd forgotten to disarm it. She felt the weight of Barry's body against her, and for a moment wondered what on earth had happened. Then partial recollection came to her. She sat up with care, to stare down at the naked shoulders of the man who was sharing her bed.

Her chief feeling was embarrassment. Because, of course, she was planning to go out now and head for the nurseries of Exo-produce near Burnham-on-Crouch. She couldn't change her plan. She had to see her mother and her daughter. She wasn't used to being separated from them. Besides, there were important things to discuss.

Gently she eased herself out of bed. Snatching up a kimono,

she crept downstairs to call the car hire firm. She showered and brushed her teeth in her mother's bathroom so as not to disturb Barry. She dressed in jeans, cotton sweatshirt and deck shoes.

She wrote a note for Barry: 'Terribly sorry, I have to be out today. Tracy will give you breakfast. I'll call you later.'

For Tracy she left a note on the kitchen table. 'I'll be out all day. There's an overnight guest in my room. See that he gets something to eat before he leaves.'

She went out of the house very quietly about a quarter past six. The sky was light, the sun was coming up. The whole neighbourhood was still asleep, the streets empty except for a scavenging cat. She walked up Putney Hill to the Green Man, and there she sat on a bench until her hire car arrived. She was driven to Liverpool Street, where she went in and out of entrances until she was utterly certain no one had followed her – but she'd not even expected it, no one was up and about at six o'clock of a Sunday morning in Putney. Anyone who was would have been noticeable.

She had time for coffee and rolls in a workman's caff before catching the eight-twenty for Wickford. She'd already arranged for a taxi to pick her up there and drive her to the nurseries, which lay somewhat to the southwest of Burnham with a view of the River Crouch and the marshes.

The spring morning was warming up, the mist was clearing from the long low levels stretching out to the estuary. A flight of geese flew overhead. Lindsay felt a surge of confidence and energy. God's in his heaven, all's right with the world, she quoted to herself.

She was delivered through some rather imposing wrought iron gates to a small brick building across which a wooden board announced in black on yellow: 'Exoproduce, Suppliers of Gourmet Veg.'

As she got out of the car, her daughter erupted from the door of the building.

'*Mummy!*' She was grabbed round the waist and hugged as if they'd been parted a month.

More slowly came Celia, holding in her arms a toddler of about two, with jet black hair and solemn eyes. 'Hello, dear. This is Govi. Have you had breakfast?'

'Yes, thanks, at Liverpool Street. I say, this is quite a place, isn't it!'

Acres of glass seemed to spread away into the clouded sunlight. Somewhere out of sight a tractor engine was throbbing. A young man in dungarees came round a corner pulling a trolley full of boxes of greenery.

'Oh, you'd be surprised. It's big business.' Celia watched the trolley go by. 'That's coriander. It'll be in the supermarkets by eight tomorrow morning. Come along in and meet Mr Goswami Senior.'

Mr Goswami Senior was sitting before a computer screen looking vexed. He rose as Lindsay was shown in, a wide smile of welcome banishing the vexation, a small bow creasing his embonpoint. 'Welcome, Mrs Dunforth. My nephew has told so much of you! I am most pleased and interested to meet you in person.'

'Thank you, Mr Goswami, and I'm pleased to meet you and very grateful –'

'No, no, we only return the favours you have already given. Who warned Sudin of the rumours concerning South Continent Bank? Who foresaw the crash and saved us from ruin? Ah, we owe much, and to give shelter to a child moreover, that is a holy duty.' He shook hands vigorously, in the European manner.

'Mr Goswami has a goat,' Alice announced. 'It gives milk and it eats everything you give it. I tried. It ate paper.'

'Alice!' her grandmother rebuked. She looked an apology at their host. 'I'm sorry, will that harm her?'

'No, no, Nini eats everything, as Alice says, and comes to no harm. Now, Mrs Dunforth, you would like tea? Coffee? And of course you wish to speak with your mother about your affairs. Come, Govi, come to Grandpa.' He took the silent toddler from Celia's arms. 'Come, Alice. We will go and visit the parrots.' He went out, calling on a radio handset in Gujarati for someone to fetch refreshments for their visitor.

'Parrots? Goats?' queried Lindsay.

'Oh, the parrots are wild. Escaped from some bird park a couple of years ago, seem to like it hereabouts. The goat's for Govi, he's got an allergy or something. This way.' She led through a covered walkway to the house, where they were greeted by a smiling elderly woman in cotton skirt and sweater but with a red good luck mark on her brow.

'This is Mrs Goswami Senior. The rest of the family is out and about among the greenhouses. My daughter, Mrs Dunforth.'

Mrs Goswami made the gesture of greeting with joined hands. 'Delighted to meet you. We are so grateful –'

'Please, please, I was only too glad to be some help to Sudin. And *I'm* grateful –'

They spent some minutes trying to outdo each other in gratitude. A younger version of Mrs Goswami appeared with a tray of tea things and some solid looking squares of sweetmeat.

'Now I will leave you to talk –'

'But please, don't let us drive you out of your living room –'

'No, no, I have to supervise the cooking – a large family here, Mrs Dunforth, and always hungry because of hard work.' Smiling and bowing, she took her departure.

Lindsay sank down into a lushly cushioned sofa. 'Well, as a cave in which to hide, this isn't bad.' The living room was adorned with gilt-framed mirrors, tapestry curtains with festoons and loops, a glass-fronted cabinet displaying Oriental silver.

'They're so *kind*, Lindsay – nothing's too much trouble. And they don't mind a bit when Alice pokes about and tries to alter the irrigation! Patience – I've never seen anything like it. There are at least six children under ten, and nobody ever seems to raise their voice to them. Well,' she ended, pouring tea, 'what's the news?'

'The photographer left a message on the answering machine –'

'Oh!'

'Nothing gruesome, he was just backing up the scare. I taped it for possible future use.'

'What else happened?'

'Nothing.' She decided not to mention to her mother that Barry had stayed the night, because that wasn't strictly relevant. 'Perhaps nothing will happen for a while. Unless I can figure out what steps to take, the next move's got to be up to the photographer.'

'That was actually him on the tape, you think?'

'He said it was his "artwork". I didn't know the voice. Of course when I got in on Friday I took a good look at the people in the office but nobody was looking guilty. But when you come to think of it, if somebody's running a scam, he could easily have a partner – one or more.'

'Doesn't that extend the risk?'

'Yes, but it might be unavoidable. Oistrav's is divided up into departments. Somebody in one department might need help from somebody in another to get transactions through.'

'What sort of transactions?'

'That's what I don't know yet, but I think I ought to try to find out. It's a pity you don't have your computers here, Mother.'

Celia coloured a little and looked guilty. 'Well, as a matter of fact . . .'

'What?'

'You said not to pack. But there was something I was working on and wanted to finish.'

'So?'

'I brought my Fujitsu in my handbag.'

The Fujitsu was an ultraportable Pentium processor, used by Celia in summer weather when she wanted to work in the garden. Clipped to an enhancement unit, it could do anything that a desk setup could do. Yet it was small enough to fit into a capacious shoulderbag, of the kind that fashion allowed these days.

Lindsay laughed. She might have known her mother couldn't be parted for long from the technology she loved. 'Is there somewhere here that you can link up?' she inquired.

'Oh, I drove into Burnham on Friday afternoon in the Goswami van and hired a multimedia – it's in my bedroom. I'm all set up if you want action.'

'Great!' Lindsay swallowed the last of her sweetmeat, which had proved to be chewy with a creamy centre tasting of pawpaw. 'Come on then.'

The bedroom allotted to Celia was at the back of the house, which had clearly been extended and re-extended to suit the growing family. They went up and down two flights of stairs, along various passages, but at last Lindsay was ushered into a cosy room with a mansard window looking out on a yard full of sacks of fertilizer. There was a bed, a built-in wardrobe and dressing table, a bureau with textbooks about horticulture, and two chairs. Clearly the room belonged to one of the Goswami teenagers.

'This is Vijia's room, she's away at college,' Celia explained.

She had cleared the dressing table to set up her equipment. It was switched on but the screen had only a logo and a winking cursor. 'What do you want me to do?'

'Can you get into Oistrav's main departments?'

'Any passwords?'

'Some. I don't know them all. And of course I don't know passwords for private or confidential files.'

'Give me some clues, Lindsay. This could be a vast thing. What am I supposed to be aiming for?'

'Well, unusual transactions. It's possible somebody's siphoning off money into a foreign account –'

'But, sweetie, that must happen all the time – I mean transferring to a foreign account –'

'Yes, but these transactions would have something fishy about them. I mean it wouldn't be one million transferred from the account of Bloggs & Co to Simpkins International for one million shares. It would go through several exchanges probably – or it would go in bits and pieces but quickly –'

'Hm,' said Celia, looking grim. 'It's going to take forever. And I might not recognize it when I see it. Any time span? I mean, how far back should I look? A month? Six months?'

'Since the middle of March,' hazarded Lindsay, naming the time at which Tad Tadiecski had joined the bank. She felt she was being unfair, for there was absolutely no hard evidence against him, but they had to start somewhere.

'What'll I do with anything I think you should look at? E-mail it to the computer at home?'

'Yes, that's a good idea.'

'Mummy!' Alice came running in. 'Mr Goswami said he thought you'd have finished your covver-sating so come on, come and look at the things in the glasshouses – I'll tell you the names of things, I'm going to do show-and-tell when I get back to nursery 'cos no one else has ever seen so many things growing –'

Lindsay allowed herself to be tugged towards the door. 'Are you coming?' she asked Celia.

'No, I think I'll make a start,' her mother said, her fingers clearly itching to get at this novel task.

So Lindsay went for a tour of the plants with her daughter. The rows of deep troughs filled with soil held all kinds of strange leaves and tendrils. People were at work, bending, snipping, gathering, tending. A warm, protected, peaceful haven. She felt herself relaxing into a serene enjoyment.

Barry Wivelstone, waking at about that time in Lindsay's room in Putney, stretched luxuriously then rolled over to take his lover in his arms. All he found was an empty pillow. Disappointed, he sat up to look for her, but she wasn't in the room and when he peeped into her bathroom it was empty.

Then he espied the note propped against the lamp on the night table. 'Terribly sorry, I have to be out today. Tracy will give you breakfast. I'll call you later.'

It took him a moment to understand the message. Then something like rage seized him. He tore up the note, threw the pieces on the floor, and grabbed up his clothes.

Tracy, in the kitchen lazily getting together the ingredients for a good old Sunday breakfast, heard thunderous footsteps on the stairs. Next the front door slammed, and then a car zoomed off from a tremendous racing start.

'Seems he doesn't want breakfast,' Tracy said to herself.

Chapter Seven

Sudin arrived at the nursery farm in time for lunch, with a dozen relations in a minivan. The meal stretched on for hours, with members of the family arriving to eat then leaving to go about the day's work.

Lindsay saw Alice into bed at about her usual hour, soothing her to sleep with a section of the much-read Pullein-Thompson which she recited from memory. She took leave of her hosts, had a conversation with her mother (no results so far, Celia was working up a campaign for tomorrow). Then she went home with Sudin in the minivan with a different collection of Goswamis, some having stayed and their places having been taken by some who were going to London.

He deposited her at the end of her road about nine-thirty. 'See you tomorrow,' he said as they parted.

Tracy came to greet her as she put her key in the lock. 'It's the dry-cleaning firm tomorrow – I've brought down the green and dark blue, do you want the black to go too?'

'The black – I wore that Friday, did I? Yes, that ought to go.'

'I'll fetch it down –'

'No need, I'm going up, I'll bring it down in a minute.' She went upstairs, showered, wrapped herself in a towelling robe, then took the black silk down to her housekeeper.

Tracy put the dress in the plastic bag for the cleaner's van. 'You want something to eat?'

'I'll just make myself a sandwich,' Lindsay said, hurrying into the kitchen ahead of her housekeeper. Tracy's sandwiches were generally of the kind that her husband Eddie enjoyed, six inches thick and oozing tomato ketchup.

The sandwich made, she took a tray and a drink up to her room. As she was pouring lager from the tin into the glass, she had a glimpse of visual memory. Something in the hall as she handed the dress to Tracy.

Oh lord! The blue hairclasps Barry had left last night for Alice!

She'd said she'd phone him and she'd forgotten all about it.

She looked at her bedside clock. Nearly ten. Was it too late to ring?

She went to the landing. 'Tracy?'

'Yeh?'

'That guest that stayed overnight – did you give him breakfast and everything?'

Tracy came halfway upstairs. 'Didn't want anything.'

'He didn't?'

'Nope. Galloped out of the house like the end of the Grand National.'

'What did he say?'

'Not a word. Didn't even see him, he just stormed right out.'

'Oh.'

Tracy was dying to ask if the guest had been Mr Wivelstone. The blue hairclasps were the kind of thing he brought for the kiddie. But Mr Wivelstone was usually ever so polite. It couldn't have been him crashing out of the house without a word of goodbye.

Lindsay went into her room, overcome with guilt. How could she have *forgotten*? She looked again at the clock. It was still a minute before ten. She must ring, even if by her own standards it was late: Barry was more of a nightbird than Lindsay and was probably watching television without a thought of ending the day.

She tapped the memory button on the bedside phone. At the other end the phone rang without being picked up. Then the answering machine clicked in: 'This is Wivelstone, I'm not available at the moment so please leave a message.'

'Barry,' she said, 'it's me, Lindsay. I'm sorry it's so late. If you're there, please pick up.'

She waited. No response. 'Barry, I know you're angry. I want to apologize. Please pick up the phone.'

No response. 'Barry, I'm desperately sorry for having to rush out this morning. It was unavoidable. I should have rung you earlier but I got caught up in things. Please show you forgive me by picking up the phone.'

Nothing. She sighed and put down the instrument.

Barry, at the other end, glowered at the answering machine. Did she think she could smooth things over with a two-minute call at ten o'clock? He'd waited all day to hear from her – not that he'd intended to answer, he wanted her to know he was very, very angry.

She had insulted him, disregarded him, and disappointed him. He had been expecting a lovely lazy Sunday morning in bed together and then a leisurely stroll to some pleasant pub for a drink. Perhaps a late lunch and an afternoon browsing through the thicknesses of the Sunday papers, and then an evening of enjoyment before she insisted – as she always did – on getting to sleep. He would have driven home to his flat contented at a weekend of pleasure.

Instead everything had been ruined. Presumably she'd had to rush off to one of her boring one-day seminars – 'Profit Margins as Measures of Activity' or 'Global Trading – Reality or Mirage?' If she imagined he was going to let her off lightly, she was mistaken.

Next day, at a reasonable hour, Lindsay rang Barry at Meneman's. His secretary told her that Mr Wivelstone was in a meeting. She rang again an hour later. Mr Wivelstone was with a client. Lindsay, who had played this game herself with unwelcome callers, asked her secretary Millicent to keep trying the number.

'But if you're told he's available, don't ask her to hold.' She could imagine how Barry would hate to pick up and be kept waiting while Lindsay was put through. 'If he's there, I'll ring him myself afterwards.'

Aha, thought Millicent, a lovers' tiff.

But Mr Wivelstone wasn't available all that day at his office, had switched off his mobile, and had left his answering machine in charge at his flat. Incommunicado.

Lindsay's sense of guilt grew with every passing hour. She had seriously offended him. Looking back, she realized her behaviour had been thoughtless, but she'd apologized and was trying to apologize again – what more could she do? Send him flowers?

Well, not flowers. But something – a bottle of port? At about two-thirty she nipped out to go to a City wine cellar. There she ordered a bottle of Old Crusted to go by hand with a note she'd brought ready written: 'I know I was inconsiderate, and I'm really sorry, Love, Lindsay.' He wouldn't get this until he reached home in the evening, usually about seven. She'd ring then, to see if he had relented.

But a panic blew up in the office just as she was about to leave at four. Chicago had gone into a spin about wheat futures after a poor forecast at the Board of Trade, which threw the Russian government into a state of alarm because they were intending to buy at harvest time to make up for domestic shortages but would now find it hard to meet the cost, which in turn caused the Bourse to have a heart attack because French banks had been manoeuvred into advancing money to the Russian government and would now be asked for more.

Several of Lindsay's big investment portfolios were affected at various points along that line. She had invested clients' money in American companies owning grain silos but if the harvest was poor they would have fewer takers. That meant a loss in profits and a fall in dividends. She had clients with money invested in bonds at French banks: she'd been uneasy for some time about losses that might ensue when they began lending to the Russian government.

On the other hand, she had funds invested in the commodities market, some of it in wheat. The price of wheat futures was about to go up. It was up to her to retrieve the losses and garner the gains as quickly as she could. She and her team stayed at their desks, watching the screens flicker with changing prices. A delicate balancing act was in progress. Sell wheat now, and take the profits? Wait, and see them go higher tomorrow?

The value of the grain in the silos would increase. But the value of funds invested in French bonds might go down. Yet the French government would be keeping an eye on that, for prestige reasons. Her main angle must be the wheat futures.

Tad Tadiecski had experience of the Chicago futures market. He joined Lindsay's team, shaking his head at Ellaline's nervous questions, making guesses that were justified by subsequent prices.

'The wheat market will keep fluctuating until Wall Street closes,' he said. 'The first steady upturn will be around quitting time, it'll settle for a bit and they'll all go home.'

'Then what?' Lindsay asked.

'Then they eat dinner, have a drink, realize that there's a *lot* of grain in the silos to meet the Russian buys, and the price will drift down to a reasonable level by mid-morning.'

'So stand fast now at the profit we've made on sales, right? And buy in the morning to replace what we've sold if we want to.'

'You got it.'

She studied him as he bent over Ellaline's screen. Why should she trust him? And yet, it would be utterly foolish of him to give her a bad steer over an open crisis like this. Whatever his reason for coming to work in London, it could hardly be part of his plan to show himself losing money for Oistrav's.

She glanced at the clock. Seven-thirty. Mid-afternoon on Wall Street. The Bourse was closed long ago, it was about ten o'clock in Moscow so those two centres would probably do nothing more for the moment. In the morning when the Bourse reopened, that would be the time to consider the French angle. If Tad's view of Wall Street was correct, this was the point at which to take a rest.

She decided to trust him. 'Okay, we stand fast, chaps,' Lindsay said to her dealers. 'We'll close out now.'

'I could do with a drink!' exclaimed Nan Compton.

'Hear hear! Dandy's, everybody!' The men on the team were leading the way. Everyone picked up briefcases and handbags in a rush for the door.

In the hall the night porter, Gresham, glanced up from his copy of the *Mirror* as they threaded cards through the machine to check themselves out. ''Night, 'night,' he replied to their calls as they hurried past, and went back to his paper. They dashed out into Pewter Lane, round the corner into Cornhill and round the next turning into the welcoming dimness of Dandy's.

Dandy's was 'their' winebar. The bar staff knew them all by name and could without being asked provide what they wanted. When they were all settled round an old oak table in a corner, their drinks were brought at once. 'Is this a celebration?' the waiter inquired, but knew better than to expect a truthful answer. Oistrav's people played their cards close to their chests.

Ellaline had one glass of wine then said she must fly, because Tony was waiting. 'Ring him and tell him you've been delayed,' they suggested, but she smiled, waved and hurried out.

'Young love,' said Mac Lockhart with a grin.

Lindsay found she was sitting opposite Tad. This didn't displease her, for she'd been thinking for some time she ought to get to know him better. With her own team, she could suggest a drink together or a lunch, but with Tad it was different – he was a junior member of staff but not directly of her trading team.

'I was hoping for a nice quiet day,' Nan remarked from her left.

' "All hope abandon ye who enter here," ' Tad quoted.

'What's that? Part of one of those dungeons and dragons games?' asked Alec Joyce, who played them on his computers.

'Sounds like the Bible,' said Mac.

'A glass of champagne for the one who guesses right,' Tad offered, laughing.

'*Lasciate ogni speranza*,' Lindsay murmured.

'Italian!' cried Nan, already too drunk to think straight. 'Liberace?'

'That's it. Champagne for Nan for guessing Liberace,' Tad said.

'Liberace played the piano, he didn't play dungeons and dragons,' protested Alec.

'You've no idea what Liberace did when he wasn't playing piano,' Tad said. 'In fact, nobody knows what anybody does when they're not on view.' There was an undernote to the remark.

'Now that is true,' agreed Milo Makionis seriously. 'That is very philosophical, Tad.'

'Champagne for anyone who can spell philosophical!' Lindsay offered.

'Filo –' Alec began.

'No, that's a kind of pastry,' she objected.

'Speaking of pastry, how about some food? I'm famished,' Tad said.

'No sandwich at lunch time?'

He looked directly at her. She saw that he'd picked up the challenge in her question. For a moment she saw something like admiration in his gaze.

'Food, good food,' called Nan. 'Can we have a menu, Tim?'

The waiter brought menus. Lindsay settled for tortellini al pesto. The men, predictably, wanted steak sandwiches. Nan settled for steak too after waiting to see what Tad would choose.

The promised champagne was brought and opened. Lindsay protested that you couldn't drink champagne with steak but was overruled. The meal was protracted by quiz games, a favourite pastime when things were slack in the dealing room.

Milo and Mac at length called it a day. Alec Joyce went to join a friend from another firm on the far side of the room. Lindsay was slowly sipping the last of her champagne. It seemed to her that Tad was staying on because she was staying, and that Nan was waiting for her to go so she could have Tad to herself.

'Shouldn't you be at home, Lindsay, reading a bedtime story to Alice?' she inquired, with a glance at the clock over the bar.

'Not tonight.'

'I thought you read to her every night, like the good mum you are?'

'I do. But she's away at the moment.'

'Away?' Nan said, in surprise made over-vehement by too much champagne. 'I thought you were never parted!'

'She's spending some time with friends in the country.' Lindsay picked up her handbag. 'But it's time I told myself a bedtime story, I think. Goodnight, friends.'

'I'll get a taxi for you,' Tad said.

'No need, I go by Tube from the Bank.'

'Well then, I'll walk you to Bank station.'

'Hold on there, Sir Galahad,' Nan protested, 'it's only nine o'clock, you know. No werewolves or bandits abroad.'

Tad laughed. 'You're right. Seems like midnight, but us financiers are in a different time warp from the rest of the world. Still, I'll see you to the Tube, Lindsay, if that's okay.'

'We'll all go,' Nan said, getting up unsteadily.

Lindsay had already settled the bill. They went out together into the cool May evening. Although Nan generally went home to her flat in Wapping by bus, she strode past her bus stop to accompany Tad and Lindsay to the Bank.

There Lindsay said goodbye, thinking that Tad was going to have a hard time getting rid of Nan. That is, if he wanted to get rid of her. For all she knew, Tad and Nan were an item by this time – though she'd heard no gossip to that effect in the gossipy dealing room. Still, she didn't hear everything these days. If rank had it privileges, it also had its drawbacks.

She was coming out of Putney Bridge station when she realized she'd once again forgotten to ring Barry. She nearly got out her mobile phone, but she didn't much approve of people who stood on the pavement in the dark chatting into phones. She'd ring when she got home.

But once again all she got was the answering machine. She'd thought the bottle of port would have had a softening effect but evidently not. She apologized once more to the machine, saying she'd been trying to reach him all day without success and was very downcast at her failure.

She went for a swim. Since she was on her own, she swam

naked, revelling in the feel of the water smoothly slipping past her skin. She let her thoughts drift.

For all that there were still problems to be faced, it had been a good day. She and her team had coped with the emergency, had enjoyed an evening together. She'd made some sort of contact with Tad Tadiecski so that she might be able to build up a character portrait.

If it wasn't that he made her uneasy, there was much about him she could like. His ability to cope with a complex problem at work, for instance, and the good sense in his advice. His sense of humour, too, and the way he hadn't shown up Nan's ignorance over the quotation from Dante.

Tomorrow she would have to deal with the aftermath of the grain problem – try to find out how the French banks were feeling and whether her portfolios could benefit. She found she was relying on Tad's verdict that Wall Street would calm down when it reopened tomorrow.

For the rest, Barry was being difficult but she would keep apologizing until he came round. Lindsay was good at apologizing, she did it a lot. It was part of her management technique. Sometimes in the heat of the action at work, she could speak sharply, or misjudge one of her traders. When that happened, she always apologized as soon as she realized what she'd done. She never allowed ill will to fester and become an incurable sore.

She knew she still had a lot to do to find out who had threatened her family. She looked back at the group around the table at Dandy's, and found it hard to think any one of them could have sent that photograph and its cruel message. Not Nan, her friend of many years. Not giggly little Ellaline, still afloat on the joy of a happy marriage. Not Mac, too cerebral and detached. Not Milo . . . well, Milo . . . Milo was an immigrant from Macedonia or some other region of Greece, difficult to know but seemingly concerned only with earning a place for himself in British society. As for Alec Joyce, he was really still a schoolboy, playing his computer games. A clever schoolboy, and perhaps there was deviousness in the games that he loved . . . But no, he was harmless.

It couldn't be one of her immediate team. But Oistrav's employed many people. Someone in some other department, some spider spinning a web in some corner out of her sight . . .

Whoever it was, she had made her move and blocked him.

Her family were safely tucked away where no one could harm them. She pictured the serene, hardworking scene at the nursery farm. People everywhere, with Celia and Alice lost among them, almost invisible. A protective cover that was almost impossible for an outsider to penetrate, and moreover how could he guess where they had gone? Yet they were close, because she could be in touch with her mother instantly.

She dived to the bottom of the pool, pulling herself along for a few yards against the old marble to test her stamina. Then she barrelled upwards into the air, shaking water from her face and hair.

Through the glass roof she could see moonlight, a silvery glow among oyster-coloured clouds. From somewhere on the Heath she heard the faint call of an owl.

She climbed out, wrapped herself in a towel and, barefoot, trotted back indoors. She showered and dried her hair. In her kimono she went along to her mother's room.

It was a big room and needed to be so, for it housed her mother's computers. Celia actually slept in what had been a dressing room, a cell-like place with a bed and a mirror and a wardrobe and an ornamental oval window.

The computer room had a long solid table along one wall and a roller-chair. On the table were four computers, two printers, a stack container for disks, phone and a modem. Here Celia worked, sometimes on two or more projects at one time.

Lindsay checked her e-mail and printed out what Celia had sent her. She took it into her bedroom to glance at while she got ready for bed. There were six rows of names and a short column of figures. Nothing jumped out at her – names of firms moving money about, perfectly legitimate. Sighing, she folded up the paper and got into bed.

Next morning Sudin had little snippets of news from the market garden. 'Alice complains there is nowhere to swim. It is true – the farm is not far from the estuary but we could not let her swim there.'

'Much too cold,' Lindsay agreed. Water in a pool was always warmer than river or sea water.

'Moreover, dangerous,' Sudin said. 'There are currents there. However, Babaji says he will take her to the town where there is swimming bath. Your mother says she will buy swimsuit.'

'Thank you, Sudin, your family are very kind.'

'Alice is very good at picking vegetables. She enjoys it very much. Yesterday she picked a kilo of okra, what you would call lady fingers, she was very proud when it was put in the box to go to market.'

'I can imagine. Perhaps she'll take up market gardening as a career,' Lindsay said, laughing.

In the office she switched on her screens to find out what was happening in Far East markets. French banks had strong links with some of the banks in what had been French colonial territories, and it might be that if the Russian loans were to be extended, the finance could come from there. She spent an hour keeping an eye on the Eastern exchanges while she mapped out a plan for the day's work.

Then she had to consider what to do about Barry. Should she send him some other peace offering? And if so, what? She was still pondering this problem when the mobile phone rang in her handbag. She got it out and responded. Celia's voice came through at once, without greeting or preamble.

'Are you alone, Lindsay?'

'Yes – why?'

'I've something important to tell you.'

Lindsay frowned to herself. A clue at last? 'About what?'

'I linked up with your office computer when I was doing a general sweep of all our data. You know your program logs dates and times of call-up? It shows someone's been into your private files on your office computer.'

Chapter Eight

Lindsay went cold.

It was an invasion of privacy. Shocking, hurtful, frightening.

'Are you there?' Celia asked.

'Just a minute.' She didn't want to talk. She had to get her breath back first. To her own surprise, she was trembling.

After a long moment she said, 'I can't talk about it here, someone might come in. I'll ring you back in about half an hour.'

'All right, I'll be waiting.'

She went out to the trading floor. It was about nine o'clock, business was brisk. Tad was standing by Mac's desk studying his screen and saying, 'But in a few hours when Wall Street opens you'll see a dip . . .'

Lindsay went to Nan, her senior trader. 'I'm just going to nip out for some breakfast –'

'Want some company?'

'No, thanks, it's just going to be a quick cup of coffee and a croissant. Watch what's happening on the Bourse –'

'Yes, I saw they were showing interest in wheat futures. Are we hanging on to ours? I've got Pellerton on the q.v.' Pellerton was their commodities broker.

'Commodities aren't our thing really, okay? So we'll sell if the price goes up by three-quarters or half per cent – but wait to see if we can get three-quarters, we're not in a hurry to unload. Tell Pellerton to play it long if he wants to, and make sure of a profit.'

'I get you.'

Studley gave her a smile as she went through the hall. 'Breath of fresh air?'

'Yes, shan't be long.'

It was an unwritten law at Oistrav's that phones shouldn't be used for personal calls. This was because every phone conversation was supposed to be on tape. Studley was quite accustomed to staff members popping out for ten minutes to telephone a bookie or a boyfriend.

She went to a bookstore in Leadenhall which had a cafe at the back of the shop. As yet business was slack. She chose a table in a corner, ordered a mug of coffee, and rang the number of the smallholding. She was expected and put through at once to Celia.

'Tell me what you found out, Cecie,' she said.

'It was early this morning. You know how I am when I've got a new problem, I like to get at it as soon as I'm awake. I'd used up all the passwords you'd given me for the big departments and was just fiddling about, thinking about private passwords. I thought I'd try yours, to see how long it would take from a remote.'

Lindsay changed the password on her private files often. She was using characters from Greek mythology at present, had worked her way through the Nine Muses and was now on the goddesses. She recalled telling her mother she'd soon have run through them, because she'd reached Selene, the Goddess of the Moon.

'So what did you find?'

'Well, of course, at first I was just looking at data. But then I decided to do some trawling and suddenly saw – somebody had been in the file on Sunday night. Now you were *here* on Sunday and you couldn't have got to Oistrav's on your way home in time to make this entry.'

'No, I went straight home.'

'So I tracked back, and there have been two other visits, one at about 2200 on the 4th April and one about 0100 on a day in the last week of March but it's difficult to be sure of the date because he's covered his tracks both times very neatly.'

'Can you tell if the file was accessed in my office or from a remote?'

'In your office on your desk computer, I'd say, but that's just my opinion.'

Lindsay was prepared to take her mother's word on anything to do with computers.

'Is there anything unauthorized before the last week in March?'

'Not that I can see.'

The last week in March. Just after Tad joined the staff.

'What are you going to do?' Celia asked.

'Change the password.'

Celia gave a snort of laughter. 'Don't leave any clues about, then. This chap isn't dim. He got your password not once but twice, because you changed it between March and April.'

That was true. In March the password had been Pallas, in April she'd changed it to Persephone, in May to Selene. She got these names from an alphabetical list in a little book she'd bought at a secondhand bookshop in Charing Cross Road, *Discovering Greek Myths*. She kept it in an unlocked drawer in her desk among other apparent trivia.

Someone had been in her office, looked through her desk, found the little book and recognized its purpose. How he had worked out which of the gods and goddesses she'd chosen, she couldn't imagine. Perhaps he had sat there and laboured through the list until he found one that worked. He had done it not once but twice – well, the second time not too hard if he thought alphabetically.

She was sure it was Tad who had snooped in her files. It was instinct that told her, instinct as certain as the one that led her to take protective action for her investment clients or urged her to back an outsider for profit. Tad would have had the wit to work out the reason for the Greek mythology book in her desk drawer.

But what good had it done him? There was nothing of great importance in her private files. Some information about her bank accounts, some investment plans, a calendar of proposed work on the house reaching two years ahead and giving the costs, some notes on the performance of her team for the past twelvemonth, and a few other things she couldn't recall without checking.

'Whoever it is, I can't see that he's gained anything by snooping,' she said slowly.

'Perhaps not. But you do think it's this man who sent the threat?'

'I don't know, Mother.' She almost groaned the words. She'd had a big fright when she first heard the news, but now she'd had time to think about it, it seemed to teach her nothing. She didn't know who and she didn't know why. She seemed to be no further forward.

'You want me to go on with this?'

'Yes, please.' Because what other plan was there?

'Into private files, or shall I work on getting the passwords for the other departments?'

'I don't know . . . It seems to me that if anybody's up to tricks, they wouldn't record them on a private file at Oistrav's. Stick to the departments. If money's moving, there's *got* to be a trace somewhere.'

'You're the boss,' Celia said, and rang off.

The first thing Lindsay did when she got back to her office was to take *Discovering Greek Myths* out of the drawer and drop it into the wastepaper basket. There it was quite visible to anyone who came in, and she wanted it so, she wanted the intruder to know she'd caught his tracks.

The second thing she did was to ring her bank to check that no one had used the information in her files to make any transactions. All was well. She asked to have the balances transferred to new account numbers and this was accepted without demur.

Next she typed 'Selene' into her computer, touched the delete key, then entered a new password, 'Segovia'. Segovia was her favourite guitarist. From now until further notice all her passwords were going to have something to do with guitar music. She was fairly sure no one would work that out easily: few people knew that she was an amateur guitarist, because she never played except in private.

For the rest of the day she worried away at the problem of the intruder in her computer files. It had to be Tad Tadiecski, had to be. But what use was he making of the information he got? Why did he want it? Was she the only one he'd snooped on?

Why was he here?

The day ended much more quietly than it had begun. Yesterday's flurry over the Chicago wheat forecasts and the silo companies died away: the French banks dealt with any problems over loans to Moscow with utter discretion. Lindsay left for home about three-thirty.

She had her swim, had a pot of Tracy's strong tea, then dialled the number of an old friend in New York. Buddy Tromberg was well into his fifties now, retired from Wall Street but writing a monthly financial column that was syndicated to several weekend supplements. He had a fine overview of the financial district and a long memory.

'Honey, how *are* you? When're you coming over again to see your Uncle Buddy?'

'Soon as I can get included in a seminar on your side of the water, Buddy. How are things with you?'

'Great, great. You know I was nominated for an award for Best Financial Columnist?'

'Did you win?'

'Hell, no, but it looks good after my byline – Nominated Best Columnist.'

'That's almost fraud, Buddy.'

They spent some time catching up with news. Then Buddy said, 'This is all very well, but you didn't call me to chew the fat about trivia. What's the beef?'

'I'm trying to find out something about a man who joined us at Oistrav's recently, Buddy. His name is William Tadiecski – I'll spell it, it's difficult.' She did so.

'Got it. What about him?'

'He's our Research Analyst. I wondered if you knew him.'

'What's up? He's no good?'

'No, not that, he's very good at his job. He came from Hurley Gounett with very good references.'

'So what's the problem, dear?'

'I'd just like to know something about him. It bothers me that if he was doing so well as a dealer in a major Wall Street firm, why would he come to a merchant bank in London?'

'Didn't you ask him?'

'Of course. He told me he had a father living now in Provence –'

'Provence, France?'

'Yes, trying to be an artist after retiring from the real estate business with a fortune. Something about a dicey marriage with one of his models – Tadiecski's trying to keep an eye on him from London.'

'It's possible, I suppose – some father-and-son relationships are warm and close no matter what Freud said. What was the real estate business of Tadiecski Senior?'

'Mainstream Property Developments, as I recall, or it might have been Mainstream Realty. Trading in Florida.'

'Well, that's likely, Florida is the place for making money in real estate.'

'Could you make a few discreet inquiries, Buddy? Just to set my mind at rest? Nothing that would attract any attention, though.'

'For you, sugar-pie, anything. Take me a day or two, okay?'

'You're a darling, Buddy.'

'I bet you say that to all the boys. I'll get back to you, Lindsay.'

'Thank you, Buddy. And Buddy . . . ring me at home, will you? If I'm not in leave a message and I'll ring you back.'

'No problem.'

Two days went by. Lindsay still hadn't managed to speak to Barry in person but on Thursday, he suddenly relented. 'I'm putting you through,' his secretary said, and next moment Barry was saying, 'Lindsay, is that you?'

'Barry! At last! I thought I was going to talk to your machine for the rest of my life.'

'I've been busy,' he said stiffly. 'There's a big sale coming off in ten days' time, Mogul carvings. So how are you, Lindsay?'

'Not bad.' The truth was, she felt tired and restless. She didn't know what steps to take, if any. Frustration was wearing her out. But she was used to living with tension in her business life so she didn't think it worth mentioning. 'How are you?'

'As I said, busy. By the way, thank you for the port.'

'Is it any good?'

'I haven't decanted it yet. But I'm sure it's excellent.'

She could tell from his tone that she still wasn't forgiven. Time for yet another apology. 'Barry, I hope you'll forgive and forget about Sunday. There's an explanation – I'm sure you'll understand when I tell you about it.'

'I know you're a busy person, Lindsay. I quite understand.' His voice told her that he didn't understand a bit.

She stifled a sigh. 'Shall we be seeing each other again soon?'

'Well . . . The weekend, perhaps?'

'Not the weekend,' she said hastily. 'Saturday's the Derby and Oistrav's are taking a party of guests.' And Sunday she planned to go down to Essex again. 'The weekend is difficult for me.'

'I see.'

No you don't, she thought. But she said aloud, 'Monday evening, Barry?'

'Monday I'll be supervising the unpacking of some of the carvings.'

'Tuesday, then.'

'Very well, Tuesday. I'm pencilling it in. If anything comes up that changes things for either of us, we can be in touch.'

'Of course, Barry.'

There had been no thaw in his manner throughout the telephone conversation. She could only hope that by next Tuesday he would have got the better of his ill humour.

She went home ruminating over Barry. She was fond of him, and she didn't want their relationship to end. It had its importance in her life. Moreover, her mother approved of him and often hinted that she hoped a marriage would ensue. And Alice adored him. If for no other reason than he filled a huge gap in Alice's life, was a sort of surrogate father, she didn't want to be on bad terms with Barry.

As she went into her house, Tracy and Eddie came rushing to meet her.

'Oh, Mrs Dunforth dear, oh, isn't it terrible, can you smell it? What a fright it gave us! But it's all right,' cried Tracy, 'my Eddie saw to it, and no great harm done, but what a thing, really these days, vandals and hooligans everywhere, I do declare!'

'What?' demanded Lindsay, her heart leaping up into her mouth. 'What's happened?'

'See for yourself, Mrs Dunforth, a rotten trick, isn't it?'

Eddie led her to the drawing room door. By the walnut bureau in the window overlooking the back garden a wastepaper bin of beaten brass lay on its side. Around the bin was a wide expanse of stained, soaked carpet. A fire extinguisher had been laid across a chair.

'What on earth –?'

'The minute we opened the door we could smell it, burning, you see, it hit you right in the face. So Eddie ran in here and saw the smoke coming up and fetched the extinguisher from the hall cupboard –'

'Mostly paper,' Eddie grunted, 'but there's a wooden photograph frame in there and some cracked glass so that kept it going a bit I daresay –'

'A fire?' Lindsay gasped.

'Huh!' said Tracy in scorn. 'Done just to make a mess, if you ask me. Kids, I s'pose –'

'But how did they get in? Weren't you here?'

'No, well, if you remember, today was the day I was going to see about that cherrywood banister, I mean, something to replace it, at that chap I told you about with a place at Guildford, buys in all these bits of good old wood, antique you might say, you know I rang him and he said he had some lovely rosewood. So Trace and I, we were to make a day of it, have a look-see, and you said good luck and buy whatever you think would do –'

'But the locks – and the alarm, didn't you put the alarm on?'

He looked sheepish. The truth was that Eddie found the alarm too complicated and relied on the locks. As for those, he often failed to check that the windows were secure although he usually deadlocked the front door.

Lindsay trod carefully into the drawing room. The carpet was a mess and would have to be professionally cleaned. She looked about but nothing seemed to be missing. How strange – a break-in by some young hooligan who yet failed to spot the valuable Medge and Dutton clock on the mantelpiece.

Her eye was caught by the paperweight on the bureau. It was out of place. She moved gingerly towards it. A piece of paper from the writing drawer was held there. She pulled it free.

'This could have been a really serious fire. BACK OFF. YOUR LAST WARNING.'

Chapter Nine

Tracy was coming into the room after her, craning to see what she was reading.

'What's it say?'

'Oh, just dirty words,' Lindsay said, crumpling it up and tossing it on the bureau.

'Really, kids these days! Are we calling the cops?'

'Nah,' said her husband, who truly believed the police were useless because they never caught boys who broke into his van. 'Nah, leave it. Who wants the hassle?'

'Quite right, Eddie. We'll get somebody in to clean the carpet and that'll be that.'

'I dunno,' mused Tracy. 'P'raps we oughta report it.'

'Nah,' repeated Eddie, nudging her – and it dawned on her that he'd have to confess he'd left the alarm off.

So that was the end of it. Tracy went to look in the *Yellow Pages* for a carpet cleaner, while Lindsay took the note upstairs to examine it in private.

Same black capitals as before. Same underlining of 'Back off.'

But the message itself . . . 'This could have been a really serious fire.'

Those were not the words of a professional heavy, surely. A man used to making threats would have said something like, 'I could have burned you out.' But: 'This could have been a really serious fire.' It was like a bank manager speaking: 'This could have been a really serious drain on your resources.'

And the fire itself. The man had had the house to himself, could have done anything, smashed the furniture, cut up the cushions, thrown the antique clock through the window. What did he do? Made a fire in a metal bin. She could almost picture him, pushing sheets of paper in and setting fire to them with his Bic cigarette lighter. Not enough fuel so he pitches in a photograph from the bureau, a photograph of Peter Gruman accepting his retirement present.

This was no professional frightener. An amateur, nothing more. If only the alarm had been set – she could picture him, fleeing the house in terror at its shrieks.

Who was he? Who were his fellow conspirators?

She locked the sheet of paper in her dressing table drawer along with its predecessor and the tape of the voice on the phone. She went along to her mother's room, wondering if he had come up here and perhaps done some damage, but no – as far as she could tell everything was in order. He had not come upstairs. Too scared, she knew instinctively. Too scared to go up the staircase, away from the downstairs window through which he'd entered and through which he must leave.

Tracy called up: 'Carpet firm can come tomorrow, no problem.'

'Good.' She went down to the hall. It had struck her that though this man, whoever he was, was an amateur, he might cause a big drama if he tried to break in while either Tracy or Eddie was there. Eddie would go for him, that was certain. Eddie was the type who would always 'have a go'.

'The day after tomorrow is Derby Day,' she said. 'I'll be going with a group from the office. What do you say, we lock up the house securely and all go to Epsom?'

'Oh, now, that would be nice,' Tracy said, delight on her plump features.

'In fact, why don't you and Eddie take a few days off? It's hardly worth your while doing much in the house for only me.'

'But Mrs Dunforth, we couldn't leave you here on your own – not after that!' She nodded towards the drawing room.

'Oh, I'll be away too – I thought of going to stay with my mother and Alice in the country. So it would all fit quite nicely.'

'Oh. In that case . . . yes, why not? I'll go and ask Eddie.'

Eddie's Aunt Maisie had a caravan on a site somewhere near Brighton, almost always available for weekends and holidays. Everything was soon fixed up: on Derby Day they would each betake themselves to Epsom, Lindsay in one of the hired limousines which would collect the Oistrav's party at the Savoy, Tracy and Eddie in Eddie's van. Lindsay would see to it that the Taylors were provided with a little bonus with which to bet on the favourite. They would then drive on to Brighton for a week's holiday. By this means – providing the opportunity for a small celebration – Lindsay deflected the attention of the Taylors from the mini-drama of the fire. She moreover removed them from any danger.

Lindsay herself was determined to return to the house after the races, for she had no intention of going out of London. London was where the struggle was taking place, this strange, unseen, unformulated struggle between herself and her mysterious opponent.

She went for a swim to settle her mind. Afterwards she wrapped herself in a towelling robe then went to lie in the sun on a chaise longue. She put a tape of John Williams playing Villa-Lobos on her stereo and lay with her eyes closed, listening to the delicate fingerwork as the guitarist picked his way through the intricate rhythms of South America.

She was called into the house by Tracy. 'Telephone, Mrs Dunforth.'

She took the call upstairs in her bedroom. It was Buddy Tromberg. 'How you doing, sweetness?' he inquired. 'Made a million today?'

'Almost. You?'

'Well, it's early in the day here but I'm going to back a little something on the market later. Now, Lindsay, about your friend Tadiecski. Maggie says he's on the personnel files at Hurley Gounett as a trader but she's never seen him and can't think who he is.'

'What?'

'An invisible man.'

'Who's Maggie? Does she know what she's talking about?'

'She's the friend of a friend – in fact, the secretary to the Personnel Officer at Hurley Gounett. I've got friends in a lot of spots, Lindsay – you can't run a financial column without inside information.'

'But what does it mean, Buddy? He's a member of the staff at H.G. but this girl doesn't know him?'

'Well, it could be what you Brits call a fiddle. Some Vice-President owes this guy a buck or two so he gets him on the payroll of the firm.'

'He draws a salary but doesn't do anything for it?'

'It happens. Especially if the guy has something he can hold over somebody.'

'Blackmail?' Lindsay breathed, aghast.

'You can't discount it. *But . . .*'

'But what?'

'There's hardly any entry in the file,' reported Buddy. 'In fact, Maggie says she's almost sure it's a late insertion in the lists, with just enough on it to pass muster if you were screening through the staff records.'

Lindsay took a moment to consider the idea. 'In other words, it's a computer forgery?'

'She thinks so.'

'But who could do that, Buddy?'

'Aw, come on! Guys hack into company files every day of the week, often just for fun. What could be easier than to get into the personnel register of Hurley Gounett and provide yourself with a career record?'

It was an alarming thought. She left it for the moment. 'Did you look into the father's firm – Mainstream Property Development?'

'Yeah, looked them up. No problem, got a copy of last year's accounts – a good investment, head offices in Miami. But it was never owned by anybody called Tadiecski. In fact, dreamboat, all the names on the board of directors are Spanish.'

'Spanish.'

'Yeah, and you know . . . Florida . . . Half of Florida's owned by Venezuelans and Colombians.'

'What are you saying, Buddy?'

'A lot of funny money gets invested in real estate, and Colombians have got a lot of funny money.'

'This is too far-fetched, Buddy –'

'I'll tell you something else. I looked up Mr Tadiecski in the phonebook –'

'The phonebook!'

'Why not? The guy's supposed to work on Wall Street, knows enough about it to convince *you*, ten to one he's a New Yorker, and in the phonebook. Sure enough, an address on West Eighteenth, used to be a tough neighbourhood but in the last ten years it's become desirable. I rang the number, a girl answered, said she was sub-letting from Mr Tadiecski who was abroad. Knew nothing about him except that she had to pay rent to him. So I cabbed over there last night to talk to the neighbours. It's an old brownstone made into four apartments, not bad, wouldn't mind living there.'

'Did you find out anything?' she asked, to urge him on.

'Mr Tadiecski lived there until he went abroad. I got a description – tall thin guy, thirty-six, thirty-seven, dresses well, a load of laughs. I think the divorcee on the ground floor takes a special interest in him, if you know what I mean.'

'Enough to know what he does?'

'Oh, he's "on Wall Street". She can tell that by all the newspapers and magazines in his trash can.'

'And the father?'

Buddy cleared his throat, heralding something important. 'Mr Tadiecski Senior died about five years ago. A nice old guy, had a bad heart. The janitor went to his funeral.'

She was silent for a moment. Then she said, almost sadly, 'So everything he told us was a pack of lies.'

'Seems so, honey.'

'There's always been something about him . . .'

'A crook, that's what.'

'But you don't understand, Buddy. Peter vouched for him!'

'Peter?'

'Peter Gruman, our former Chairman, I mean Chairman of Oistrav's. He rang somebody at Hurley Gounett to check on Tadiecski and got the all clear.'

'Who did he ring?'

'Wait a minute, let me think . . . Blebel? John Blebel?'

'Yeah, that's right, Senior VP – old style Stock Exchange type, very straight arrow. He vouched for Tadiecski? That's weird, huh?'

'Buddy, the whole thing is weird. What's this man doing at Oistrav's?'

'Nothing good, I'd imagine. Listen, Lindsay, I think you ought to be a bit careful. This guy quoted Mainstream Property Development as a background detail, which kind of makes you think that if you'd called them, they'd have vouched for Tadiecski Senior too. And I mean it when I say there's underworld money in Miami.'

'I'll be careful, Buddy. And you too – maybe you should warn your friend Maggie not to make waves over those false entries in the personnel files.'

'Oh, sure! She cottoned on to that herself – said she thought she'd forget she ever saw the entries. Is there anything else I can do?'

'Perhaps it's best to leave well alone. But thanks a million for all the trouble you've taken.'

'If you uncover a juicy fraud, sweetness, don't forget I get first dibs at it in print.'

She laughed and hung up. But she was perplexed beyond measure by what she'd heard.

She thought about it with total concentration until Tracy came up to say dinner was ready. It proved to be a frozen gourmet meal from Harrods' food department, asparagus chicken in a cream sauce. She ate it without noticing what it was.

At her daughter's bedtime she rang the market garden to listen to her account of the day – 'We went to the swimming bath, I did five lengths' – and to say a long goodnight. Then her mother came on the line.

'Cecie, have you got anything useful on the computer files yet?'

'Nothing that seems very big. There's somebody in the Accounts Department who seems to be skimming off small amounts on very active clients, I'll send it through on the printer in a minute. How are things with you?'

'It's got a bit more serious.' She related the story of the fire, and was interrupted at once by her mother.

'That's a lot worse than sending a photo! You've got to go to the police, Lindsay – that's twice you've been threatened!'

'I didn't take it too seriously at first, because it all seemed so inept. But I had a talk with a New York friend and . . . I don't know . . . It seems more and more certain that it's something to do with the bank.'

'Well, that was always the supposition –'

'Yes, but it may not be some small fiddle by a clerk in the Accounts Department. I've been thinking, and I remember speaking about that estimate we got for the cherrywood banister – remember?'

'Cherrywood banister?' Celia echoed, at a loss.

'And how Eddie was making a trip out to some junkyard in Surrey today to rake around for something there. It made an amusing little story, I'm famous for always having something done to the house. I've been racking my brains to recall who I said it to. And . . . and . . . I think it might have been in the conference room when we were waiting for the Chairman to start a meeting.'

'I don't follow, dear –'

'Don't you see, I let it be known the house would be empty

today. So whoever it is knew he could send his minion to throw another scare into me.'

'But . . . you're saying . . . it might be one of the *directors*, Lindsay?'

Lindsay sighed. 'That could tie in with what my New York friend was saying. He was talking about really big money – it makes me think it could be somebody important who's at the back of this.' And as she said it, Peter Gruman's name flickered in her mind.

'I know you're going to argue against it, but I really think you should go to the police –'

'No. But to be on the safe side, I've given Tracy and Eddie a holiday.'

'A holiday? So what will you do? You're not going to be there on your own, Lindsay – I *forbid* it!'

'No, perhaps not,' she agreed, thinking about Buddy's guesses at the Colombian Mafia. She'd at once tried to discount that, but Tad Tadiecski was here in London under false pretences for *some* reason, and it couldn't be something negligible.

'Come and stay here with us. Mr Goswami would love to have you and there's plenty of room –'

'It's too inconvenient, Cecie, I need to be in London –'

'But not at the house! Please, dear.' There was an agony of anxiety in her mother's voice and for a moment Lindsay saw it from her point of view. How had she herself felt when Alice was threatened?

'All right,' she conceded, thinking quickly. 'I can move into one of the courtesy flats, at least for the time being. There's one at Canary Wharf – will that do?'

'Anything's better than having you in that great house on your own –'

'Calm down, Mother. Getting in a panic isn't going to help.'

'Neither is getting knocked on the head by some scary burglar! Please, I think you ought to call in the police.'

'But we've been through all that! I've no idea why I'm being targeted like this, but whatever the reason, it's nothing that the local police would understand. It's something to do with Oistrav's, Cecie. The only way to get it sorted out is to find out what they're up to at the bank.'

'You know, I could probably do a lot better if I had comments from you,' Celia said, having been reassured enough to start thinking straight. 'I'm thrashing about in the dark half the time. Wouldn't it make a lot of sense if I were to come back to London?'

'But you just said a minute ago that the house isn't safe –'

'I mean to this flat you mentioned, in Canary Wharf. Is it big enough for two?'

'Oh, of course. It's meant for VIP visitors – oil sheiks and German bankers.'

'Right you are then, I'll come back –'

'But what about Alice?'

'She'd stay here. She loves it, Lindsay. She gets to pick the crops in the glasshouses and thinks it's terribly grown up, and she gets to look after Govi and for her it's like having a live doll to play with.'

'But it's asking too much of –'

'Not a bit, dear, I mean it. The Goswamis are delighted to do anything at all for you.'

She couldn't deny that it would be a help to have her mother close at hand. Celia knew so much more about computers than Lindsay. Besides, it would be good to have someone with whom she could talk. Part of the pressure upon her was that she had no one she could trust at the bank.

While she was still considering, her mother broke in.

'It would be perfectly simple – the boys here are always driving to London with loads of special produce for special restaurants and shops. I could just ask them to call by Putney, put my gear in the van and be there by midday tomorrow. By the time you get home I'd be set up and running.'

'But I'm not moving into the flat until after Eddie and Tracy leave for Brighton –'

'Which is when?'

She explained about the trip to Epsom and how the holiday would follow on from there. 'I don't want to move to the flat because it would mean packing my Derby Day dress and it would get crushed –'

'Good heavens,' her mother cried, divided between amusement and anxiety, 'only a woman would bother about a thing like that!'

'All the same, it will save a lot of explanations to Eddie and Tracy if I wait until they're gone before I move out.'

'All right, but you move at once, is that understood?'

'You win, you win. I'll pack on Saturday – that'll seem quite right to the Taylors because I told them I was going to stay with you and Alice in the country for a few days. Sudin can collect my things and no one will ever know where I'm staying. The girl who handles accommodation will think I'm setting up a love nest when I ask her to keep quiet about it. If he *happens* to think of asking about the courtesy flat –'

'Is he likely to?'

'I don't think so, Mother. But if he does, Melissa will tell me and then . . . we'll know who he is, won't we?'

'How you can talk about it so calmly –' her mother began in a fluster of anxiety.

'What would you prefer? Hysteria? That's just what Mr X is hoping for. But I'm coming to the conclusion that this chap isn't very bright –'

'He must be, if he's involved in some kind of fraud –'

'Perhaps he himself isn't clever. Perhaps he's got someone pulling his strings.'

'Someone who *is* clever . . .'

'Clever enough to see I've left the house, and perhaps clever enough to think about the VIP flats. But even if he does, what can he actually do? There's good security at both of them – I mean, Oistrav's don't put up visiting tycoons where they can be got at!'

'But it's such a lot to handle on your own. Couldn't you ask for help? Discuss it with Peter Gruman? He always seems to know what to do.'

'I'm thinking about Peter,' she said, and with that comforting remark her mother was content.

But if she'd known what her daughter was thinking she wouldn't have found it comforting at all. Lindsay was looking back at her visit to Peter when she'd had her first doubts about Tad.

She'd shown him the CV. He'd been quite satisfied, had tried to persuade her to take it at face value. When she'd gone on being anxious Peter had offered to ring John Blebel at Hurley Gounett.

Blebel, Buddy assured her, was above suspicion. If he vouched for Tad, that should be the end of any doubt.

But . . . Had Peter actually rung New York?

She re-ran the events of that evening. Peter had offered to make the call, had gone into his study, and from there she'd heard him speaking with his usual clarity and force. In other words, she'd heard his end of a conversation.

But what proof had she that he'd ever put the call through? How did she know he wasn't talking to an empty line?

She shuddered at herself. She was thinking the unthinkable. Peter Gruman? Ex-Chairman of Oistrav's?

Yet there he was, cooped up in a flat high in the Barbican. Able to see his beloved City but yet no longer part of it.

She could imagine how boredom and frustration might lead such an active mind to dishonesty. It had happened before. Men played against the City, mostly for money but sometimes also to prove that they could do it and win.

Peter had seemed more than ready to accept Tad Tadiecski. What if he had summoned him to Oistrav's? Or connived at his coming?

The threats to Lindsay's family had occurred since Tad came on the scene. Now she learned from Buddy that everything about him was a fraud – the CV, the family background, the supposed reason for the move to London.

Whatever had brought him here, it certainly wasn't to keep an eye on a recently remarried father. So what was it?

She dared not challenge him outright. He seemed to have henchmen he could summon, and if he was conspiring with Peter Gruman he had a clever brain as his support. One threatening move on her part, and any evidence of wrongdoing would vanish. One *wrong* move on her part, and Oistrav's could be brought down in ruins.

She woke next morning from a troubled sleep at the unwelcome call of her alarm. She had a throbbing head and an avid longing to rid herself of the problem.

Suspect Peter? Her friend and mentor of five years? Impossible.

On her drive with Sudin to Pewter Lane, she put the new plans before him.

'There was another upset at my house yesterday, Sudin. Someone set a little fire in the drawing room –'

'A fire! Good heavens, are you all right? Was anyone injured?'

'No, no, it was only a baby fire in a metal container – but it's worrying. I think it's best to move out of the house for a while. Will you collect my case on Saturday, and take it to an address I'll give you in Canary Wharf? And don't mention it to anyone?'

He gave her a troubled glance from his brown eyes, but his faith in her was complete. 'Yes, certainly, Mrs Dunforth, anything to help.'

As soon as normal businesses would be in operation, Lindsay rang a security firm often used by Oistrav's and asked to have their automobile patrol keep an eye on her house as from today until further notice. 'My housekeeper and her husband are still in the house for the moment but we will all be leaving mid-morning tomorrow, Saturday. The alarm system will be permanently switched on from then – can it be routed so as to sound in your headquarters if it's set off?'

'Of course, madam, no problem.'

Next she went to Oistrav's Public Relations office to ask for the use of one of the courtesy flats. She explained that her house – well known to most of her colleagues as being in a permanent state of 'improvement' – would be unlivable in for a week or two.

No problem. Oistrav's had the lease on two flats, one in Canary Wharf, one in Mayfair. The Mayfair flat was in use at the moment; its occupants would be of the party going to the Derby on Saturday. As she expected, she was given the keys of the flat in the docks.

She made a list on her organizer: go at midday to let her mother into the flat, take a supply of milk and bread with her. Tomorrow key in the telephone number to which telephone calls should be rerouted on her answering machine at home, pack her case ready for Sudin to collect, lock up and set all the alarms before setting off for the Savoy, from which she would be driven to Epsom. Somewhere in there she ought to find time to get her hair done. Derby Day was a special occasion for Oistrav's, there would be important guests to entertain.

She felt a pulse of anger, of bitterness. This man, whoever he was, had the ability to spoil everything. He had parted her from her little girl, chased her out of her home, wrecked her peace of mind, even tainted the simple pleasure of a day at the races. The dress hanging in her wardrobe was a special dress, a shimmering pale blue, quite unlike the demure silks she wore at the office. She'd been looking forward to wearing it but now it seemed merely one more detail to attend to.

If Tad Tadiecski was part of this scheme, if he had caused this upheaval in her life, she'd see that he was locked up for a thousand years.

On Saturday at Epsom, she found herself thinking of yet another suspect. Peter Gruman was of the party: it was he who had instituted this annual event as a means of paying off some of the bank's social obligations, and though he was no longer an official his influence was still strong. He was invited this year because he was the past Chairman, and would always be invited because he was still active in the financial markets, although as a private investor now.

He came slowly towards Lindsay to greet her. 'My dear, what a pleasure to look at you.' He took her hand in both of his, and raised it to his lips.

Surely he couldn't be behind the attacks on her home. She watched him as he chatted with old friends. His aristocratic profile, his mane of white hair, his elegance of bearing, all picked him out as a grandee of the business world.

He had been her friend, her mentor. She owed her career to him, for he had singled her out. Impossible to believe he was a swindler, a fraudster. If that were so, the foundations of her world would crumble.

All the same – and this was one more loss inflicted on her by what was happening – she decided not to go to him for advice on how to handle things. She couldn't trust him any more.

Chapter Ten

When she got to the flat after Epsom she found her mother waking from a nap on a huge chesterfield in the living room.

'Hello,' she said, yawning. 'Back any winners?'

Lindsay laughed. Years ago she'd evolved a technique for these occasions. She always asked one of the male guests to make her bets for her. This they found flattering, and it saved her the trouble of reading any of the tipsters' recommendations.

'I gave the job to M Jusquenard of Utrecht, who came out ahead by about four pounds. How about you – what have you been doing?'

'Well, I set up a program for the computer to do a search and then went out for a walk. It's interesting round here, isn't it? Those big stretches of water – keep the place cool in a hot summer, but I wonder if the wind doesn't come whistling off them in winter . . . Are you hungry? I bought some food at the shops.'

'No thanks, I've been nibbling all day – pâté de foie, all that nonsense. Wouldn't mind a cup of tea if you're thinking of making one.' She walked into her bedroom to get out of her race-going clothes – the shady hat of blue straw, the dress of hyacinth voile and matching shoes, very attractive to look at but tiring to wear.

The bedroom had windows looking out on the lagoons. She stood for a moment staring out at the reflection of the buildings, darker shapes in the dark waters of evening. Of Oistrav's two VIP flats this one was the more sedate. The decor was nineteenth-century-merchant, lots of dark wood highboys and lamps with brass fittings and dark green shades. Impressive, but a world away from the light, country-life style she was aiming for at the Putney house. She couldn't really feel at home here.

She splashed cold water on her face to freshen up, hung the blue voile in the fitted wardrobe then donned a denim skirt and a chambray shirt. When she came out into the living room Celia was putting a tray of tea things on a low mahogany table. The teacups were Derby, the pot was Delft. 'Nice things,' Celia acknowledged. 'There are enamelled tea caddies in the kitchen with names on – this is Assam.'

'Anything as long as it isn't Earl Grey!'

'That reminds me, how was Peter?'

'Looking very handsome in his pearl grey silk cravat and topper.'

'Must be rather splendid in the Queen's Stand with all the men in morning dress and all the women in high fashion. How's Peter's arthritis?'

'Worse, I think, but he never lets you talk about it.'

'Did you speak to him about this problem of ours?'

'It was hardly the place or the time, Cecie.' She knew she was avoiding the truth, but she couldn't face the thought of actually telling her mother that Peter might be a villain.

As they drank their tea Celia imparted some news. 'You know that search program I was talking about?'

'Yes?'

'I directed it to trawl through some of Oistrav's departments – those I had codewords for.'

'Looking for what?'

'Well, you said not an accounts clerk taking the odd pound or two off somebody's balance. I decided to look for a pattern of large amounts moving about very actively. I mean, we're not looking for somebody who deposits a million and lets it sit there earning annual interest, are we?'

'No, we're looking for somebody who's working the bank system to his own advantage.'

'Right, so I thought the money would probably be moving about very quickly. And I think I've found something.'

'Really?'

'Come and look.' Celia set down her teacup and led the way to the dining room. On the dining table she had set up her computers, first taking the precaution of covering it with a blanket for fear of scratching its expensive surface.

She pointed to a print-out. Lindsay picked it up and read it through. Nothing unusual: it showed two accounts held by companies in the Banking Section, sums of money coming from the tax-free Antilles, remaining in the Oistrav accounts for a couple of days or sometimes less, and then being transferred elsewhere. One account seemed to prefer Switzerland as its destination, the other liked Liechtenstein.

'This is quite acceptable, Mother,' she said. 'Companies use their bank accounts to move money around to the most profitable places. Plenty of our clients do that. I move money myself, on behalf of pension funds and so on, if I see a way to increase the income.'

'But then the money comes back to the pension fund accounts in the end, doesn't it? It doesn't go to some other account.'

'But in the course of trade –'

'I just thought it was strange. These two accounts keep accepting money from deposits made in the Antilles but never keep it, the money just passes through and out to somewhere else. I mean, it's a pattern. I was looking for a pattern where big money was concerned.'

Celia called up a screenful of data. It showed the movement of money in the first of the two accounts from about eight months back. There was no doubt about it. Arranged by Celia in a graph, the money movement made a definite pattern.

She tapped a key and another screen came up, for the second of the accounts. The same pattern was evident.

'Um,' said Lindsay, sitting down in front of the computer. 'Let's list the destination accounts for this one.'

The screen twinkled and rearranged itself. Lindsay asked the computer to sort the destinations. Another twinkle and it was done.

'Yes . . .' She leaned back. 'Every one of those destinations is a country with laws favourable to secrecy about bank accounts. And the money comes from yet another country where "confidentiality" is all-important.'

Celia looked pleased. 'Well, I didn't know that. That's significant, isn't it?'

'Well . . . The fact is, darling, that quite a lot of highly respectable people send their money flitting about in Monserrat and Panama and the Antilles. It doesn't mean they're up to anything wicked.'

'Then why do they do it?'

'Tax avoidance . . . High interest rates . . .' She paused. 'All the same, who, one wonders, is National Northern Concentral Inc?'

'Sounds American.'

'Yes, doesn't it? I could do a little investigating on that. And the other one, Global Soundfast . . .'

'That might be all right. Global – sounds big and important.'

'Darling, you could set up a company to make penny sticks of rock for Blackpool seafront and call it Global. There's no law against it.'

'But surely there must be some rule –'

'Not at all. That's why investors ought to take care what they put their money in. Big names don't necessarily mean big business . . . Although Global Soundfast seems to deal in big sums.'

'So you'll look into it.'

'Yes, on Monday. It's easier to do it from the bank, we've got all the special software that lists companies, and there are rows of directories and reference books in the library.'

'You could go in tomorrow –'

'Tomorrow's Sunday and I'm going to Essex to see Alice,' Lindsay said firmly. 'And so are you. You've had your nose glued to a computer screen long enough.'

Sunday was enjoyable. Sudin collected them in his minivan and drove them together with yet another group of friends and relations to the market garden. Alice greeted them with a catalogue of activities undertaken since last she saw them – another visit to the swimming baths, the care of a special row of tomato plants which were to be hers entirely, the discovery that the estuary was only half an hour's walk away, a great place to find shells and strands of weed and pieces of driftwood.

'Babaji says I can't go there on my own, but Tapti likes to go there, he fishes off the end of the jetty but he doesn't catch anything. He has two fishing rods but he won't let me use the one he's not using 'cos he says the hooks are dangerous – they're not really, are they, Mummy, they're only small?'

'Yes, they are, and he's quite right not to let you meddle with them. When shall we get tomatoes off your tomato plants, love?' she inquired, to change the subject away from dangerous hooks.

'Not for ages and ages, but Babaji says patience is one of the greatest Vishnus –'

'What? Oh, virtues – my word, you are learning a lot!'

'Yes, aren't I,' the little girl said proudly.

'Wait till she does show-and-tell back at the nursery school,' Celia said with a laugh to Lindsay afterwards. 'Growing her own tomatoes and talking about Vishnu –!'

'When will she ever get back to nursery school?' Lindsay cried, suddenly attacked by a feeling of helplessness. 'This thing might take weeks and weeks to sort out –'

'Don't worry about it, dear,' her mother soothed. 'She's well and happy, and learning more here perhaps than she would at nursery school. And she doesn't start real school until September – by then I know you'll have it all worked out.'

Lindsay was a lot less certain, but said no more.

At mid-morning next day a message appeared on the intranet screens that the pictures taken at Epsom were now on display in the loggia. The Public Relations Department always put up a display after any public event in which the bank was involved, and esprit de corps demanded that everyone should take a look. As soon as she could spare a minute, Lindsay made her way there.

She found a group surveying the photographs. 'Lady in the emerald green must be Herr Lautenbard's wife,' someone was saying.

'Very smart. I must say I think compared with her, Lindsay looks a bit too garden-party in that floaty dress and pale straw hat.'

'Don't knock it, feller,' said a voice she recognized. 'New York girls would die for that look.'

'Thank you very much, Tad,' Lindsay said. 'Can I have that in writing?'

'Oh – didn't know you were there –'

She was surprised to see that he, usually so debonair and self-possessed, was quite flustered. Now was the moment to catch him off guard and ask if he knew anything of National Northern Concentral. But that was too big a risk. It could put him on his guard.

Conversation turned to what Naismith was reporting about conversation during the races. Although it was a social occasion, snippets of information were always welcome. Lindsay slipped away, choosing this moment to go to the library. The usual search tools – the Dow Jones, Standard & Poor's – had failed her. She'd looked at SEAQ, the Stock Exchange Automated Quotation system, but had found nothing. Perhaps in the less high-powered realms of the handbooks she might find some reference to National Northern Concentral and Global Soundfast.

All she knew so far was what was in Oistrav's records. The two accounts had been opened one after the other in September of last year. The companies had provided the necessary references (four impressive firms, one of them a top-ranking Japanese bank). They had also provided the high-level deposits needed to establish an account with a merchant bank. On the face of it there was nothing to prompt further inquiry.

Yet the fact that she could find nothing about them in the standard indexes was odd. Only rather small firms were left out so completely. And neither of these two could be small firms judging by the money transactions they carried out. A cash-flow of millions of dollars every few weeks meant big business. So where were the references?

She found them at last in the credit agencies' ratings. Both National Northern Concentral and Global Soundfast were given the highest rating, AAA. So there was an end of her anxieties. Any company that was given such a rating must be above reproach. Besides, she was needed back in the conference room to take part in an international TV linkup.

Now and again throughout the day she let her mind travel back to the two companies. What exactly did they produce? Global Soundfast might be in the music business, or in communications – there were thousands of new communications firms these days. But National Northern Concentral . . . What did they make? Were they in logging? Production of oil pipeline for Alaska?

She returned to the problem when she had time next day. She called up contacts in New York who came back with the information that NNC Inc was a fund-managing company in Colorado. Global Soundfast was in marine equipment. Who were their directors? Well, take some digging to get that for her, NNC Inc and Global Soundfast were subsidiaries of other companies, don't hold your breath.

It began to seem that it was very, very difficult to find out who owned or managed Global Soundfast and NNC Inc. Which was worrisome. Companies with ghostly directors should never have been accepted as clients by a respectable merchant bank.

Had their references been checked, she wondered? After all, it was easy enough to forge references. The more so if one of the references was supposed to be a Japanese bank. That in itself would be taken as proof of probity.

Yet even Japanese banks, she reminded herself, could have less than honest members. Only a few days ago four banking officials had been arrested for arranging loans to Tokyo gangsters known as *sokaiya*. If loans could be arranged, so could references.

She needed to step back from this for a day or so. Her thoughts were ranging too far, things were getting out of focus. And anyhow, this evening she was to have dinner with Barry. She must stop thinking about banking and think about Barry.

He rang soon after lunch to finalize the arrangement. 'I thought we'd go to that new place on the river at Richmond –'

'Oh, Barry, I wonder if . . . Could we go somewhere within the London area? It would be a lot easier for me –'

'But I've already booked, and anyhow I'll pick you up –'

'No, I won't be at the house, Barry, I'll be coming from the City –'

'Oh, really, you're not going to be kept at some tiresome conference –'

'It's nothing like that, I assure you. I'll explain everything when I see you. Can we meet somewhere in Town?' She was thinking not so much of the journey to a Richmond restaurant but the journey home afterwards. She liked to be in bed by eleven at the latest, but travelling all across London would take at least an hour.

It dawned on her, as she considered the journey home, that she was ruling out any episode at Barry's flat. Yet this was supposed to be a meeting of reconciliation. What was she going to say to Barry if he suggested a romantic interlude to seal the bargain?

She hurried on: 'I hear there's a very good new Indian restaurant in the City – the Lal Fort – I know you enjoy Oriental food –'

'The Lal Fort! It's practically in the East End, I gather –!'

'Well, you choose –'

Barry was clearly not pleased at having his plans disrupted. His tone had changed from the indulgent, I-forgive-you tone of the beginning of the conversation to irritation. She knew she would have to fall in with his next suggestion, whatever it was.

'Very well, then, we'll go to Eloise, they know me there so I'll be sure to get a table even at this late hour.'

'All right then, Barry, Eloise at what time? Seven-thirty?'

'Better make it eight,' he said huffily, 'it's quite a way for me to come, you know, not nearly as convenient as Richmond.'

She didn't reply that Soho was quite a way for her to come also. She was anxious to keep the peace.

Her mother was pleased that she was going out for an evening with Barry. 'What will you wear?' she inquired, thinking of the limited wardrobe that her daughter had brought from the house. Business dresses and casual clothes . . .

'Mm . . . It'll have to be my Derby dress but without the hat.' It was too good for a Soho evening, and might give Barry the idea she was trying very hard to please, but it was the only semi-formal item at present available.

'Oh, that *will* be nice!' And Celia, ever hopeful, wondered if her daughter expected a proposal this evening.

Barry was first at the restaurant, as always. He was determined that nothing would make him lower his standards of politeness, not even the sudden change of plan from an award-winning new place to an old familiar haunt. Restaurant Eloise was pleasant, decorated in the manner of a provençal farmhouse and famous for food to match. Since today was Tuesday, the tables were rather sparsely occupied. The music system was playing old-fashioned *bal musette*.

'How charming you look,' Barry said rather formally as she joined him.

'Thank you. I hope I haven't kept you waiting?'

'Not at all, not at all.' He summoned the waiter for pre-dinner drinks. That done, he gave his attention to the menu. 'The chef recommends the smoked chicken timbales,' he murmured. 'I thought we could have a chilled Montrachet with that, if you agree, and if we start with the tartine au saumon we could have a little Malescot Blanc, just a half bottle.'

'I leave it to you, Barry.'

'Very well.' The waiter returned, the order was given, and Lindsay nerved herself for the apology she knew he was waiting for.

'I'd like to say again how sorry I am about what happened last week, Barry. I hope you realize that I would have explained I had to be away –'

'At some one-day conference, I suppose – where was it this time? Brighton? Paris?'

'No, it was nothing like that. I had to visit Alice and my mother –'

'Visit them? But you said . . . Didn't you say Alice was with a neighbour?' he said in surprise.

'No, she'd gone to some friends in the country. It was a rather sudden arrangement.'

'I must be very stupid,' he said, frowning, 'but I don't understand why you should tell me she was at a neighbour's when she wasn't.'

'It just seemed the simplest thing at the time. I didn't expect it would turn out the way it did.'

'But why did you have to rush off to see her –'

'I was worried. She'd never been away from me before and even though Mother was with her –'

'Your mother had gone too?'

'Yes, and we had things to discuss so I had to –'

'I can't see that it necessitated a dawn departure –'

'Barry, I'm sorry, I know it seemed thoughtless –' She had a sudden mental picture of herself, silver-haired and aged ninety, getting down on arthritic knees and quavering, 'I'm sorry about that Sunday fifty years ago, darling, can you ever forgive me?'

Barry said with sharpness, 'Do you find something amusing in this?'

'I'm sorry,' she said, 'it was just a passing thought. And that must be the twelfth or thirteenth time I've said I'm sorry. I wish you'd accept my apologies.'

'It's an explanation I want,' he returned, his mouth tightening. 'You behave like a giddy goat and expect me not to be put out. Why on earth should your mother and Alice suddenly depart for the country? And why couldn't you just tell me that?'

'I didn't want anyone to know –'

'What?'

'Wait, let me explain. We got a threatening message –'

'Who did? Threatening? Who did it threaten?'

'Alice and Cecie. So I shipped them off straight away to some friends –'

'Did the police recommend that?'

'I didn't call the police. Just let me explain, Barry. The threat seems to have something to do with Oistrav's, so –'

'I'm not following you, Lindsay,' he said, his irritation growing at the mention of the bank. He always shirked the thought that she had a high-powered job at a merchant bank.

'If you'd just let me tell you without interrupting –'

'If this is how you go about business at the bank, I can't understand how you come to be such a success. You're not making any sense!'

'Barry, my mother and my little girl were threatened by

someone who seems to be connected with the bank. I got them to a safe place at once –'

'Somewhere you decided on by yourself? And where, may I ask, did you decide they'd be safe without the police being informed?'

'It doesn't matter where I chose. They're tucked away –'

'Excuse me, it does matter. I want to know.'

'But why on earth should you?' she countered, astonished.

'It would be a demonstration of trust –'

'A demonstration of –?'

'Have you any idea how insulting this is? You lied to me at first, now you come out with this weird yarn about a threat which seems to have happened *days* ago yet you never told me a word of it, and now you don't have enough confidence in me to tell me where they are! Your attitude is just so self-centred –'

'Self-centred? But for heaven's sake, Barry, I've been trying to make things right between us for days and you wouldn't even take my calls!'

'Oh, so it's all my fault, is it?' he said, leaning back in his chair and glancing around as if to ask other diners to witness how unreasonable she was. 'You walk out on me without a word, you keep all this from me, and it's my fault? You insulted me, you disregarded me, you disappointed me – and now you're *blaming* me?'

Lindsay made no reply. She was filled all at once with a great weariness. Why should she expend so much thought, so much time and energy, on mollifying this man?

'Well?' he said, waiting for her response.

'Barry,' she said, 'I've apologized and you haven't accepted. Nor have you said a word about how worrying this has been for me, not a word of sympathy or concern –'

'How can I be concerned when you don't trust me?'

'Is it a test? If I tell you where Alice and Cecie went, that proves something?'

'It would certainly make me feel I counted for something in your life. I thought we were building a relationship, Lindsay. I thought you wanted me to take the place of that missing father for Alice, and I've played the role as best I can –'

'Thank you,' she said. 'I didn't quite understand you were giving a performance. I thought you really liked her.'

'Well, good lord, you don't really think I have anything in

common with a child of four-and-a-half? I did what I could because I knew it was what you hoped for – a father figure for Alice –'

'Alice can get along quite well without play-acting –'

'Oh, of course, you can be everything – mother, father, big career woman –'

There was so much resentment in his tone that she stood up. 'I don't think this evening is going to be a success,' she remarked. 'I'm sorry I dragged you into Town on a mistaken idea –'

'Sit down. I'm not having you walk out on me again!'

'Barry, don't give me orders. It's a big mistake. Goodnight.'

She had reached the door and opened it when he caught her arm. 'Just a minute. Understand this. If you go now, it's the end.'

'Oh, I understood that when I said goodnight.'

'And you can just do it? You don't feel that you're throwing something away?'

'What I feel, Barry, is a great sense of relief.'

He was utterly taken aback at her words. He stared at her, struggling to say more, but a waiter came hurrying up. 'Is anything the matter, monsieur, madame? The service? The menu?'

Lindsay gave him a smile. 'I'm sure the food would have been excellent,' she remarked, and walked out of the door and away.

Outside she grabbed her mobile phone. She called her mother. 'I'll be home in about twenty minutes, Cecie –'

'*What?* I thought you might –' Celia had half-expected not to see her daughter till morning.

'I haven't eaten yet – have you?'

'Well, I've just taken some things out of the freezer –'

'Put them back. As soon as I've got out of these glad rags, we'll go out for a meal.'

When she reached the flat Celia was hovering in the hall, waiting for her. 'What on earth happened?'

'Barry and I had a disagreement.'

'But what about? I thought you and he –'

'No, Mother,' Lindsay said, going into her bedroom to change.

Celia followed her.

'What do you mean, no? I thought it was an understood thing, practically –'

Lindsay was unzipping the Derby dress and stepping out of it. 'No, it wasn't.'

'But *Lindsay* –'

'Where shall we go to eat? Have you noticed any good restaurants on your walks?'

'Lindsay, please talk to me. What's happened between you and Barry?'

Lindsay was carefully putting the dress on its hanger. 'I just . . . found out I didn't like him much.'

'Didn't like him? Don't talk nonsense! You're very fond of him, and he's *devoted* to you! And he thinks the world of Alice –'

'No he doesn't.'

'What are you saying? He dotes on her, and she adores him.'

'Mother,' she said, kicking off the pale blue shoes, 'believe me, he doesn't give two hoots for Alice. It suddenly came to me that she'd had one father who walked out on her and I might have given her a second one who'd just use her as a way to manipulate me.'

'Lindsay!' Celia sat down slowly on the dressing table chair. 'It sounds as if . . . as if . . .'

'Yes, it's over.'

'But I thought you and he would be getting married!'

Her daughter pulled on jeans and a shirt. 'We don't seem to have too much luck with men, do we?' she said, with a smile that only half-masked her disillusion. 'Come on, I'm starving – let's go.'

'What's Alice going to say?' Celia said mournfully as she followed her out to the hall. 'He's become so important in her little world.'

Lindsay turned to face her. 'It was all a sham. He doesn't care about her. Alice will have to manage without him.'

They were silent as the lift took them down to the lobby. There Celia linked her arm comfortingly through her daughter's. 'We managed before,' she said stoutly. 'We'll manage again.'

Lindsay relaxed at the consoling gesture. By and by she would explain what had parted her from Barry, but for the moment Celia was concerned to be supportive to her. Yes, they had managed before and would manage again.

But before, they had had no anonymous enemy threatening them.

Chapter Eleven

Celia decided to go to Essex next day to visit Alice, since Wednesday was one of the days the contract cleaners came to attend to the flat. She knew she wouldn't be able to work at her computers with vacuum cleaners around her. Besides, the idea that the little girl was to lose Barry from her circle of grownups somehow made her seem vulnerable, in need of comfort.

'But don't tell her about Barry,' begged Lindsay. 'I'll do that when the time comes.'

'All right,' Celia agreed, relieved. She wouldn't have wanted the task of breaking such bad news, anyhow.

Lindsay was up and out to work long before her mother set off for Burnham-on-Crouch. Sudin, who had refused to be parted from Lindsay even though she had moved to Docklands, collected her as usual at six-thirty. The journey to Pewter Lane was much shorter so there was less time for conversation. But he had news to impart.

'I drove by your house in Putney yesterday,' he said. 'Just to make sure everything is all right.'

'Oh – that's very good of you, Sudin, but I've got a security firm looking after it –'

'Really? Well, that is very sensible, I should have thought of that. Probably that is who it was.'

'Who what was?'

'The man keeping watch.'

'Where?' she said, immediately alarmed. She'd hired general surveillance, but that meant a drive-by every so many hours and an immediate response to the alarm system. There should have been nobody keeping watch.

'Well, he was sitting in a car a few yards down the road, looking at the gate to your drive. This was about four-thirty yesterday afternoon. I had had my sleep. I was going out to buy an evening paper and thought I might as well just drive past –'

'But Sudin, you don't live anywhere near –'

'Oh, in a car, what does that matter? But when I drove by, there was this Rover, a little way from your gate on the opposite side. It seemed strange.'

It was indeed strange, for the few houses neighbouring Lindsay's had capacious garages so there was no need for anyone to park in the road. Occasionally at night courting couples took advantage of the leafy quietness. Now and then a birdwatcher would leave his car there while he went up with his binoculars on to the Heath by the footpath in which Lindsay's road ended. But in general the short length of Edgefold Road was quiet and deserted.

'Did you get the car number?' she asked.

He looked abashed. 'Alas no. I didn't turn into the road, you see, I drove past the end of it, and by the time I had found a place to turn and come back, he was gone.'

'I wonder if he's been there before?'

'I am afraid I cannot help you there. Yesterday was the first time I thought of driving past. I wish I had thought of it before –'

'Why should you? No, no, it was very kind of you to think of it but don't go back.'

'No?'

'No, I don't want to alert him.' She thought about it. 'The first time, when he sent a threat though the post, he rang next day to see how I reacted. This last time, he didn't ring next day, or at least if he did he left no message on the machine. But he may have rung since then and got the information on the answering machine – which tells him all calls should be referred to another number.'

'That may have made him think you had gone away.'

'And he went to check. Yes, that's probably it.'

'And now he knows you are not living in the house at the moment.'

'Yes.'

'Is that a good thing or a bad thing?'

'I've no idea, Sudin. The fact is, I've no idea why he's threatening me in the first place. He seems to think I'm a danger to him, but in what way I haven't been able to work out.'

They drew up in Pewter Lane. As she prepared to get out he said, 'Take care, then, Mrs Dunforth.'

'I will. See you tomorrow.'

Part of the morning was taken up with a team conference over whether or not to part with U.S. Lennox, whose price had risen considerably since Lindsay bought the shares at launch. Then there was the planning of an environmentally friendly portfolio for a millionaire client who had unexpectedly developed a conscience. She was preparing to leave for a business lunch when her mother rang.

'Thought you'd like to know – your daughter's unlikely to grieve over the loss of Barry when she hears of it.'

'Really? What makes you think so?'

'She's fallen head over heels in love with someone else.'

'Good heavens! Anyone I know?'

'No, a new arrival, from a branch of the Goswami family in Birmingham. His name's Jamnu and he's ten years old.'

Lindsay burst out laughing. 'Well, that's a smaller age difference than between her and the others she's adored. How does Jamnu feel about it?'

'As far as I can see he thinks she's a pest. She doesn't seem to mind, she follows him around and lets him order her about. He arrived here after we left on Sunday, he's convalescing after doing himself some damage in a bust-up with a skateboard.'

'It's wonderful, isn't it, the way they just take people in?'

'They've invited me to stay overnight, but I think I'll come home – I've moved all my computing stuff there and though I could borrow Mr Goswami's, they need it for business. See you around tea-time?'

'I may stay on a bit, Cecie. I want to make a few inquiries about those American firms.' She was speaking on her mobile phone, but all the same she avoided mentioning the names NNC Incorporated and Global Soundfast.

'I thought you had people in New York doing that for you?'

'Yes, but they've come up with nothing so far and time's going by. I thought I'd do a bit myself this evening.'

'Okay, then. Shall I cook? I'm being given a basket full of Oriental delights to bring home.'

Lindsay gave her blessing to the project, but her attention was on the lighthearted information Celia had given her. She felt encouraged by it. After all, children could be fickle: they fell into adoration of pop stars and cartoon characters and footballers, yet soon switched to some new hero. Barry might very soon be shut away in some mental attic along with the Lion King.

The lunch was in the directors' dining room of a prestigious financial company. Rather austere, high-ceilinged, with quiet waiters in old-fashioned tails to serve them. No wine, only mineral water, because financiers ought to keep a level head even after lunch. This gathering was a regular engagement, simply to keep friendly contact going. The Chairman of Oistrav's, Henry Wishaw, always deputed the task to someone else because he was fond of good food and Noovie Naismith always avoided it if he could because he was a wine buff. Lindsay went oftener than others because she didn't mind cuisine minceur and mineral water.

She walked back to the bank afterwards, partly for the exercise and partly to buy a sandwich to take into the office; she'd need sustenance until she got home to Celia's Oriental goodies. She intended to stay on late into the evening.

As she entered the foyer of the bank, to her dismay Barry rose from a chair to meet her.

'Barry!'

'I've been waiting here,' he told her. 'They wouldn't let me in without verification –'

'I'm sorry,' she began, and caught herself up. Here she was, being wrongfooted again by Barry. She went on in a less apologetic tone, 'There's a strict security routine here. No one gets in without either an identification card or an appointment.'

'Utter nonsense! And very bad manners –'

'What are you doing here, Barry?' she interrupted.

'I came to take you to lunch and sort things out –'

'There's nothing to sort out. That was all dealt with last night.'

'I can't allow things to end that way. We've got to talk.' He glanced about the lobby, taking in the porter at the entry desk and a gardener snipping dead leaves from the bougainvillaea in the island display of leafage. 'This isn't very private. Can we go up to your office?'

'My office is even less private,' she said, thinking of that fish-bowl of glass walls. How the dealers would love it, to have a lovers' quarrel going on in full view.

She could have invited him in, and taken him to the quietude of the loggia. But that would mean having him fill out an information form and pin an identification tag on his lapel. She could see he was in no mood to accept any of that.

'We'd better go outside,' she said.

'Outside!'

'There's a nice shady seat under the acacia tree.' Without waiting for his assent she led the way out of the bank and across the small paved courtyard to the bench. There she sat down, and after a hesitation Barry sat also, but upright and unrelaxed.

She waited, looking at him. He said, 'What did you mean last night, when you said you felt relief?'

A bubble of laughter rose up within her. So he hadn't come out of a desperate passion, he'd come out of pique. She'd made a slighting remark, which he couldn't accept. He was going to take her to task.

But there was no laughter, only seriousness when she made her reply. 'I meant I was glad that we were parting.'

'Glad?'

'Yes, I'd begun to find our relationship a terrible burden.'

'I don't understand you! A burden? When we've had such good times together, when we've been so *right* for each other?'

She sighed. 'If you mean in bed, I have to tell you that to me there are more important things –'

'Oh yes, your career, the all-important world of money! Let me tell you I found it very offensive when you wouldn't even try to explain your problem last night. The implication is that I'm too dense to understand anything to do with the bank –'

'I've never said or thought that. But the fact is, when I've tried to talk to you about the bank, your eyes glaze over. You've never wanted to know.'

'That's absurd! I've been to gatherings with your friends, I've never had any difficulty in holding conversations with them –'

'They talked to you about junk bonds, did they, or copper futures?'

'What?'

'If we had a tape-recording of the conversation I bet it would prove to be mostly about generalities, or your subject, fine art. You never listen when the talk is about finance.'

'Well, if you must know, I find conversation about money rather gross.'

'Exactly. And that's why I was relieved at breaking up.'

' "Relieved" – it's an extraordinary thing to say –'

'I found I was tired of being made to feel inferior because I deal with money. After all, you deal with money too –'

'I do? What an absurd thing to say!'

She ignored the fact that he was calling her absurd and tried to be reasonable. 'When you're up there on the podium calling for bids for some ancient piece of carving, don't you ask for money? Don't you want as much money for it as you can get?'

'Yes, but that's on behalf of my client –'

'Whose money do you imagine I'm dealing with? It's not my own, it's other people's money.' Other people's dreams, she thought, but didn't utter it aloud because she had a feeling he would once again call it absurd.

'So you're telling me you're glad to be breaking up because I wouldn't take an interest in your career? I might have known it would be something like that.'

'Oh, it's nothing like that!' she said, getting to her feet. 'This is a waste of time, Barry. I've got to get back to my desk –'

'Just stop where you are! I haven't finished –'

'But I have. Goodbye, Barry, and this time it's final.'

He grabbed her wrist to hold her back.

Tad Tadiecski, coming into the courtyard from Pewter Lane, was presented with an extraordinary sight. Lindsay Dunforth, in her demure dress of black and cerise silk, was having a wrestling match with a big, square-built guy in a Savile Row suit. Really weird. But different strokes for different folks, he said to himself, and prepared to pass without appearing to notice.

At that moment Lindsay gave a little gasp. Her handbag dropped at her feet and the little plastic bag with the sandwich shop logo flew out of her hand, across the flagstones, to land at his feet.

Hard to ignore a thing like that. Besides, that gasp had been one of pain.

He reached them in one stride. 'Excuse me,' he said, laying a hand on the well-tailored arm.

The man rounded on him. 'Get out!' he snarled. 'This is none of your business –'

'Seems like it is,' Tad said, taking away his hand but staying close. 'Can't let you manhandle the head of the Investment Portfolio Department.'

The formality and weight of the title made Barry pause. The crimson tide of rage receded from his features. He became aware of where he was and what he was doing. He squared his shoulders and fingered his tie as if to straighten it. He made a sound as if he were about to say something but decided against it, and with a glare of anger marched out of the courtyard.

Lindsay sank down on the bench again.

'Are you all right?' Tad inquired, leaning over her.

'Yes, thanks.' But she was rubbing her wrist.

'He hurt you?'

'Oh, it's nothing.'

He gathered up her handbag, retrieved the sandwich carrier, and brought them to her. It was to give her a moment to recover. 'Okay now?' he asked.

'Yes, quite all right.'

'Er . . . was that something personal or was it a disgruntled investor?'

That brought a faint smile to her lips, he was glad to see. 'He was certainly disgruntled. But it wasn't to do with investment.' Except of time and emotion, she added inwardly. A year of investment in a friendship that had seemed to hold promise. Why had she not seen earlier that it was never going to work?

Because her little girl had liked him, because he was a *man*, a heroic figure in Alice's small world. Because Celia had approved of him. Because he had seemed dependable, established in his career, a settled and reliable figure – unlike her missing husband, unlike the lover she'd chosen when she was first left alone. A good choice, 'husband material' – husband material, perhaps, but not for her.

She went with Tad Tadiecski into the foyer. She felt his eyes on her as she ran her card through the machine and made a special effort not to let her hand tremble. She very much wished he would disappear tactfully, but there was no escape from going up together in the lift.

Should she ask him not to mention the episode to the others? She was already under an obligation and shrank from asking him for a favour. And besides, what did it matter if he gossiped? Sooner or later her colleagues would guess that she and Barry had parted. Romantic relationships seldom remained unknown among the dealers.

As they stepped out of the lift together he said, 'You okay? Want a coffee or anything?'

'I'm fine, thanks. And thanks again for the rescue.'

'Any time.' He ran his card through the lock of the department door, standing back to allow her to enter. She gave him a smile before walking across the dealing room to her office.

Boy, she was cool. Most women would have had the shakes after a tussle like that. And who was the man? It was very interesting.

Luckily for Lindsay it was a quiet afternoon. After a decent interval she got her secretary Millicent to fetch her a cup of coffee from the machine. The caffeine revived her. She dictated letters and the last part of a report for next day's board meeting. Routine chores, very reassuring.

The big room began to empty by four o'clock. Lindsay too went out, her sandwich having disintegrated due to its impact with the flagstones. She ate a quick meal at a nearby snackbar already preparing to close as the City denizens headed home. She went back into the bank at five, greeting Gresham the night porter as he came on duty.

'Evening, miss,' he said, and he was already unfolding the sporting columns of the *Evening Standard* before she'd finished threading her entry card through the machine.

At her desk she switched on her computer again to access the software that would give her some of the search indexes of the financial world. Over her meal she'd scribbled down a few headings: it was no use forging through every level of search, she must make a basic premise and work from that.

The premise she'd chosen was that in working back from subsidiary company to parent, she must always expect the parent to be yet *another* subsidiary. She might come in time to the originating firm, but she was almost sure she would find a dummy board of directors.

In other words, she was seeking the spider in the centre of the web – but when she found it she expected it to be less than helpful. What she sought to prove was that a fraud was actually taking place, by a means nicknamed in financial circles a 'layer cake'. Layer after layer of deceit, until in the end those claiming the money were so far distanced from its beginnings that no one could prove anything – and then the funds could be withdrawn from the last bank, cleansed, untainted, apparently honest.

She was so taken up by her pursuit of information that the hours slipped by. The cleaning staff arrived. A turbaned head was put round her door and a muffled, 'Oh, 'scuse me' disturbed her. The big Jamaican woman said apologetically, 'I can come back later.'

'Give this room a miss for tonight, would you mind? I'm busy on something.'

'I'll just empty your wastepaper basket, then, eh?'

She did so, peering edgily at the computer. 'Never understand 'em,' she muttered as she went out, and whether she meant computers or people who stayed late to work at them, Lindsay wasn't quite sure.

It was the tension in her own shoulders that brought her to a pause at last. She knew, as everyone who used computers knew, that it was wrong to sit too long without a break. She rose, stretched, bent two or three times to touch her toes.

And while she was touching her toes for the fourth time, she heard a sound out in the big office.

She stopped dead. Silence. Then a moment later a faint thud as if someone had walked into a chair.

Lindsay stayed bent down. Carefully crouching, she moved to the glass wall of her office. She raised her head to look over the waist-high opaque glass through clear panes at the dim vastness beyond.

The light in the big trading room was always shaded by perpendicular blinds at the windows. This was so that the computer screens could be read without strain. Now that evening had fallen over the City, the light was even lower. She could see nothing.

Then a faint illumination sprang up. Someone had switched on a computer screen.

She crawled back across her own room to switch off her machine. Luckily its screen faced inwards into her office, not outwards towards the trading floor, so the newcomer hadn't noticed it.

She sat on the floor by her desk, thinking.

So, someone had come in at ten minutes past nine to use a computer. Well, there was nothing criminal in that. People did come in sometimes, to contact a country whose time zone was different from London, to finalize a deal, to tidy up some report or just pursue an idea.

On the other hand, someone unable to hack into the bank's system, someone without the computer know-how of, say, Celia, needed access to information on Oistrav's files. It would have to be something that would look odd if accessed during ordinary working hours, something not available on the ordinary company intra-net.

Lindsay crouched, inactive, considering her next move. She very much wanted to know who was sitting at that computer. And after all, she herself had a perfect right to be here. All she need do was stroll out of her office and say, 'Hello there, working late too?'

Right, that was the course she would follow. She stood up, walked to her office door, and opened it.

It creaked in the stillness before she had it fully open.

There was a muffled exclamation of alarm. The screen was switched off. A figure leapt up from a chair. There was the thud of footsteps running on the carpeted floor.

Lindsay darted among the desks, trying to reach the department's door before the intruder. But the door opened and swished shut while she was entangled with a length of cable two-thirds of the way across the room. When she got to the door and pulled it open, the corridor was empty.

Where had he gone? Where *would* he go? Out, of course, but by what route? She dashed to the lift. It took so long to come it was clearly a long way off, perhaps on the ground floor. Had he gone down to the hall? He would have to pass Gresham and run his card through the machine to log himself out.

But that seemed to be the obvious route. She went down in the lift. Gresham had put away his newspaper and had phones in his ears, listening to a Walkman. She had to walk round in front of him before he was aware of her.

'Oh, hello, Mrs Dunforth, off home?'

'Not just yet. Has someone else just gone out?'

He took the earpieces out. 'Gone out? Not recent, miss, not since the cleaners left at seven-thirty.'

'Can I see?' She came round behind the desk to look at the screen which recorded who was in the office. According to its listing, only herself and Gresham were now in the building. She called up the last exits, all grouped around the time-recorder at seven-thirty: they showed cards with the identity code of the cleaning staff. In the hours before six a clump of clerical staff and messengers had left and before that, in dribs and drabs, department heads and dealers.

The twenty-four-hour record would be wiped off at midnight and would start again, recording those who arrived at seven or seven-thirty in the morning.

So . . . No one was in the building except herself and Gresham.

Everybody had gone home by six p.m., then the cleaners had come at six-thirty and left an hour later. Yet she *knew* a third person had been, perhaps still was, in the bank.

She was totally puzzled. How had he got in in the first place? How had he tricked the computer into letting him into the bank?

Perhaps . . . Perhaps he had never left the bank.

Between the hours of four and six the bank staff left in a disorderly muddle. Some left early because the deals were finished for the day. Some worked a measured nine to five and went home with the rush-hour crowd. Some stayed on to work out some problem. All had to log themselves out with their electronic card.

But the vestibule of Oistrav's was an elegant, decorative place. The teak desk for the porter faced the entrance, a little right of centre as you came in. Here you had to offer yourself for the recording machine and, if you were a visitor, be given a name-tag with the time of your arrival printed on it.

To the left of the porter's desk was a big island display of greenery in a great trough of earth with a marble surround. The plants it contained were luxurious, Mediterranean or semi-tropical – agave, yucca, bougainvillaea and palm. A beautiful indoor garden. But if you looked at it another way, a perfect screen to hide from the porter's gaze.

All you had to do if you wanted to sign out and come in again without being seen was walk round the island while one or two others shielded you momentarily. Then you could quietly walk to the back of the hall, go through the door of a ground floor department, thread your way through corridors, and wait in one of the cloakrooms – or even the comfort of a secluded corner of the loggia – until the building was deserted.

It was as security consultants kept telling them – a building was only as safe as constant vigilance made it. A night porter reading the racing columns, a momentary crowd in the lobby . . .

But if he had signed out and quietly slipped back in, where was he now? She had interrupted him in whatever he'd intended to do in the dealing room. His swift flight might have taken him anywhere.

Should she institute a search? Call up the security firm who provided the messenger staff and the porters, and have their men look in every room?

It could take all night. And besides, the intruder might have gone out by a fire door while she was questioning Gresham. The fire doors were required by law. They opened from inside and for security reasons could not be opened from outside. If he had gone out of a fire door, he was long gone by now.

Whoever he was, he had been thwarted for this time.

Gresham was staring at her with some bewilderment. It was to say the least of it unusual that one of the biggies, a departmental head, should come round behind his desk to stare at the security screen. 'Is anything wrong, Mrs Dunforth?'

'I thought I heard someone a minute ago, upstairs in the dealing room.'

Gresham flicked a hand at the screen. 'Nah,' he said, 'everybody's gone. Probably a draught – those long blinds at the windows, they flap sometimes if there's a draught.'

Lindsay forbore to point out that the dealing room was air-conditioned because of the computers, and had no draughts.

'I'm going back upstairs to get my handbag and then I'll be down again in a minute,' she said. Meaning, If I don't come down again in five minutes, hit the alarms.

But though the lift felt constricting and the vast dealing floor very spooky, she reached her office without molestation. She picked up her handbag and hurried out.

'G'night,' said Gresham as she signed herself out, his Walkman already back in operation.

She chose the security of a taxi home to the flat rather than the Docklands Railway. As she came in, delicious aromas were floating in the air. It was somehow very comforting, like coming home from school to find Mummy in an apron baking a cake . . . She went to the kitchen, to find her mother measuring cornflour into a bowl. She put her arms round her waist to give her a hug.

'What's that for?' Celia said, and turned in her embrace to look at her. 'Hi, what's wrong?'

'I had a bit of a scare at the bank.'

'What? Something you found out on the computer?'

'No, somebody came into the dealing room and when I walked out to speak to him, he ran off.'

'Who?' Celia demanded, dropping the measuring spoon into the bowl to send up a little cloud of cornflour. 'Who was it?'

'I don't know. I didn't get a proper look, only a sort of silhouette in the dimness. Somebody about medium height, fairly stocky –' Tad, she thought. Was it Tad? But surely Tad was taller than the man who had run from the desk. Walking beside him at lunch time, she'd felt he was a head taller than herself. The man who had run out of the room – had he been that tall?

'You'd find out who it was from the desk,' Celia said. Though she'd never been to the bank in business hours, she'd gone there for social occasions such as Peter's retirement party. She knew you had to sign in and sign out.

'No, according to the computer the building was empty except for me and the desk porter.'

'That's not possible, dear. The security system –'

'The security system can be hoodwinked if you just nip round the plants in the hall. Or perhaps –'

'What?'

'One of the cleaners? No, because they all signed out correctly at seven-thirty.'

'Lindsay,' her mother said, taking her hands and drawing her to a kitchen chair, 'this is getting too serious. You could have been hurt tonight!'

'I don't think so, Mother. Whoever he was, he was as scared as I was, he ran like a deer the minute he heard my office door open.'

'All the same . . . Shouldn't you speak to someone about it? I thought you were going to speak to Peter?'

She said nothing. Celia frowned. 'What's the matter? What is it about Peter?'

'Mother, *he* might be involved in this.'

'Who? Peter?' Celia was aghast. 'Don't be silly.'

'I'm not being silly. I told you a while ago, it could be someone at director's level who's behind all this. Why not Peter?'

'But Peter . . . Peter . . . it's unthinkable!'

'So are the people behind most insider deals.'

'But what reason have you for . . . for even beginning to suspect Peter Gruman?'

'He was keen for Tad Tadiecski to be taken on. When I went to him to express some doubts, he even took the trouble to ring a contact in New York to get verification for me.'

'Well then!'

'But I've checked it out through a friend in New York and Tad's entire story is a fiction.'

'But you said –'

'I said Peter rang a contact. But I never saw the number he

dialled.' Briefly she sketched in the events and the subsequent information supplied by Buddy. 'The long and the short of it is, Cecie, I don't know who to trust now.'

'But it wouldn't have been Peter in the dealing room tonight,' her mother pointed out. 'Peter can hardly walk, let alone run.'

'No, but it could have been some henchman.'

Tad Tadiecski, she thought. It's essential to find out more about Tad Tadiecski.

Chapter Twelve

The first thing Lindsay did next morning when the main office staff arrived was to phone the housekeeper. 'I think you ought to have the floral display in the hall cut back a bit,' she said.

'I beg your pardon, Mrs Dunforth?'

'The plants obscure the porter's view from his desk. Someone could slip in without his being aware of it.'

'Oh, I hardly think –'

'Aren't we always getting memos telling us to be security conscious?' she broke in.

'Well . . .'

'Have those plants thinned out.'

'Yes, Mrs Dunforth.' She could almost hear the housekeeper muttering, 'Fusspot,' as she rang off.

Millicent appeared as she put down the instrument. 'Millicent, there's something I want you to do immediately. You know that conference at Marseilles?'

'Yes?'

'Ring through to them, will you?' She issued her instructions, then turned her mind to other matters for the next half hour. When Millicent appeared at her door with the folder of information about the conference, she rose and took it from her. 'I'll be in Tad's office if you need me.'

She tapped at his open door. He looked up from the papers he was examining. 'Department stores,' he remarked. 'Never believe anything you read in the balance sheet of a department store if the work's done at year-end. Keeping track of their Christmas sales sends the accountants into such a tizzy they make amazing mistakes.'

'What's that you're looking at?'

'That new chain in Australia.'

'Aha. Might be interesting.' She came farther into the room, giving the folder a little flourish. 'Tad, I feel I owe you a little something for that knight-errantry yesterday. So I thought I'd give you an all-expenses-paid trip to see your father.'

He stared. 'My father?'

'In Arles, isn't he? There's a conference this weekend on Investment in Wetland Crops – it's about the Camargue, of course, but it could have relevance to other warm-climate marshland, of which we know there's a lot in Pacific Rim countries. The conference is in Marseilles, so you could make a side trip to visit your father. Nice, don't you think?'

'But . . . so late in the day . . . getting a booking . . .'

'No problem. Oistrav's generally books up for anything that seems likely to be interesting. I thought of going myself,' she lied, 'but something's come up and I can't go, and my second in command – that's Nan, of course – she's already signed up for a thing in Prague this weekend.'

'I don't know if –'

'I've made you a little list of the questions I'd have asked if I'd been there myself.' She'd typed them up the minute she got into her office. 'I'd really like to have them asked.' She held out the folder with the slip of paper sticking out at the top.

Tad recognized the voice of a head of department speaking. 'Yes, of course,' he said, rising to accept the documents.

'Airline tickets, hotel booking, it's all there. The hotel's the Ste Lucienne, I think you'll like it. Of course the booking is for two so if you like to take along a friend . . . ?'

'It's really kind of you.'

'Not at all. I believe you haven't had much chance to get over to see your father so far? At least, I haven't heard you mention it.'

'No . . . Settling in at a new job, in a new city, you know . . .'

'I hope you find everything is going well with him. Give him my regards, and bring back one of his paintings if you can.'

She saw him suppress a smile. She couldn't quite read its meaning. It was almost as if he knew he'd been finessed.

So far, so good, she thought.

It was a busy day. She gave her report at the board meeting, she supervised the sale of U.S. Lennox and with the profit began a re-investment programme. She checked that the half-yearly statements would be ready for despatch to her clients at the end of the month. Then came lunch time.

Soon after one o'clock the dealing room was almost empty. It was a very warm June day. The girls were in summer dresses and sandals, the men had taken off their jackets to work in shirt sleeves. When going out to lunch, it seemed right to leave jackets slung on the backs of chairs.

In Tad's office, his jacket hung in just that way. Lindsay went into the room with a reference book in her hand as a pretext. But the few people still at their desks didn't even look up.

She put the reference book on a shelf behind Tad's desk. She accidentally bumped into his chair. His jacket fell off. She picked it up to hang it back in place.

Her hand flickered into the inside pocket. No card case or wallet, he'd taken them out with him to lunch. But there were two or three envelopes. They would do just as well. She plucked them out to read the address.

Flat five, twenty-two Burslow Street, Islington.

She returned the letters to the pocket, brushed an imaginary speck of dust off the jacket sleeve, and left the room.

After that felonious interval she herself went to lunch. Then she had a long conversation with an Inland Revenue adviser on a problem concerning windfall profits. Mr Wishaw called her in at three for a review of her client list – could she take two more, as a special favour to him?

She went to the City leisure centre on her way home for a long swim and a massage. She sat with Celia while she went through some of her tricks on the computer, took her out to dinner, went to bed early, and slept like a log.

On Friday she checked to see that Tad had brought a flight bag with him for his trip to Marseilles. She would dearly have liked to see him off at Heathrow, but that would have been going a little too far. However, she rang the airline immediately after flight time to ask if a message could be put through to Mr Tadiecski before he boarded.

'Oh, I'm sorry, madam, the flight took off ten minutes ago –'

'No!'

'I'm afraid so.'

'Was Mr Tadiecski on it? He might have waited for the next one.'

'Well, I'll put a message out, but if he does not respond I'm afraid we must assume Mr Tadiecski was aboard at take-off.'

'Oh never mind . . . I'll try to reach him in Marseilles.'

'I hope you do, madam. Good evening.'

So he was gone, safely gone to Marseilles. Not due back until Sunday evening.

'You're coming to Essex tomorrow?' Celia inquired over a home-cooked meal that night. 'I want to get some more of those marvellous cucumber things.'

'No, there's something I want to do tomorrow. I'll join you there on Sunday.'

Celia didn't query it.

On the grounds that those bearing gifts are always welcome, Lindsay stopped at a shop in Holborn at mid-morning on Saturday. She bought an 'executive toy', a good-looking affair consisting of magnets, metal bars, and little mirrors. She asked for this to be wrapped in blue metallic paper with gold ribbon bows. She then took herself to twenty-two Burslow Street.

The address was an old-fashioned but sturdy block of flats. There was a lobby with an entryphone. She rang the buzzer for Flat Five, but there was no reply. She rang the buzzer for Flat Six, and after a little delay got a crackly voice. 'Hello?'

'I've got a parcel for Mr Tadiecski in Flat Five but I can't get an answer. Could I leave the parcel with you?'

'Eh?'

'A parcel for Flat Five. Could you take it in?'

'Are you Parcel Force?'

Do I sound like Parcel Force, thought Lindsay. 'No, I'm a friend of Mr Tadiecski. Could I come up, please?'

'Oh, I s'pose so.'

The buzzer sounded and the door gave way to her push. She went up to the third floor in a reasonably active lift. At the door of Flat Six an elderly gentleman in a Noel Coward dressing gown was waiting. He had clearly started his day only recently. His eyebrows went up when he saw the parcel.

'Oh, a present?'

'It's his birthday,' Lindsay said, putting on a simpering smile.

'You don't say.' He held out his hands for it.

'I suppose you haven't got a key to let me into his flat? It would be nice to leave it somewhere . . . you know . . . intimate . . . On his bed, perhaps.'

The neighbour woke up a little and began to get into the spirit of the thing. 'I'd love to help, dearie, but I don't have a key. Used to have Mrs Goodyard's, just in case, she having a tendency to fall over, poor dear, but when I suggested it to Mr Tadjiki, he didn't seem to want to.'

'Oh, what a pity. I suppose your own door key doesn't fit?'

'No, no, all separate locks.' He paused in thought. 'Tell you what – the lady that does the cleaning – Mrs Amalia – she's got a key, she'd let you in.'

'Where is she, then? In this building?'

'No, no, darlin', the rent here would be a bit steep for the likes of Mrs Amalia. But she lives . . . let's see . . . it's above a shop in . . . Oh, I know, I've got the telephone number, no problem, we can ring her up and ask her to pop round with the key.'

She was invited into an untidy flat whose furnishing had seen better days. Many posters of bygone vaudeville acts adorned the walls. Her host began to look for the telephone but it seemed to be lost under magazines and copies of *The Stage*.

'You could use my mobile,' she offered, producing it.

'Oh, I say! Dinkie little thing. Just a minute.' She half expected another search for the telephone number but when she followed him into his kitchen she saw that the door of one of the kitchen cupboards was his telephone book.

He read off the number aloud as he tapped the buttons. After a moment the call was answered.

'Mrs Amalia? Mrs Amalia, is that you?' He turned to Lindsay in exasperation. 'Can't hear for some kid wailing.' Then to the phone, 'It's me, Mr Fotherill at Burslow Street – yes, Flat Six – no, not this time, no spills to mop up. Listen, Mrs Amalia, could you pop round with the key to Number Five?'

A long pause. Mr Fotherill shook his head at her. 'She's not keen. Saturday's shopping day, she's getting ready to go to Sainsbury's.'

'Tell her I'd make it worth her while,' prompted Lindsay.

'Right you are. Mrs Amalia? Mrs Amalia? This young lady here, she's got a surprise present she wants to leave for Mr Tadiyok, she says it's worth a quid or two to you to let her in.'

That seemed to be entirely different. Mrs Amalia said she would be there in ten minutes and in fact was there in only a little more than that. 'I don't stop, I got baby in the hall in baby-buggy.' She looked pointedly at Lindsay, who at once opened her handbag.

The coins dropped into Mrs Amalia's plump hand. The key to Flat Five was put into Lindsay's. 'You live it on ledge in the hall when you go, I pick it up on my way home from shops.'

'Yes, thanks a million, Mrs Amalia. And listen, don't mention this to Mr Tadiecski, I want him to be mystified.'

'Missto fie?' said Mrs Amalia, in her impenetrable Croatian accent. But she nodded as yet another coin fell into her palm. 'I say nodding,' she agreed.

Mr Fotherill gave Lindsay a conspiratorial wink as he went back into his flat. Lindsay put the key in the lock of next door. The door opened. She stepped in, closed it, and stood holding her breath.

Not a sound. She waited for a full minute, listening. Nothing. The flat was empty.

Of course it was. She'd sent Tad to Marseilles to ensure it would be empty.

She moved from the tiny vestibule into the living room. It was furnished in an old-fashioned way. Perhaps the tapestry-covered armchairs and oak bookcase had belonged to the lady who lived here before. She set down the gift-wrapped package on the coffee table, glancing through the magazines there – financial journals, the *Economist* for this week and last, two or three American magazines, a copy of the *New Yorker*. She examined the room. The books in the glass-fronted bookcase must have come with the flat, they were mostly classical novels and out-of-date travel books.

What she wanted was to look through his desk, but where was it? She went out of the living room and into what was clearly the dining room. Old-fashioned oak table, four matching chairs and sideboard, empty decanters, the air still and rather musty as if the room were never used.

There were two other rooms. The next was the bedroom, but a glance showed her the same dark 1930s furniture, a double bed with its Indian cotton counterpane neatly spread, a big wardrobe with linenfold panelling, a dressing table with triple mirrors. She shied away from the thought of going in unless she had to and went instead to the next room.

Here she felt she had struck gold. This too had been a bedroom. The bed was pushed against the far wall. On its surface various cardboard boxes and cartons had been piled but they were clearly empty. What held her immediate attention was the trestle table that had been set up in the space cleared by pushing the bed aside.

On its surface was ranged a formidable array of computer equipment, including add-ons whose use she couldn't guess at. She saw a printer, a sound system of more than average range, a modem, a stack container for CD-ROMs, a scanner and a calculator. She walked almost timidly into the room, and sat down in the chair facing the mainframe. She switched on.

The screen came to life. A logo flickered and vanished. A word appeared: Enter. She tapped Enter. The screen said: Who?

Who?

Of course it would be Tad Tadiecski. She typed in Tadiecski.

Incorrect Entry, said the screen.

She tried Tad.

Incorrect Entry.

She used up all the variations of his name she could think of – Mr Tadiecski, Mr Tad Tadiecski, William Tadiecski, Mr William Tadiecski, William, Bill . . .

The screen was obdurate. She had failed to find the entry code.

She sat for a moment in thought then tried all the famous names of American history that occurred to her: George Washington, Benjamin Franklin, Davy Crockett, Orville Wright, Franklin Roosevelt. She even tried Frank Sinatra. It was no use.

She switched off. She needed Celia here, to clue her up as to how to unearth the password. But she had come here really to get some clues about Tad's out-of-the-office life. Who was he, what did he do in his spare time when he wasn't snooping round Oistrav's? If the computer wouldn't let her in, she must try elsewhere.

There was a tallboy in the room which might once have served as a dressing table. She opened the drawers one after the other. Stationery supplies in the top, instruction manuals for the machines, still in their polythene wrap, in the second, various electronic gadgets in the third, some in slender zipped cases.

She recognized one of them as a Psion organizer, got it out, and switched it on. It seemed to be a diary mainly, with initials at some of the dates and cryptic numerals at others. There was a small calculator which showed up much what you'd expect from someone in a bank – calculations of interest, notes of differential rates.

She closed the last drawer and stood in thought. Nothing in the tallboy to help her. Her eyes wandered round the room.

A printer. Where was the print-out?

Almost everybody she knew who owned a computer and printer left print-out lying around. But there was nothing in the printer's carrier nor in the drawers of the tallboy when she looked through them again.

There was a wardrobe. The door was locked but the key was in the lock. She unlocked and opened it. It contained three airline suitcases neatly stacked but when she painstakingly got them out one by one they proved to be empty.

She put them back and relocked the wardrobe. Once more she stood at a loss.

Nothing. Empty. Innocent.

Too empty. Too innocent. It was as if Tad quickly disposed of anything that would give insight into his activities.

Where was the print-out from the printer? If he disposed of it at once, where did it go?

She went to the kitchen to look in the swingbin. An empty coffee jar, two or three tinfoil trays that suggested take-away meals, yesterday's *Evening Standard*, some empty plastic bags . . . He didn't get rid of the print-out paper in the rubbish, that was clear.

She went back into the living room. She looked among the pile of magazines but there was no print-out interleaved with any of them. She looked in the sideboard but found only stacks of old-fashioned crockery and a walnut box of silver cutlery.

The fireplace? Did he burn it? She went to it, knelt on the rug, and examined it. But the grate was filled with imitation coals and when she looked further she realized that it was an electric contraption simulating a real fire and that the chimney was blocked off.

She was still kneeling on the hearthrug when she heard a key in the door.

Chapter Thirteen

Lindsay froze. For a long moment her breath deserted her.

Flight? She stared wildly round. The windows – but she was three floors up with a hard pavement below.

Take cover? She could hide behind an armchair. And then what? If with any luck the newcomer went straight past into the bedroom, she still had to tiptoe to the door, open it without noise, and get out.

While these thoughts were still tumbling about in her mind, she heard something being dropped in the vestibule – a travel bag, perhaps. Footsteps.

She rose from her kneeling position on the rug. Whoever it was, she was going to face him standing up. She dusted the knees of her jeans, pulled the collar of her shirt straight.

Tad appeared in the living room doorway.

She expected an exclamation of surprise but nothing of the sort.

'In my home town, there's a saying,' he remarked. 'Somebody helps you on with your coat, check for your wallet.'

'I beg your pardon?' she said. For a moment the meaning didn't come to her. Then she understood: he'd wondered why she was being so good to him with that free trip to Marseilles.

'How'd you get in?' he inquired. He came into the room, throwing his jacket over a chair back. He was clad in clothes suitable for the Mediterranean – linen shirt open at the neck, chinos and deck shoes.

Whenever possible, tell the exact truth. This was a business rule she'd followed all her life. So she said, 'Your cleaning lady let me in.'

'Mrs Amalia?' He shrugged, but she saw a certain grimness in his eyes. Mrs Amalia was going to suffer for it.

Another business rule: go on the attack. 'Why aren't you in Marseilles?' she demanded.

'I wanted to know why I'd been sent away. Seems this is –'

'Sent away?' She tried for amazement mixed with indignation. 'You get a nice trip to the South of France in June and you fly straight back? What a curious way to behave!'

'Hah,' he said, glancing about. 'Talking of curious behaviour . . . what are you doing in my apartment?'

Whenever possible, tell the truth – or at least part of it. 'I was leaving a welcome home present.'

'What?' His raised eyebrow said, Tell me another.

'Or a thank-you-again present.' She made a gesture at the glinting package on the coffee table and blessed her stars that she'd bought it.

'You don't say.' He came to the table, picked up the package, turned it over in his hands. There was a certain caution as he untied it, as if he half expected a bomb. The metallic paper parted, the box containing the desk toy appeared. He opened it to reveal the intriguing collection of little mirrors, magnets and metal bars.

'What do you know,' he said in wonder. 'It really is a present.' He put it down on the coffee table, twitched the bars about to see them immediately form a pattern reflected in infinite repetition in the mirrors. 'Well, thanks.'

His features were lit up by a sudden grin. 'Neat,' he said. But whether he meant the present, or her excuse, she wasn't quite sure.

'Do you like it?' she said in a tone that she hoped held innocent inquiry.

'It'll be a big thing in my life. But you needn't have taken the trouble to come all the way here with it, you could have given it to me at the bank.'

'What, and have everybody in the dealing room staring at us?'

'Well, that's a good point. It would puzzle them to see us here together like this – they all think you don't take to me much.'

'Oh, that's nonsense.'

'Really? I must say, I thought the same myself.'

'No, no, I try to be on good terms with all my colleagues.'

'Yeah,' he replied disbelievingly. 'Well, since you're here, can I get you anything? Tea, coffee, Coke?'

'A cold drink would be nice.'

He went to the kitchen, came back with two opened bottles of ice-cold Coke with moisture forming on their surface. It didn't occur to him to bring glasses, apparently. Lindsay hated having to sip from a bottle but didn't say so.

'Want a look around? Let me give you the conducted tour.'

'Oh, no, I –'

'I took this place over, furnished. I've still to get around to buying a few things, so don't judge it too hard. This is the dining room, never use it. D'you know, there's a full set of silver knives and forks in the sideboard, what the agent calls a canteen of cutlery.'

He ushered her on to the bedroom, and for a moment she was uneasy, but they merely looked in from the doorway. 'Great bed – plenty of room for two.'

'So I see.' She thought about Nan Compton and her evident liking for Tad. Had she shared the bed with him?

He took her elbow to lead her on to the next door. 'This is my hobbies room,' he said, waving the Coke bottle at the array of machines. 'I'm a computer nut.'

'Oh, my goodness!' She pretended that she'd never seen it before. 'You're really into it, aren't you?'

'I do a lot of analysis here, I've got all kinds of software with specialist programs.' He wandered into the room, set down the Coke bottle, and laid his hand fondly on the mainframe.

And she knew at once that he was trying to find out whether it had been switched on.

A machine heats up when electricity is flowing through it. She had switched off the computer about forty-five minutes ago after her failure to get into the system. Would it still be faintly warm? Yet it was a June day, the room itself warm from the sun shining through the windows. The only air conditioning was the floor-standing electric fan. Why shouldn't the casing be warm?

She held her breath. He might say, 'Why have you been snooping in my computer files?'

But he let his hand slip off the top, turning away without comment. 'Can I show you something?' he said 'It's produced by a little set-up in Deming, New Mexico. Automatically graphs losses over gains as you enter them, then formats them in any balance-sheet pattern to match the style used by any firm these days.' She listened more to the tone than to the words. He was filling in time while he decided what to do.

Go on the attack. 'I ought to be cross with you for throwing away the chance to ask my questions,' she said, leaving the computers and heading for the living room. She wanted to be on safer ground. She'd come here to find out more about him, and now they were face to face – what better opportunity could there be? But not surrounded by the machines that held his secrets.

'Yeah, I suppose I should apologize,' he agreed, appearing embarrassed.

'You really thought I'd sent you to Marseilles for some ulterior motive?'

'Well . . . yes.'

'Do they do that kind of thing on Wall Street?'

'All the time!'

'And what motive was I supposed to have?' This was a dangerous question, but she wanted to get him off balance.

'A little bit of jiggery-pokery with my research figures?'

'I beg your pardon?' She was genuinely surprised. She suspected him. The thought had never entered her head that *he* might suspect *her*. 'Why would I want to meddle with your research figures?'

'My results influence what the bank does with its money, right? For all I knew, you might have some scam in mind.'

She knew she had coloured up at the suggestion. She was hot with indignation. How dare he! And yet . . . if he were an honest man who felt he was being manoeuvred out of London, mightn't he be justified in thoughts like this?

He said, 'Who was the big guy giving you a hard time the other day?'

'Barry?' Now he had taken her aback once more. 'Barry's an old friend of mine.'

'That was the famous Barry Wivelstone?'

'What's famous about him?'

'The folks at the bank say he's lasted a long time with you, even though he's a real bore.'

This wasn't going the way she wanted. She said with coolness, 'My relationships outside the office are nothing to do with them.'

'That was some relationship, by the look of it. He was roughing you up.'

'Oh, that was . . . that was unlike him. He was in a temper.'

'And that gives him the right to play Tarzan?'

'I really don't see why I have to –'

'What was the quarrel about? He trying to get you to do something you didn't want to? Insider tips from the bank? That sort of thing?'

'Barry?' She burst into laughter. 'Barry wouldn't know an insider tip if it danced the cancan in front of him. He's a financial ignoramus.'

'Ignoramus, huh?' An odd note in the way he repeated the word.

'In fact, it was because he's always despised crude money-making that –'

'What?'

Now she sighed. 'I suppose everybody will guess it sooner or later. Barry and I have broken up.'

'Oh, *that's* what it was about.'

'Well . . . yes.'

Once again he gave that unexpected grin that seemed to light up his narrow face. 'Good,' he said.

He set down his Coke bottle on the coffee table next to his present. As he straightened he turned towards her.

Next moment she was in his arms.

Surprise held her immobile for a second. Then she stiffened and pulled away.

'What are you –'

'Come on, just a friendly little kiss to say thank-you for my present.'

'Let me go, you dolt!'

'Let's try it first, see if you like it.'

She still had the Coke bottle in her hand. Her grip on it tightened. She was going to hit him with it if he tried.

But as her hand came up, he grasped her wrist. By a simple movement he caused the bottle to slip out of her grasp.

The kiss that followed was strange. Soft, almost casual. 'Mm . . .' he murmured. 'Not bad. What do you think?'

'No, stop this –'

'Lindsay, it's just a kiss.' His mouth touched hers again, this time with more force, savouring the contours of her lips as if they were a new country he was exploring. He pulled her hard against him.

Between her body and his there was only the thin barrier of her shirt and his, the thin clothes of summer. She could feel the warmth of his flesh, sense the rising rhythm of his heartbeat.

Or was it hers that was quickening? Something within her was melting, responding. She closed her eyes, tried to will herself to draw back. Instead her arms went about his shoulders. She found she was pulling him closer.

For a strange, unearthly moment, they seemed to be one. It was as if their bloodstreams mingled, their pulses beat together with one pounding insistence. She felt his embrace change, as if to lift her off her feet and carry her – to what? To the towering completion of this upsurge of passion?

What strength came to her then she never knew. She wrenched herself free. Snatching up her bag, she ran from him, from the room, from the flat, from the building.

Routed, defeated, overpowered. Utterly vanquished by some traitor within herself that had almost handed her over to the enemy.

Chapter Fourteen

A bus happened to be stopping at the end of the street. She stumbled aboard. She must put distance between herself and what had happened – physical distance, mental distance. She gave the driver a pound, sat down, and with her eyes closed tried to calm her breathing.

She tried to think but her mind, usually so obedient, refused to function properly. Thoughts and feelings whirled within her, a maelstrom in which she felt lost, overpowered.

Time went by. When she looked up, it was to find herself being borne through North London, to no good purpose. At the next stop she hurried to get off.

There was a minuscule park with a sundial and two or three benches. She sat down and, using her mobile phone, rang the firm whose vehicles normally conveyed her around London. Lindsay didn't actually own a car, she used taxis, minicabs or public transport within the London area, then if she wanted to go further, hired a self-drive. She knew she could depend on them for quality and swift service.

Within minutes she'd arranged for a car to be delivered to a rendezvous in Docklands. Next she rang the market garden to let the Goswamis know she was coming. She flagged down a taxi to take her home to the flat. There she spent only a few minutes throwing things into a travel bag so that she was waiting in Cabot Square when the hire car arrived.

It was a capacious new black Passat with a VR6 engine. She signed for it, tipped the delivery driver, and got in. She drove out of London, slowly at first because of the Saturday afternoon traffic but soon with greater ease as she left the city behind her.

Comfort came to her with every succeeding mile that she put between herself and the flat in Burslow Street. She drove well; handling the car restored something of her self-respect.

How could she have been such a fool? To let herself be swayed, be tempted – and just when she should have been at her most watchful. Because Tad was an adversary to be feared.

She knew now that he was under no illusions about her presence in his flat. He had guessed she was there to pry. That unexpected embrace was his way of punishing her. 'Think you can just walk in here and look around? I'll show you!' That had been the message.

Very well, message received and understood. She must never take risks with him again. He was too quick, too ruthless.

Ruthless? But then, she'd felt his response to the moment, as intense as her own. That wasn't ruthlessness, surely.

No, but it was opportunism. He'd seen an opportunity and tried to take it. After all, he knew she had broken up with Barry – she'd admitted that to him herself. Here she was, available, taking risks by being in his territory. Why not grab the chance?

She should have been angry, but what anger she felt was directed against herself. She'd been scared silly when he first walked in but she'd pulled herself together, had handled it quite well by taking him to task for coming home. Why hadn't she stayed on the attack? Why had she been so weak?

It was no good saying to herself that he would never know he'd got under her guard. That telling moment had been as clear to him as it had been to her. He knew she'd wanted him then, as much as he wanted her. Such things couldn't be disguised, couldn't be denied.

But it had been only a moment, one moment in time, a tick of the clock, an infinitesimal movement of the earth's turning. It had happened, but it was past.

She would discount it, shrug it off. Anyone can feel a momentary impulse of desire. A physical thing, nothing more. She had escaped from it. She could say, if challenged, that it had meant nothing.

And of course that was true. It meant nothing. It couldn't mean anything. She had no feeling for Tad, except wariness, suspicion, anxiety.

All the same, if she were to draw up a balance sheet, this morning would count as a loss. She had gone to the flat to learn something about him, and had failed. Worse than that, she'd been caught in the act. He had given a demonstration of his ascendancy over her by almost sweeping her off her feet.

Between now and the next time she saw him she must think how to compensate for that loss, must set the balance sheet right.

It was necessary for her self-image. She was Lindsay Dunforth, respected by all those around her in her workplace. Never let it be said that one of her colleagues was grinning to himself at almost having got her into bed with him.

The urban part of Essex went by unnoticed, Romford, Harolds Wood . . . But when the gently rolling fields began to spread out on either side, their freshness and tranquillity calmed her little by little. She caught glimpses of the streams that fed the land and nourished the trees whose shade was so welcome on this hot June day. At Wickford she turned east for Wansea Island, no island in reality but framed by the rivers that flowed out to Foulness Sands and the North Sea.

The quiet roads were a little busier than on earlier visits, for the holiday season was beginning. She was slowed down by a car trailing a caravan but by and by it turned off into one of the many mobile-home parks. The yachting season was waking up: she saw sails moving on the Crouch, their gentle movements advancing them towards the waters of the estuary and the breeze from the open sea.

By the time she reached the nursery garden the combination of landscape and seascape had brought a state of equilibrium. She was able to think calmly of how things stood at the moment. There were almost forty-eight hours before she need see Tad again. If in the meantime he tried to contact her by ringing the house in Putney he would be referred to another number. At that number the phone would ring unanswered. She was telling him, we have no reason to be in touch, we really have nothing in common.

Except a luminous moment when they might have reached paradise together. But that was all over.

Celia and Alice were waiting for her as she drove into the nursery grounds. 'I thought you had something to keep you in London?' her mother remarked.

'Well, that got cut short. Hello, darling.' This to her daughter, who was clearly bursting to tell her something. 'Just let me park the car then I'll be with you.'

Alice followed in her wake as she manoeuvred round corners to the parking area. When she got out of the car the little girl announced proudly, 'I can tie shoe laces now, Mummy!'

Lindsay looked down at the little sandalled foot. 'But you're not wearing shoe laces, love.'

'Jamnu taught me to tie *his* shoe laces.'

Lindsay burst out laughing. Her mother said, 'The power of love!' Alice, delighted with herself, rushed at her mother and hugged her round the knees. Lindsay swept her up into her arms.

How normal, how serene everything was here . . . The community of family and friends worked in harmony, the youngsters tending the plants, their parents driving vans or handling complex equipment, the elders running the office or the catering. She'd seldom witnessed any disagreement, and if one arose it was soon settled. In its way it was as complex as Oistrav's Bank, but there seemed almost no competition, no striving to be preeminent.

It was balm to Lindsay's troubled spirit. She allowed its healing to penetrate deep within her during the rest of that day. She went to examine her daughter's special row of tomato plants, she had a long conversation with one of the senior Goswamis about how to finance yet another extension to the glasshouses, she helped one of the teenage nieces to write an application for a college place.

In the late evening, over a glass of wine, she sat with Celia under the boughs of what had once been an apple orchard, enjoying the cool breeze from the estuary.

'Anything wrong?' Celia inquired.

'No, why?'

'You seem a bit subdued.'

For a moment she longed to confide in her mother. But what words could she use, what images could she conjure up? She hardly knew how she felt about the episode in Tad's flat: how could she describe it to anyone else?

'Oh, it's been a tiring week,' she said. 'The City's always tiring once it starts to get warm.'

'True enough. But it's nice here. Try to unwind, darling. Things have been so hectic recently . . .'

So she avoided any confidences, and was half-glad, half-regretful.

Next day Tapti was taking Jamnu fishing off the end of the jetty about a mile away on the estuary. Alice looked bereft on hearing this. Jamnu, considering it a manly triumph to be lent a fishing rod by his teenage cousin, clearly didn't want his devotee tagging along.

'I'll tell you what,' Lindsay suggested when she saw the

trembling underlip and the tearful gaze as the others picked up their gear. 'Let's join them at lunch time, eh? We'll take them a lovely picnic lunch.'

'Would you really?' said Tapti, surprised and pleased. 'That's awfully nice of you, Mrs Dunforth.'

'We'll bring you some special sandwiches,' she promised. 'Won't we, Alice?'

'Oh yes, and some of Auntie Nita's special peshwari nan –'

Celia said in her daughter's ear, 'You should be in the diplomatic service.'

At lunch time they set off carrying the picnic in a pair of carrier bags. Their way was along a leafy lane which led to a footpath across a marshy meadow. Across the river the tower of St Mary's at Burnham could just be distinguished in the heat-haze of noon. The terrain here was flat, with few dwellings and with something of a Dutch landscape about it, light reflecting off the muddy foreshore and the rivulets of brackish water.

The jetty was long and needed to be so, to reach water deep enough for the anglers' lines or for the rowboats which were tied to the supports. The tide was coming in, causing the thread-like nylon to sway sideways from the rods towards the boats. Tapti muttered complaints about their owners. 'They use them at the weekends. It's the same every Saturday in summer, they row across from the other side and hang about for hours doing nothing. Why can't they go somewhere else?'

'Why don't you get down in one of the boats and fish from there?' Lindsay suggested.

Tapti looked startled. 'But . . . suppose the owner came back?'

'Well then, he'd row away and you'd have more clear water.'

Jamnu, untroubled by problems about ownership, was already clambering down into the nearest boat. After a moment's hesitation Tapti followed him. The two anglers cast their lines. In a moment they were sitting in great content waiting for a bite, oblivious of the womenfolk on the jetty.

Alice looked longingly at the water. 'Couldn't we go in for a swim, Mummy? Babaji says I mustn't because it's dangerous, but it wouldn't be dangerous if you were here.'

'I don't know about that,' Lindsay said, eyeing the fast flow of the tide as it surged past the rickety pier. 'I don't think it would be much fun, and besides we haven't brought swimsuits.'

'And anyhow we're going to have lunch, and doesn't Mummy

always say you mustn't swim after a meal?' Celia put in. 'Or don't you want any of this lovely food we've brought?'

Alice of course wanted her share of the goodies, and moreover wanted to show her devotion by making sure Jamnu was looked after. The idea of swimming was forgotten. They sat with legs dangling over the edge of the jetty, passing down sandwiches and iced fruit juice to the anglers. By and by the water was almost washing at the shoes of the grownups, and Tapti and Jamnu in their boat were at eye level with the jetty.

'Doesn't it change *fast*,' marvelled Alice. She leaned forward to offer peshwari nan to her idol, her grandmother meanwhile holding her safe with a firm grasp on the waistband of her shorts. Two mallards drifted past, looking hopefully at the eatables.

A world away from the City of London and all its problems.

When it was time for her mother and her grandmother to leave for London, Alice for the first time showed some restlessness. 'Why can't I come home with you?' she demanded, pouting.

'I thought you liked it here,' Lindsay said.

'Oh, I do, but I want to have swims in the pool and I want to see Eddie and Tracy.'

No mention of Barry, Lindsay noted thankfully. 'Well, Granny and I aren't living in the house at Putney for the moment. Eddie and Tracy are away –'

'Away!' Alarm sounded in the child's voice. Eddie and Tracy were fixed stars in her firmament.

'Oh, just on holiday,' Lindsay assured her. 'You're having a holiday, so Eddie and Tracy are too. But if Eddie's away, there's no one to look after the pool –'

'Eddie's the mimtemus man,' said Alice, summoning the thought from her memories of home.

'That's right, Eddie's the maintenance man, and if he's not there to maintain the pool we can't swim in it, so you see it's no good going home for swims.'

'Babaji will take me to the swimming pool in Bishop's Stotfot tomorrow p'raps,' mused Alice. 'And he says I've to pinch out my plants. You take little bits off, but he says it doesn't hurt them.'

'No, they know you're doing them good,' Lindsay said.

'Like Dr Milner when he gave me a jab?'

'Exactly.' They hugged goodbye. Celia looked back to wave until they were turning out of the gateway. Lindsay said, looking in the rear mirror to the last, 'She's not crying or anything, is she?'

'No, she's fine. Don't worry, dear, it was partly the grand new car that made her want to come. She wouldn't really want to leave Jamnu.'

'Poor Jamnu, every time he turns around she's there wanting him to play with her.'

'He's a nice boy, really. But I suppose ten-year-old boys always feel five-year-old girls are a nuisance.' She glanced about at the interior of the Passat. 'Why the car, dear? Were you avoiding Saturday crowds on the train?'

'I just thought I'd like to drive for a change.'

'Could we keep it a while? I hate not having wheels and I'd like to get to know the neighbourhood round the flat. There must be more shops than I've found so far.'

'We'll keep it if you want to. There's garaging under the building. But this is a bit different from your old Citroën, you know.'

This caused a disagreement about driving skills so that at the next lay-by they changed places, to allow Celia to get the feel of the big estate car on the comparatively quiet roads of Essex. They reached Docklands as night was falling.

Next morning Lindsay was driven to the bank as usual, leaving the hire car for her mother. She had put behind her the doubts and perplexities of Saturday, and felt equal to anything the day might bring.

Sudin had learned through the family grapevine that she'd spent the weekend at the nursery. 'I hear you went fishing,' he remarked, smiling at the thought. To him, Mrs Dunforth was an icon adorning the temples of high finance. He couldn't picture her carrying sandwiches to two young anglers.

'We didn't catch anything, though. I half expected to see you there, Sudin.'

'No, yesterday we had a birthday party for my youngest.' He paused. 'However, in the evening I went for a drive past your house.'

'Oh, Sudin, please – don't put yourself out –'

'No, no, it's nothing. I just thought I would tell you – I turned into Edgefold Road and almost immediately afterwards the security patrol turned up.'

'Well, they're supposed to drive by every so –'

'I just wanted to tell you, so you won't be alarmed – the driver of the van asked me what I was doing there and I told him I was a friend of yours. I expect he'll report it so when you hear, you will know it was me. He asked me for identification, very efficient.'

'Well, that's reassuring,' she said. 'Thank you again, Sudin.'

Much of the morning was taken up with phone calls from clients: newspaper coverage of the 'windfall' from a building society's privatization had caused an unwarranted interest in their shares. Lindsay assured her clients that the shares would be overpriced at the outset, persuaded them to wait until things calmed down and then see if they still wanted to invest.

She was signing off from the last of a batch of calls when the door of her office opened and Tad entered. 'Lunch today?' he suggested. 'Let's go early to avoid the crowds.'

Lindsay was utterly astounded. She was still trying to find her voice when he added, 'Not Dandy's. Somewhere quiet.'

'No. I . . . have other plans for today –'

'You and I have got to talk, Lindsay –'

'I don't see the need.'

'Oh, come on! What about Saturday? You're not pretending –'

'You must excuse me, I'm busy, Tad,' she said, very coolly. As if to enforce this, her phone rang.

'See here, don't pull rank on me –'

'I've someone calling –'

'Let it ring,' he said, raising his voice above the trilling of the phone.

Millicent, from her office one door down, could hear the raised voices. She came to see the cause. She hovered in the doorway. 'Is anything wrong, Lindsay?' she asked, looking anxiously at the unanswered phone.

'No, everything's fine. Mr Tadiecski is just leaving.'

Millicent retreated, waiting to one side for Tad to pass. He followed her, but in the doorway turned. 'Well,' he said above the sound of the telephone, 'can you let me have back the key to my flat? My cleaning lady needs it.'

If he had been looking for a stroke to lay her low, he had found it. She stared at him in dismay, while interested heads were raised at the desks nearest her office door. Even the loyal Millicent looked intrigued.

Tad, completely insouciant, walked away.

The phone continued to ring. Lindsay picked it up, glad of the excuse. Heads were bent once more over desks, eyes were directed towards the figures on the screens. Millicent returned to her office.

About an hour later, when the phone calls abated, Lindsay got out her handbag. She tipped it up over her desk. Among the last things to fall out, among the usual debris of till slips, crumpled tissues, sunglasses and used travel cards, was the key to Tad's flat.

She put it in an envelope then summoned Millicent. 'Please go along to Mr Tadiecski and give him this.'

Millicent, wordless, accepted the envelope with the key obviously inside. She went out.

About sixty seconds later she returned. 'Mr Tadiecski says thanks, and asked me to give you this.'

Unwillingly Lindsay accepted the folded sheet of paper she held out. If it was an apology from Tad for his behaviour, she didn't want to read it.

All the same, she had to know what it was he had sent her. She unfolded the sheet of paper and there before her, neatly typed, were the answers to the questions she'd thought up for Tad to ask at the Marseilles seminar.

Once again she was taken by surprise. He had flown back again to Marseilles after that momentous Saturday morning! While she was imagining him ringing her house, ringing the Docklands flat, trying to get in touch, he had been sitting complacently in the conference hall taking notes.

So now she knew. What to her had seemed so important, so shattering, to him was a mere nothing, a little bit of fun.

A strange feeling shook her for a moment. It was a mixture of intense relief and . . . disappointment.

She found her secretary still waiting, watching her. She handed the sheet of paper to her. 'File this,' she said. 'Put it under "Conferences, Marseilles." '

Put it under 'Misapprehension', she should have said.

At lunch time she went out because, as she had said to Tad, she had plans of her own. She needed to buy some clothes. She had packed very little when she first closed up the Putney house and she didn't want to go back there to pick up additions to her wardrobe. Sudin had told her that the security patrol was watchful but all the same, she preferred to stay away. But this evening she had a dinner at one of the livery companies' halls, and nothing suitable to wear.

Contrary to the general belief, the City isn't all banks and financial houses. There are good shops intermingled with the premises of insurance companies and investment houses. In an hour and a half Lindsay bought a plain black skirt of raw silk, a lace camisole top, a pair of evening sandals, and while she was at it two summer dresses of pure cotton to cope with the warm weather. These wouldn't have been her choice if she'd had time to go to her usual shops – Harvey Nichols or Liberty. But their big flower prints pleased her well enough, and there was amusement at this break from tradition. She left these packages in the foyer with Studley rather than cart them up in the lift and when she got up to her office, rang her mother.

'Cecie, I've bought a clump of new clothes so it'd be a bit difficult to come home on the train. Could you collect me in the car?'

'I say, what got into you?'

'Well, it seemed the simplest way to extend my wardrobe. Everything I brought with me needs to go to the cleaners.'

'What time shall I come?'

'Er . . . better make it five-ish. I've been practically tied to the phone dealing with clients who want to buy building-society-bank shares and they're still calling.'

'Righto, see you five-ish.'

She'd barely put down the phone when Tad appeared in the doorway of her office. 'Sorry to interrupt,' he said with a smile that was only faintly apologetic. 'How about a drink after the day's end?'

'No thank you.'

'Oh, come on. Don't be stand-offish, Lindsay.'

'No, someone's collecting me at five –'

'Don't tell me you've made it up with the Big Bruiser?'

'What business is it of yours?' she exclaimed. 'Go away, please.'

Heads were once more being raised to observe what was going on – *again* – between the head of the Investment Portfolio Department and Tad Tadiecski. Tad's back was to the dealing room so he was perhaps unaware of the interest they were arousing. Or perhaps not. There was a glint in his eye that could have been mere mischief.

'Sure, it's my business,' he countered. 'If it's the Wrestling Champ, I ought to be around to –'

'If you must know, it's my mother who's collecting me,' she said. 'Now if you don't mind, I'm busy.' She bent her head to the papers on her desk and didn't look up until she was sure he'd gone.

As the day drew to a close she began to regret asking her mother to come. It was hot and sticky. A swim at the leisure centre before going home would have been good. Moreover, to arrive at five o'clock Celia would have to battle with the rush hour traffic. She debated ringing to cancel the arrangement but if she did so she'd have to call a taxi. While she was musing on this point, she saw Tad making his way across the dealing room and remembered she'd told him her arrangements. She mustn't change them, or he'd think she'd just been making excuses to avoid him.

She saw Nan Compton detain him by her desk. Nan was always quick to take any chance to chat with Tad. Screens were being switched off, the dealers were thinking of heading for home. A little group gathered by Nan's desk; a foray to Dandy's for a cooling drink was clearly being planned. Ellaline gestured towards Lindsay's office. Tad was shaking his head and explaining that Lindsay had other plans. She saw his lips form the words, 'Her mom's picking her up.'

'How do you know?' Nan demanded, loud enough for Lindsay to hear her through the glass wall of her office.

Tad made smoothing motions with his hands. She could see him say, 'I already asked her.'

Frowning, Nan got up, picked up her handbag, and flounced off to the cloakroom.

Lindsay sighed inwardly. Just as well to steer clear of them all by going home as she planned with Celia.

When Studley rang to say her mother was waiting, she went down in a lift full of homegoers. Celia had had to park some way off. They shared the parcels between them. 'This is a shoebox,' Celia remarked as one of the plastic carriers was bumped by a pedestrian hurrying by.

'Sandals to wear tonight –'

'What's tonight?'

'Dinner of the London Resource Group at the Farriers Hall –'

'Oh, Lindsay, you were going with Barry!' mourned Celia. 'What will you do for an escort?'

'Do without,' she replied. But in some recess of her mind she saw herself going into the Farriers Hall on the arm of a man, and the man had something of the look of Tad Tadiecski.

At that point they reached the parking lot and the fantasy was banished. On the way home Lindsay asked to be dropped off at a hairdresser. When she got to the flat an hour later her mother had hung up her purchases for her and was admiring the Italian sandals.

'I wish I could wear skimpy shoes like that,' she sighed.

'Nothing's stopping you, Mother.'

'Except the likelihood of turning my ankle. I say, Lindsay, those cotton dresses – are they to wear at the office?'

'Yes, this one I'm wearing is the last of what I brought and they all need cleaning.'

'But they're so different from your usual office clothes, dear . . . ?'

Lindsay shrugged. 'I really didn't have much choice. I was dashing around in my lunch hour and had to take what was available. I thought they were rather nice.' She sighed a little. 'Everything's different at the moment,' she said. 'Why shouldn't my clothes be different too?'

There was plenty of time before she had to bathe and change. Lindsay made tea. They sat in the kitchen to drink it while Celia pored over a sheet of paper that contained the recipe for her evening meal.

'I got it from a friend on the Internet,' she explained. 'He's a teak exporter in Bangkok so this should be authentic Thai cuisine –'

'Talking of the Internet, how's the search for funny money at the bank?'

Celia waved the paper at her in rebuke. 'I don't spend *all* my time chasing fraudsters, you know,' she said. 'I do have other things to do –'

'I know, I'm sorry. In fact I think you spend too much time tied up to those machines –'

'Tied up to them? What a funny thing to say. You know I enjoy it, dear. But it gets a bit samey, prowling through columns of figures, especially when I don't have your gift for making sense of them.'

Lindsay was seeing in her mind's eye the array of machines in Tad's flat. Tad had the gift for making sense of columns of figures, and those computers would give him the same access to the bank's files as Celia, always supposing he had her know-how.

'Cecie . . .'

'What?'

'Could you hack into the computer of a private person?'

Her mother paused with her cup halfway to her lips. 'A private person?'

'Yes.'

She carefully set down the cup. 'What private person?'

'I think . . . perhaps . . . the man who hacked into my files at the bank.'

'Oh. So it would be kind of tit for tat?' That seemed to make a difference. Celia looked less unwilling.

'It's someone I'm worried about. Since he first arrived on the scene, everything has gone haywire –'

'You're not saying he's the one who sent the threats?'

'I don't know. He could be. There's something about him . . .'

'Oh, in that case, I'd be more willing to –' She broke off, clasping and unclasping her hands. 'It's something I've never done, breaking into someone's *private* territory – it's illegal of course but it's also . . . not quite decent, if you know what I mean.'

'I know, I understand. If you don't want to do it, that's all right.'

'This computer of his, it's at the bank?'

'No. It's at his flat.'

It didn't occur to Celia to inquire how in that case her daughter knew of it. Instead she got the notepad that hung by the kitchen telephone to take down some details. When she'd got name and address she asked, 'What sort of computer?'

'I don't know – very impressive with lots of things connected to it –'

'What shape is it? Did it have a maker's logo?'

Lindsay tried to summon up an image of the trestle table with its equipment. Her mother wrote down the items as she described them. 'That sounds like a new-type modem. And that's a scanner by the sound of it. You say the screen came on and asked you who you were?'

'Yes, but I couldn't find the right answer.'

'Did you give it his name?'

'Of course, in every version I could think of. And then I tried various historical names and, oh, all sorts of things, but nothing worked.'

'What was the program that was working?'

'I don't know.'

'What kind of icons came up on the screen?'

'I can't remember. Nothing unusual enough for me to notice.'

Celia sat tapping the pen on the pad. 'Well, we'll worry about passwords when we come to them. First I've got to find him. And of course he would need to be on line. Do you suppose he used this equipment to break into your office files?'

Lindsay said in a rush, 'I think that's what it's *for*!'

'To break into bank files?'

'Yes.'

Her mother gave a little grimace of satisfaction. 'Well then, he'll have left tracks. I'll find him.'

Lindsay shook her head in wonder. She never understood how Celia, outwardly so ordinary, could make electronic machines obey her commands.

The dinner at the Farriers Hall was excellent and so was the company. Since Lindsay had rung to say her partner Barry Wivelstone would be absent, the seating at table had been rearranged and she found herself next to a lively Welsh architect. All thoughts of danger and computers and Tad Tadiecski were temporarily banished.

When she got home her mother was in bed. A note on her bedside table said, 'No luck so far.' In the morning she was out early as usual, with no chance to ask for details.

As the dealers arrived at the bank, she noticed heads turn in her direction. At first she couldn't understand it, but then her reflection in the glass wall of her office caught her eye. Of course – she was wearing something completely different from her usual garb of soft dark silk. Instead she had on a cotton shift with yellow and brown flowers on a white background.

She stifled a laugh. How odd they were, her colleagues. Did it really matter so much, what she wore?

Well, it seemed it did. She crossed the dealing room to head for a meeting in the Bond Department, and heard a conversation cut off at her approach: '– totally different image!'

'I suppose Tad's told her he doesn't like the prim look –'

She felt herself flushing, but didn't stop in her progress towards the door.

Did they imagine she'd changed to please Tad Tadiecski? How could they be so absurd, how could they base a judgement on such scant evidence! But the dealing room was always awash with gossip. And she reminded herself that they could have no idea of the difficulties by which she was beset – living away from her home, limited by the need for security, full of uncertainties and doubts.

When she got home to the flat that evening, Celia was waiting for her with unconcealed delight. 'I found him! I'm hooked on! Come and look.'

Lindsay followed to her mother's bedroom, where one of her computers was winking with its message.

'Who?' it inquired. It was a replica of the format she'd seen at Tad's flat.

'That's marvellous, Mother!'

'You see, he stays on line twenty-four hours – expecting important stuff Eastern Standard Time –'

'Or perhaps because the bank mainframe is always on line and he wants to know everything that goes through the minute it happens –'

'So now all I've got to do is find the answer to "Who?".'

'You'll do it.'

'Maybe . . . He's a clever chap, Lindsay. It took me a long time to track him down although I had a lot of hints about his passage here and there.'

'Don't get too obsessed about it, Mother,' Lindsay said anxiously. She could see the light of battle in her eyes, the longing for the chase.

'No, I won't, because to tell you the truth I don't know what to do next,' Celia agreed, stretching in her chair and flexing her arms. 'I've been trying all afternoon to get the password and I feel full of kinks and cramps. When that happens it's best to take a break. So I thought I'd drive down to Essex tomorrow to see Alice, get my mind completely off it, stay overnight maybe, and come back to it fresh on Thursday.'

It was an excellent idea. The last thing Lindsay wanted was for her mother to exhaust herself over the problem. Since it was still early evening she slipped out to buy a present for her to take to Alice. Docklands was quite busy, homecomers emerging from the railway stations, dropping into shops that stayed open on purpose to accommodate them. She bought a book of cut-out pictures and a pair of blunt scissors for Alice, smiling to herself as she thought of her little girl attacking it with her usual enthusiasm.

Next morning at the bank, things began badly. There was e-mail awaiting her that needed immediate action, and her team were slow to show up for the day's work. Nan Compton was particularly late.

'What's this?' she demanded when she saw the message Lindsay had left for her. She stalked into her office. 'I can't be a minute late without having you on my case?'

'Good heavens, I don't mind if you're late on an ordinary day, Nan, but Newton's sent word –'

'Newton, Newton, who's he, another of your bosom pals?'

'What's the matter with you? Newton's a friend of mine in Banca di Mercati Centrali –'

'Oh, a Latin lover? Is that how you do it? Close contact, eh, all over the –'

'Nan, have you got a hangover or something?' Lindsay cut in, too perturbed about the crisis on hand to bother about what she was actually saying. 'We've got to shift those shares in the Bimondi cruise line, Newton says –'

'Newton says, Dunforth says, we all leap to attention –'

'Nan, get on the phone and shift those shares. Or do you want me to delegate it to Ellaline or Milo?'

Nan wavered in the doorway. 'I'm second in command –'

'Well, behave as if you are. Are you going to get to work?'

'I'll do it,' grunted Nan, and walked out.

Lindsay was too busy to ponder over what had just happened. Sid Newton had let her have word that a big Italian cruise and hotel firm was bankrupt. Since some of Lindsay's clients had shares in the company, she had to repair the damage. The rest of the City would be doing the same, there was no time to lose.

Lindsay was wearing the second of her two new dresses. It was softer than the shift dress, with a flowing pattern of white petals and dark leaves on a pale green background. She herself was quite unconscious of it, but it drew approving glances from the men.

The entire morning was taken up with the problem of the Italian firm's demise. At lunch time everyone thankfully went out to enjoy a break and recharge batteries for what came next.

It appeared that Nan had decided to take a longer break than anyone else. Moreover it seemed she'd had a somewhat liquid lunch. The result was that she fumbled two or three of her deals.

Muttering in annoyance, she went to the machine for coffee to clear her head.

Lindsay came to her desk to see how she was doing. The screen in her own office had shown her that Nan had made mistakes. 'Are you feeling all right, Nan?' she asked.

'Of course I am.'

'That sale with Peramban should have gone off better –'

'I'll sort it out, just leave me alone.'

'Nan, if you'd like to go home, I'll give the folio to Alec –'

'I'll do it, I'll do it, just stop pestering me!'

'Nan!' cried Lindsay, startled. 'What's got into you?'

'Oh, *you*!' Nan exclaimed. 'Never lose your cool, do you? Always so perfect, always on top of everything! Think you're so *marvellous*, attract all the men, turn yourself into a perfect picture in your party frock, eh? I'll show you!'

And Nan threw the contents of her beaker of coffee all over the dress with its soft pattern of petals and leaves.

Chapter Fifteen

There was an audible gasp from the dealing room. Then, in that atmosphere usually so frenetic, a moment of utter silence.

Lindsay stood transfixed. She could feel the hot coffee seeping through the thin cotton. Nan was staring at her, mouth transformed into a grin of triumph.

'Nan!' cried Ellaline, springing up from her place.

Nan gave a laugh. 'Fixed her, didn't I! About time. Look at that, her pretty dress all spoilt!'

'Nan, come and sit here –'

'Keep off! I'm dealing with this. Put a spoke in her wheel at last. You!' She swept the group of horrified colleagues with an angry glare. 'You've wanted to do it, admit it – bring her down, show her there's nothing so great about being head of department!'

'Nan, you don't know what you're saying –'

'Oh don't I? I've wanted to say it for months. But of course you can't say things like that to your boss, oh no, you don't want to be thrown out on your ear. We're all cowards when it comes to losing our jobs – but I'm not bothering about that any more. It's time to tell her – tell her she's no better than the rest of us but she's always got to be on top, always got to come first, always got to have what *she* wants, take it away from other people, what does she care if she tramples over your feelings, she treats us like dirt!'

McCormick Lockhart tried to take her by the arm. She whipped it free.

'Don't you touch me! Who do you think you are?' There was so much physical force in her movement that he withdrew in haste. She looked ready to scratch at him with hands that suddenly looked like claws.

'Get Tad,' someone whispered.

But Tad, drawn by the outcry, was already on his way.

'What's going on –' He broke off at the sight of Nan standing as if at bay. He stared a moment, turned to look about and saw Lindsay with coffee all down the front of her dress.

'*You'll* understand, Tad,' Nan said almost beseechingly. 'You'll see why I had to do it.'

He came slowly towards her. He said in a low voice, 'What did you do, Nan?'

'I . . . I punished her. It served her right.'

'What had she done to you?'

'To me? Oh, everybody knows what she's done to me. I owe her everything, don't I? She gave me my job. I've got to be grateful and humble and take orders from her and apologize if things go wrong.'

'And have things been going wrong today?'

'Oh yes, today – every day – I can't bear it any more, being second best, losing out to her all along the line –'

'Nan, I've never wanted to make you feel indebted –' Lindsay began.

'No, no, of course not – Lady Bountiful, gives us assignments, shows us how to make money for all her darling clients and for ourselves if we have the wit to do it, we all know who we have to thank for our success, because she never lets us forget it!'

'You're talking nonsense, Nan,' Mac Lockhart said. 'We all know our salaries and high bonuses are thanks to –'

'Yes, you do well, don't you, Mr Highroller? Highest income on the team except for Her Ladyship here. You're all so smug, so pleased with yourselves, you don't see how you're being used to make *her* look big –'

'Come away, Nan,' Ellaline said. 'Come to First Aid and lie down –'

'First Aid? I don't need First Aid! You think I'm hurt?' She brandished her hands and her bare arms. 'Where's the cut, where's the bruise? It's not where First Aid can deal with it.' She surveyed them with a haughty gaze. 'What's the matter with you? Think I've gone round the bend, do you? And all because I'm saying aloud what the rest of you think!'

'Come on, now, Nan –' Ellaline persisted, touching her elbow.

Nan pushed her away. 'I'm not going anywhere! There's still a lot to say!'

Tad gave Lindsay a meaningful glance. She understood at once. If Nan wouldn't quit what she saw as the field of battle, then Lindsay must. Without a word she turned to walk into her office. She sank into her chair.

Millicent was at her side instantly. 'I rang the nurse, Lindsay, and told her Nan was having hysterics. She's on her way.'

'Thank you.'

'Can I get you anything?'

'A glass of water.'

'Oh, your lovely dress,' mourned Millicent. She pulled one or two tissues from a box on Lindsay's desk and made ineffectual efforts towards cleaning, but almost in tears abandoned it and went for the water jug.

As Lindsay put the glass to her lips with trembling hands, she looked over it to the scene in the dealing room. Tad had somehow managed to capture Nan's hands in his, and was making stroking movements that turned claws into passive fingers. The First Aid nurse in her grey dress and white cap was threading her way across the dealing room. Ellaline was picking up Nan's handbag in preparation to go with her to the restroom.

'No!' Nan was declaring, but her tone was less violent. 'No, there's nothing the matter with me – why can't you all see –'

The nurse gently put herself between Nan and Tad. She took Nan's hands in hers. Her soothing words were spoken too low to reach Lindsay, but Nan bent towards her as if to listen. Tad stood back, half-shaking his head. The rest of the group parted to let them through as the nurse led Nan away with the sturdy figure of Ellaline in their wake.

Milo Makionis came to Lindsay's door. 'Lindsay, you must take no notice of what she said. None of it is so.'

'Thanks, Milo, it's all right.'

'It is because of Tad,' he said, in his frank, over-earnest way. 'It is because of what she saw and heard the other day.'

'But that wasn't at all what she thought it was –'

'You say no?' He shrugged. 'It seemed clear to Nan . . . She said to me you always took what she is wanting . . . But I didn't expect of this.'

'No, it was a surprise.'

'You don't take it seriously,' he insisted. 'It is just . . . nerves, pressure of work, and the feeling for Tad not going well . . . I express myself badly but you know what I'm saying, Lindsay. She doesn't speak for the rest of us, when she says cruel things.'

'I understand. Thank you. Now shall we all get back to work?'

Milo stiffened a little, seeing it as a rebuff. But Lindsay looked so white that he at once understood she wanted to be left alone. Despite his tactlessness Milo wasn't without perception.

Slowly the dealing room returned to normal. Lindsay turned to her computer screen so as to appear busy. She stared at it as it winked and re-formed, giving the minute-by-minute state of trading. None of it meant anything. Her team could have lost ten million pounds that afternoon and she would never have noticed.

Activity slackened as it usually did in late afternoon. Screens were switched off, dealers drifted away to cloakrooms or made phone calls arranging their evening. Ellaline Maitland returned. She made her way to Lindsay's office, the rest of the team gathering behind her at the door to hear the news. Lindsay turned away from her screen to hear what she had to say.

'Nurse Timson gave her a sedative that calmed her down quite quickly. I took her home in a taxi. Timson had told me to ring her doctor and arrange an appointment tomorrow but Nan wouldn't give me his number at first. I found it in her address book and phoned him anyway.'

'She won't go,' said Alec Joyce mournfully. 'She's in too much of a state.'

'She'll come in tomorrow just to show us how tough she is,' Mac suggested.

'She'll go to her doctor,' Ellaline said with a little grimace of irritation. 'She needs a few days off to sort out what she'll do when she gets the sack –'

'Who says she's getting the sack?' Lindsay broke in, startled.

'Well, I . . .' Ellaline flushed. 'I took it for granted. After what she said . . .'

'The girl is ill,' said Lindsay. 'You don't sack someone because they're ill.'

There was a mutter, part surprise, part disagreement. Alec said, 'She's been a pain in the neck for quite a while, Lindsay. Not easy to work with.'

Milo said something in an undertone. Lindsay said, 'What was that?'

Milo looked embarrassed. 'I shouldn't say.'

'What is it? If it helps to deal with Nan's behaviour, spit it out.'

'She gambles,' Mac said. 'That's what Milo doesn't want to say. Nan goes out gambling.'

'I know she gambles,' Lindsay returned. 'She always has.'

'But she plunges . . . I think she's lost a lot of money recently.'

'You're not saying she's gone over her head?'

'No . . . But if you're on a losing streak, it makes you feel . . . edgy . . . desperate . . .' Like all other dealers in the City, Mac had had his downs as well as his ups, so he knew what it felt like.

'That's true, Mac. Perhaps that's a factor in the way she's behaved.' Lindsay turned to Ellaline. 'How did you leave things?'

'I helped her get to bed and gave her a sleeping pill Nurse Timson gave me. She was falling asleep. I left a note about her doctor's appointment on her bedside table.' She threw out her hands in appeal. 'I did the best I could. But she's so difficult sometimes . . . and recently, more difficult than ever.'

'You did fine, Ellaline. Thank you for coming to the rescue. And thank you, all of you, for rallying round. Let's put it behind us, shall we?'

'Yes . . . well . . . we're going to Dandy's to wind down. You'll come with us, Lindsay?' Mac said.

She shook her head. 'Thank you, but I . . . I think I'd rather just be quiet for a bit . . . you know, to get the better of it . . . if you don't mind.'

'Yes, of course. Yes, we understand.' With nods and sympathetic smiles they melted away.

Millicent came to say she was off home. Lindsay nodded goodbye. Still she sat on, her office silent, her only companion the computer screen's green glow.

She had no idea how much time had passed when her computer screen was switched off. She started, focusing her gaze. Tad was standing at the side of her desk.

'You ought to go home,' he said.

Yes, she ought to go home. But Celia had gone to Essex, the flat would be empty and drear in its dark wood and leather.

'I'll go in a minute,' she said.

'You look a mite fragile. Come on, let me buy you a drink –'

'No, no – the others –' She couldn't face her team at Dandy's, the coroner's inquest on the afternoon's drama.

'We won't go to Dandy's,' he said. 'Come on.'

He put a hand under her elbow so that, almost automatically, she rose. He urged her through the doorway and then linked arms to guide her through the dealing room. They waited in silence for the lift. They slid their cards through the electronic register at the porter's desk, said goodnight to Gresham, and went out. It was still a bright June evening outside, the shadows growing longer as the sun moved westwards behind the towers of the City.

'There's this little place I've found,' Tad said, 'near Finsbury Circle, has a wine list that includes California. Do you feel like walking?'

'Yes, fine,' she said, breathing in the warm air. So much more normal than the chill of the bank's air conditioning, reassuring and bland.

She thought she caught one or two interested glances from passers-by but they didn't register. She walked along, her arm linked with Tad, thankful for the ordinary streets with buses and taxis hurrying by, the newsvendor at the Tube station holding out the evening paper, the bricked flowerbeds glowing with geraniums, the signposts pointing to Guildhall and Bank and Smithfield.

The wine bar proved to be modern, with metal tables and chairs and giant sunflowers growing in pots. They sat outside under a striped awning, with a view that gave a glimpse of the greenery of Finsbury Circle.

Tad handed her a wine list. She took it and looked at it, but it meant nothing to her. When the waiter came Tad asked for two glasses of Zinfandel. It came, she raised the glass to her lips and sipped. There was a silence.

'Don't take it so hard,' Tad said at last in a quiet voice. 'She's been heading towards something like that for quite a long time now.'

'I should have noticed,' she agreed. She thought about it. 'It's my business to know if my team is under stress.'

'It's not your fault. Nan's a strange person. She has this view of herself that maybe isn't quite accurate. Trying to live up to it has been too much for her.'

'I should have noticed,' Lindsay repeated. 'She's my best friend.' Tad was shaking his head. 'She is,' she insisted, 'we were at university together. We shared digs, went out together with our boyfriends. We started out in the City at the same time. She was bridesmaid at my wedding.'

'And you got her the job at Oistrav's.'

'Yes, she was wasted where she was at Keningham Lightfoot –'

'And you streaked ahead of her and were made head of Portfolio Investment.'

'I was . . . yes, Peter Gruman promoted me . . . but Nan made progress, she's leader of my team . . .'

'You gave her that post.'

'Yes, of course.' She tried to tune in on what he was saying.

'In my home town there's a saying: "If you want to keep your friends, don't do them any favours." '

A faint smile touched her lips. 'Your home town is a very cynical place.'

'It sure is. Because it's full of people looking facts straight in the face, and one of the facts is that some people hate to be grateful.'

'Nan isn't like that.'

'Nan has a great big heavy chip on her shoulder that makes her unbalanced –'

'Unbalanced?'

'Sure, I'd imagine she's been quietly going nuts for a year or so –'

'You hardly know her!' she cried, indignation at last rousing her out of the lethargy of the past few hours.

'Believe me, I know Nan,' he replied in a very matter-of-fact tone. 'I've spent hours sitting beside her while she watches a roulette wheel spin round. I've seen her flushed with pride when she wins, and ready to throw herself off the top of Lloyds Building when she loses. And when I finally tried to back out of all that – because there are better ways to spend an evening – I discovered how hard she works to keep up the façade.'

'Façade? What façade?'

'She's a successful, top-of-the-bill City swinger with a row of cast-off lovers behind her. That's Nan's view of herself.'

'Well,' Lindsay said, 'she *is* successful. She's a member of a winning team. She merits really big bonuses. And she *has* a string of cast-off lovers behind her.'

'Yeah, right. She's a member of a winning team who all get really big bonuses – but Mac does better than Nan, am I right? And Milo is coming up behind him. Nan isn't the best dealer on the team. And as for the lovers – who did the casting off?'

'Don't talk about her like that,' Lindsay protested. 'You're trying to portray her as a loser –'

'She's certainly not a winner. Winners don't behave the way she did this afternoon.'

Lindsay shuddered at the recollection. 'I never saw her like that in my life before. She said some dreadful things . . . but she didn't mean them.'

He nodded. 'The others are really angry about that. She dragged them in, claiming they felt the same. But the truth is, it was her own troubles that caused all that. She's desperate to recoup the losses she's made at the gambling tables, and you know what that can lead to in a City firm.'

'What it can lead to?' She frowned. 'What do you mean? Are you talking about insider dealing?'

'What's your view? Is Nan capable of playing both sides against the middle?'

'Never!' she flashed. 'Don't dare suggest that! Nan's not a swindler. If something's driven her over the edge it isn't pressure from keeping things hidden, nor a sense of guilt, nor anything like that. She's straight as a die!'

In her agitation she rose. The wine was forgotten on the table. She made a move towards the open pavement, away from the wine bar's forecourt.

Tad threw some money on the table so as to hurry after her. 'Slow down there,' he said, taking her arm as she stepped unwarily off the pavement. A car turning into the Circus from Liverpool Street had to brake sharply as Tad pulled her back. 'Let's get you home,' he suggested, and had the luck to flag down a passing taxi.

'Old Flag Wharf,' he told the driver as he handed her in. To Lindsay he said, 'Are you okay?'

'I'm quite all right, thanks.'

'How long is it since you ate?'

'I don't remember . . . oh yes, a sandwich at lunch time . . .' But the memory of what came immediately after lunch time swept over her and quenched her words.

'Have you got any food in the flat?'

'Yes, of course, my mother . . . But I'm not hungry.'

'You've got to have something. You've had a big shock.'

'Yes.'

'It's not every day you see a lifelong friendship crash before your eyes.'

'No.'

'You handled it well, Lindsay.'

'I didn't handle it at all.' She had a mental picture of Tad coming on to the scene. 'You were the one who handled it. You calmed her down.'

'Yeah . . . well . . . she has this wrongheaded idea, you see . . . but it had a good effect at that moment.'

'Poor Nan,' Lindsay grieved. 'It seems nothing's going right for her.'

They reached the block of flats. Tad paid the driver. Lindsay was searching fruitlessly in her handbag for her keys. He took the bag from her, found the keycase, and opened the outer door. The lift was at the foyer, he ushered her in and pressed the button for the third floor.

By the time they reached her door she'd got enough control of herself to put the key in the lock and show him in. She had a momentary thought that it was odd he should be here, Tad Tadiecski, in her temporary home, but her brain seemed unable to supply any reason for the feeling.

'Where's the kitchen?' he asked. She pointed, then followed as he made his way there.

'What are you going to do?' she inquired.

'Soup,' he said. 'You could swallow some soup, I bet.' He glanced about the handsomely fitted kitchen. 'Lord, there's a full battery of equipment here that looks as if it's never used!'

'The people who generally stay here don't go in much for cooking,' she said. 'And my mother confines herself to two or three saucepans.'

'Yeah, right, saucepan. Store cupboard? Tins of soup?'

She shook her head. 'I think there are some cartons. In the freezer.'

'Better yet, because you don't have to use a tin-opener. Right, sit down, service will be available in three minutes.' He took off his jacket, loosened his tie, and opened the door of the freezer.

She sat down at the kitchen table. She told herself she ought to be making the meal, this was her home, she was the hostess. But it was all too much trouble.

In the promised three minutes, Tad set a mug before her. 'Now go on, drink it.' She obeyed. It was celery soup, piping hot. She swallowed a few mouthfuls.

'Better?' he inquired.

'Yes, it's good. Thank you.' And it did have reviving powers. She felt the inner coldness that had been with her since she walked into her office from the dealing room begin to thaw. 'You should have some too,' she said, good manners making a bid.

'Don't mind if I do.' He came to the table with a matching mug, and drank the soup with relish. 'What we'll do,' he said, 'is when you feel up to it, we'll go out and have a proper meal.'

'Yes,' she agreed.

'Well then, finish up your soup.'

She drank what was left in her mug.

'Finished?'

'Yes.'

'Now go and change, and we'll find a nice quiet restaurant.'

Obediently she got up. She went out of the kitchen, into the big living room, and there she paused. Where was she going? What had she been told to do?'

Tad joined her. 'Go on, then, honey.'

'What?'

'You were going to change your dress.'

'Oh.' She looked down at her dress.

And there it was, a great ugly brown stain across the front of the skirt, like a blight that had attacked the pretty blossoms. No wonder passers-by had stared at her.

Something cracked within her, and a great sob shook her.

'Oh, my dress, my lovely new dress!' she cried, and burst into a storm of weeping.

'Lindsay!' Tad exclaimed. 'Don't –'

But the dam had burst, the force of emotion carried her beyond the sound of voice or call of reason. What she longed for was human contact, human warmth. She threw out her hands in appeal.

He took them, pulled her towards him, and let her fall against him for support. Her head rested on his shoulder. Her hair caught in the collar of his shirt, her tears fell on its fine cotton surface. He held her firm, stroking her hair, murmuring soothing words.

For long minutes she wept, her body shaking with the bitter unhappiness of loss – the loss of a friend, the loss of her belief in that friend, the final parting with the good things of her girlhood, of which there had been too few.

By and by she became calm. She straightened. 'I must look a sight,' she sighed falteringly.

'Not at all,' he assured her. 'But come on now, let's bathe your eyes and get you ready to go out.'

With his arm about her, she went to her bedroom, on into the bathroom to bathe her eyes and wash her face. Tad handed her a towel. She held it close against her cheeks, rubbed hard to scrub away all dreadful memories of the day.

When she went into the bedroom Tad had the door of the fitted wardrobe open, surveying her clothes. 'We won't go anywhere high-hat,' he said. 'How about jeans and a shirt?'

She began to unzip the ruined frock. Tad turned as it fell to the floor about her feet. For a moment his gaze remained the same – a kindly adult being helpful to a hurt child. But as they stared at each other, it changed.

He stepped up to her. He put his two hands on her waist, on the bare patch between bra and slip. His touch was warm on her cold skin. She raised her hand to let her fingers trace the tendons of his throat into the opening of his shirt. Their eyes were gazing deep into each other, locked already in a joining of spirit and feeling that called for yet more, a consummation of the body. They knew without the need of words that this was why Fate had placed them here, for this moment and for this reason.

With an impulse as strong as the life force itself, they moved together to the bed. And on its welcoming surface, they made love.

Chapter Sixteen

She woke with a start. Someone was moving about in the room. But then Tad's voice said softly in her ear, 'It's all right, it's only me. I have to go now, Lindsay.'

Only half-awake, her mind told her, Oh yes, I had to do that a score of times, hurry home so as to get ready for work . . .

Drowsily she said, 'See you later, darling.' She felt his goodbye kiss as she slipped back into sleep.

When she opened her eyes again it was light, but she could tell it wasn't long after sunrise. She stretched luxuriously. Her hand encountered the empty pillow. For a moment she was surprised, regretful, then recalled he had slipped away while it was still dark.

She dragged the pillow close to her, embraced it as if it were his body. About it there was still the faint fragrance of something – shaving cream, hair gel, something that spoke to her of Tad.

Drifting in and out of sleep, she remembered the night that was just ending. A tumult of passion, beyond anything she'd ever experienced before. Mouths seeking and finding valleys and contours of delight, hands exploring and caressing, voices murmuring endearments until words ceased to have meaning and only physical triumph would serve.

And then the long, soft hour of lying together, the current between them eased into little touches, little jokes, his hand in her hair and hers on his shoulder, easy, gentle, but with promise of things to come.

The second coming-together was utterly fulfilling. They had learned each other's ways, so there was no hesitation in giving and receiving pleasure, confident enough to delay, to string out the sexual tension until at last they were one, transformed, free of the earth, a rainbow in the sky, a comet with a fiery train, a star whirling in a far galaxy.

She sighed to herself. Ah, how long it had taken her to find him, the man who was truly meant for her. How lucky she was to have found him – lucky, happy, grateful for this glow that suffused her body, her whole world. I'm in love, she said to herself, really in love at last. Everything that's gone before was second best, and I thought it was wonderful, but now I know, now I can never be mistaken again.

By and by the radio-clock on the bedside table sprang to life with music from a brash commercial station, guaranteed to waken any sleeper. She put out a hand, switched off the noise, and sat up. It was six-thirty, time to start the day.

She showered, and found that she was singing to herself: 'Oh what a beautiful mo-orning . . .' Laughing, she quenched the song in a vigorous scrub with the sponge. When it came to choosing what to wear, she decided on the new skirt of raw silk and a chambray shirt – a totally new look again, what would the office say? Even the sight of the ruined frock couldn't mar her good spirits. She bundled it up and put it in the kitchen bin.

She drank orange juice, ate some crispbread and butter, then realized she was ravenously hungry. But she had time for nothing more, for Sudin was downstairs pressing the buzzer. She ran down, greeted him with a sparkle that perhaps surprised him, then got into the car.

As she did so she had a quick mental snatch of doing the same thing last night. Tad had handed her into a taxi outside the wine bar.

And had given her address to the driver without asking her for it.

She gave an exclamation. Sudin asked, 'Something wrong, Mrs Dunforth?'

'No, nothing.' She didn't want to have to converse. She wanted to concentrate on last night.

Tad had hailed the taxi after something that happened outside the wine bar – had she nearly got herself run over? Something like that, she couldn't recall. But she remembered that he had spoken her address. 'Old Flag Wharf,' he'd said.

And when they got to the block he'd taken her into the lift and without hesitation had pressed the button for the third floor.

How did he know she was living on the third floor at Old Flag Wharf? It was a well-known joke at the bank that she lived in a wreck of a house in Putney that was perpetually under repair.

Sudin, seeing that she was thinking, tactfully made no effort at conversation. She said goodbye at the bank and went in, nodding good morning at Studley.

As usual, few people were about in the building. She went along to Tad's office to see if he was there and was glad to see that so far, he was not. She went to her own office, switched on her screen, and sat down. But she wasn't concerned with the columns of figures that showed up. She was thinking about last night.

Tad hadn't gone out with the others to Dandy's to unwind, although it would have been natural to do so. He'd waited – on purpose? – and then come to her office.

'Come for a drink.' She'd shied away and he'd said, 'Not at Dandy's,' so they'd gone to the wine bar where of course they'd be alone.

They'd talked. What had they talked about? Nan Compton, what else. She tried to remember what they'd said about Nan. Phrases and disconnected sentences came back to her. 'She's straight as a die!' She'd said that when he asked something about Nan – was she honest, was she likely to be doing something shifty.

Others began to appear in the dealing room. She waved good morning to them. Millicent arrived. She warded off inquiries as to her well-being, gave instructions for the next few pieces of correspondence, sent a message through the intra-net to her team for the beginning of business. She'd intended to go out for a big breakfast, but she found her appetite had deserted her. But she needed to have time to think, and there would be little of that if she stayed in the office.

'I'm going out for a bit,' she told Millicent. 'If you want me you can call me on my mobile.'

'Okay,' said Millicent. Nothing unusual about people popping out at odd moments.

In the streets the nine-to-fivers were pouring out of the Tube stations and alighting from buses. She walked down Moorgate and into the forecourt of the Guildhall. Later the City Flower Show would open in the great old building, but for the moment it was relatively quiet. She sat on a bench in the courtyard.

She was beginning to think that Tad had made friends with Nan Compton at first for reasons of his own. Then he had seen the signs of her coming breakdown and tried to back off.

Had Lindsay become his next target? Was he thinking she would be his accomplice, his dupe?

What his aim might be, she couldn't yet understand. But he had come to London with a purpose and Oistrav's was to be the means by which he carried it out. He had snooped around the office. She was almost sure he had hacked into the personal files on her office computer. He had come into the dealing room one night to carry out some action on the bank's equipment but she'd startled him and put him off. He'd realized she was on his track when he caught her in his flat and had somehow found out where she was living – for what reason? To return the compliment? To pry into her private life?

She was struck by a dreadful thought. Her mother's computers . . . She'd wakened in the night to find Tad up and dressed, about to leave – but how could she tell what he'd been doing while she was asleep? All he had to do was walk into the dining room and he'd see that array of electronics. And he himself was an adept: perhaps he'd broken into Celia's files.

No, not in an hour or two. Celia had weird passwords, nothing simple like Greek goddesses but compilations of letters and numbers. It would take ages to unravel, he wouldn't have had time.

But if he'd seen that equipment he probably knew that he should be doubly on his guard.

And of course he would think it easy to handle her now. She was in love with him, poor fool. She'd told him so last night.

Burning with shame, she jumped to her feet. She walked out of the courtyard and into the busy City streets. With a quick stride she covered the ground between the Guildhall and Oistrav's.

So he thought he had her in the hollow of his hand, did he?

She found him hovering near her office, tall and spare and conservatively clad in dark trousers and white shirt. 'Nan hasn't come in yet?' he asked, nodding at her empty desk.

'Evidently not.'

'Ellaline was asking if someone should ring to see how she is – not you, of course,' he added hastily as she stiffened. 'Ellaline says she'll do it.'

'If Nan is keeping that doctor's appointment, she won't be at home.'

'Oh, right. What do we do, then, just wait?'

'Seems so.'

He gave a half-smile, half-frown. 'Are you all right?'

'Yes, thank you. Did the figures from Allby Dynamo come through?'

'Why – yes – they're on my desk –'

'The Chairman will need them after lunch, we're seeing the M.D. at three.'

'Sure thing, I'll send them in. Lindsay –?'

'That's all for the moment, Tad, thank you.'

She turned in at her doorway. She had a glimpse of his baffled expression as he too turned away, and felt an impulse of satisfaction. She felt like saying to him, If you've got something in the hollow of your hand, it can slip through your fingers.

At mid-morning the Personnel Manager rang to say that Miss Compton had been in touch. She had a certificate from her doctor for a week's sick leave on grounds of mental stress. Lindsay was thankful not to have her in the office and called her team in to tell them the news, allotting Nan's work between them.

Henry Wishaw, the bank's Chairman, asked Lindsay to join him ahead of the meeting with Allby Dynamo. 'I hear there was some sort of fracas in the dealing room yesterday?'

'Yes, one of my brokers, Nan Compton. She's on sick leave for a week.'

'Er . . . em . . . the word is that she was hysterical?'

'The doctor's certificate calls it mental stress.'

Mr Wishaw groaned. It was well known that the strain of the dealing room was apt to burn out the dealers. Recently some of them had been bringing suit against their employers on grounds of undue pressure. Since many of the sufferers had been high-flyers earning large salaries and larger bonuses, settlement of claims for loss of earnings tended to be very costly.

Lindsay spent some time soothing the Chairman. Then in came the Managing Director of Allby Dynamo trying to pressure them into putting his shares back on their list of preferred investments.

Back in the dealing room her team were trying to recoup the losses of yesterday and also repair the mistakes Nan had made. They reported only partial success.

It had not been a good day.

She went to the leisure centre when she left the bank. She swam for almost an hour, using all the different strokes in her repertoire, diving from the highest step so as to feel the cleansing water rushing past. When she climbed out at last she was physically tired, and to some extent her thoughts were slowed down. But she didn't have the feeling of being restored and refreshed that usually followed.

When she got to Old Flag Wharf, her mother had returned. She was unpacking a basket of exotic vegetables when Lindsay came into the kitchen.

'Hello, love, look what I've brought.'

'Looks lovely. Had a good visit?'

'Oh yes, great, we all went to Bishop's Stortford to watch Alice showing off in the pool. She's really good, you know, Lindsay – maybe when she gets to school she'll make the swimming team, like her mother.' Celia closed the door of the fridge and for the first time turned to take a good look at her daughter. 'What's wrong? You look awfully pale.'

'Nothing serious. Mother, you went away to have a think about getting into those computer files. Did you come up with a plan?'

'No, I went over it and over it and I can't see how to do any more than I've already done. I mean, you can program a search for a password and let it run until it finds it for you, but it could take months, years even!'

'So there's nothing you can do?'

Celia shook her head thoughtfully. 'The screen just asks "Who?" It's odd. Usually it says something like "Enter Password." I don't know what to do about it.'

'I suppose we'll have to accept that he's too clever for us,' Lindsay sighed. 'Certainly he'd got some awfully sophisticated stuff.'

'Describe it to me, Lindsay.'

'I've already done that –'

'Do it again.'

So Lindsay went through the mental list, trying to picture the room as she described it.

'What was that?' her mother said sharply.

'What?'

'Did you say a microphone?'

'Yes, I think so. On one of those headsets.'

'You didn't mention that before!'

'I did.' She hesitated. 'Didn't I?'

'No, you said nothing about a mike on a headset.'

'Is it important?'

'I think it is. Because, you see, I think it means the computer expects a verbal reply.'

Lindsay stared. 'Voice-activated software?'

'It's getting better all the time.'

'I've never heard you speak to your computer,' Lindsay said, half-joking.

'No, no, I haven't bothered. But I could easily put in software that responded to my voice.'

'To *your* voice.' She thought about it. 'That means . . . if someone else said your password, it wouldn't respond?'

'No, it has to be the programmed voice.'

'So even if we could work out the password we're looking for, it wouldn't do us any good, because it would only answer to a man's voice.'

'That's the case as it stands at the moment.'

'That's that, then. The program is impregnable.'

Her mother laughed. 'Darling, anything put into a computer can be unloaded. All you have to do is find out how.'

'Could you do that? You'd unload the voice response?'

'I can certainly try.' Her forehead wrinkled in thought. She ran a hand through her wiry hair. 'I'll have to get a few things, though – the software I'm using here isn't up to the job. But tomorrow . . . yes, tomorrow I'll definitely have a go, and now I know what I'm up against I think we'll see a change.'

'Well, that's great, Cecie, that's marvellous!'

'I see it is,' Celia replied. 'You actually look better than when you came in!' Then, after a pause, she added, 'It's that important, is it?'

'Yes, Cecie, it is.'

Towards six o'clock, the phone rang. Lindsay was in the kitchen preparing a salad from the supplies her mother had brought from Essex so Celia answered. 'It's someone called Tad,' she reported, hand over the mouthpiece.

Lindsay dropped the paring knife with a clatter. 'Tell him I'm not here.'

'I'm afraid she's not here,' Celia said obediently. 'No, she's out. No, I don't know when – No, I don't. Perhaps not. Very well, I'll tell her.'

'Tell me what?' Lindsay asked as she hung up the receiver.

'He'll ring again.'

Lindsay walked over, picked the receiver off the apparatus, and laid it on the worktop.

'Oh,' said Celia, 'like that, is it?' And asked no questions.

Although Lindsay had no appetite she knew she ought to eat. Mother and daughter had a leisurely meal then resorted to television for the evening's entertainment. About nine o'clock the entryphone buzzer sounded from downstairs.

Celia looked at Lindsay with raised eyebrows. 'Could this be "Tad"?' she inquired. 'And if it is, how does he know this address?'

'It's too difficult to explain. Just answer and say I'm still not here.'

'Why don't you answer and tell him to go away?'

Because I don't want to speak to him, because I want to avoid any contact if I can. Aloud she said, as the buzzer sounded yet again, 'Please get rid of him, Cecie.'

Celia went to the microphone in the hall. 'Who is it? Oh, yes, you telephoned – No, I'm afraid she still isn't here. Really? No, I didn't know. Thank you for telling me. Yes, of course. I'll write it down. Goodbye.'

She came back into the sitting room. 'He says our phone isn't working, and when you come in will you ring him. I didn't bother to write down the number since you obviously wouldn't want it.'

Lindsay felt herself colouring up. 'I'm sorry,' she said. 'I know I seem silly but it's . . . well . . . I'd just rather not speak to him.'

'Who is he?'

'Someone from the bank.'

Her mother sat down. In the background the television was still quacking on about a resolution at the United Nations causing a deadlock. With one of those leaps of intuition that sometimes come to mothers, Celia said, 'Is Tad by any chance the man whose computer has a voice-access program?'

Lindsay said nothing.

'I see he is. Do you think he's the one who's after us?'

'Yes. No.' How could the man who had held her so tenderly last night be an enemy? 'I've got to find out, Mother! It's terribly important.'

'It certainly is. Because if he's the sender of those threats, he knows where we're living now. How did he find out?'

'I don't know.' She thought of Tad giving her address to the taxi man. 'Perhaps he followed me home one day. I just don't know.' Yet that didn't seem likely. Travelling home as she did by Tube and Docklands Light Railway, she would have been difficult to keep track of.

'It's not good, Lindsay.'

'No, I agree, but at least Alice isn't here. Nobody knows where Alice is.'

Celia nodded. 'Well, when we go to bed tonight we'll put the chain on the door –'

'He couldn't get in at the entry without a key, Mother –'

'Don't be silly, Lindsay, when I came home with my arms full of aubergines and peppers, someone coming out held the door open for me.'

Lindsay stifled a groan. It was only too true. As the consultants at the bank kept saying, security is only as good as you make it. And she, by her stupidity, had laid them open to attack.

She had brought him here – or let him come, which was the same thing. She might say she was only half aware of what was happening, because of the shock of Nan's attack. It was true. Yet it was only a half-truth.

For while she was stepping out of the ruined summer dress, he was in the same room with her. She knew it, was intensely aware of the fact although everything else that day had faded into a haze. She must surely have known what would happen. Had she wanted it to happen? Looking back, she tried to be honest in her reply to herself. But she was unsure.

The fact was, this morning she'd been blissfully happy because they'd become lovers. Now she was blaming herself, regretting every moment of that wonderful night. The contrast between how she'd felt at daybreak and how she felt now was as bitter as wormwood.

The only remedy was to put her defences back together. She had distrusted Tad at the outset, had kept a certain chill in her manner. So she would go back to the distant smile, the polite brush-off. She had to banish for ever the memory of how dear he had been to her as she lay in his arms.

She slept badly, and next morning her mirror told her so. She applied a little makeup to remedy her pallor. Today was going to be difficult enough without the consciousness of looking wan and tired. But all her colleagues were still being very kind and considerate to her in the aftermath of Nan's outburst, so that her only real difficulty was steering clear of Tad.

When he arrived at the bank the first thing he did was to stop by her office. 'Didn't your mother give you my message?' he asked.

'What message? Oh, to ring you? Was it important?'

'Important?' he echoed. She saw him frown, then make a little shake of the head. 'Obviously not,' he said. 'My mistake.'

There, it was done. She had shown him how things stood. And if she avoided him in the building, and made sure he didn't catch her alone at any time outside, she was safe.

She had a lunch date that day and a dinner engagement in the evening, both on behalf of the bank. The dinner proved very tiring because her next door neighbour on one side spoke only Portuguese of which she had only a few words, and on the other side she had an executive wife. Executive wives come in two varieties, those who share their husband's career ambition and work at it, and those who wish to shine on their own account. Mrs Bardolo was of the latter type: she was patroness of several art galleries and wished everyone to know it.

Weary to the point of exhaustion, Lindsay went home to the flat by taxi about eleven-thirty. As she stepped out at Old Flag Wharf, a figure emerged from a car parked hard by.

'Lindsay, let me speak to you a minute –'

'Tad!' She drew back in alarm. 'What are you doing here?'

'Waiting for you, of course. You've been so quick on your feet at the bank I haven't been able to get near you.'

'I've been busy –'

'So I noticed. Listen, I don't understand what your view is. I thought we –'

'If you want to talk about that little episode a couple of nights age, I think we can just forget it. These things happen.'

'They do?' he said, brusquely.

'Office romance, you know – it's never a good thing. So let's put it behind us.'

'I didn't think it was quite like that for us –'

'You weren't taking it seriously?'

She couldn't tell whether the little silence that followed was puzzlement or displeasure. Then he said, 'That's all right then. We just go on as if it never happened.'

'Right. Now if you don't mind, Tad, it's been a very long day –'

'Sure, sure, sorry to have bothered you. Goodnight, Lindsay. Sweet dreams.'

'Goodnight, Tad.'

While she was unlocking the outer door of the flats she heard him drive away. She turned to watch the tail lights of his car blink as he braked at the corner, then he was gone. She had to wait some minutes before her hand was steady enough to turn the key and go in. In the lift she leaned against its mirrored wall, hardly able to keep her feet in the undertow of weariness and misery.

She'd fended him off. It was what she'd wanted to do. Everything was now crystal clear between them. If he'd had any thoughts that she might join him in whatever scheme he was engaged in, he knew now it was hopeless. Moreover there could be no reason now for him to telephone her or come in person to the flat. The barriers were up, the sign saying No Admittance was there in very large letters.

All the lights in the flat were on. A litter of used cups and plates bedecked the kitchen table. The door of the dining room was open and from it came a subdued sound, a faint tattoo of fingers on keyboard. She went to the door to look round it at Celia, intent on her work.

'I'm home, Mother.'

'Oh yes, dear, good. Have a nice time?'

'Lovely,' Lindsay said with hidden irony. 'Do you know it's getting on for midnight?'

'It is really? Never mind. I'm on the verge of cracking this thing.'

'You've found the password?'

'No, but I've unblocked the access. I've managed to download his voice-only lock and in a minute I'm going to have it on-screen and accessible to an "Enter" response.'

'Well, that's great,' Lindsay said. 'What did you do, buy some new software or something?'

'No, I had things at home that I knew would help so I just drove over to Putney to collect them.'

'You went to the house!'

'Oh, don't worry, I switched off the alarm when I went in and turned it back on when I left. And I brought you some clothes – they're in those carrier bags you'll find on your bed.'

Lindsay was about to say she would rather her mother didn't go to the Putney house while it was standing empty. But all at once it seemed too difficult to explain all that.

'I'm going to have a bath,' she said, 'and then I'm going to bed. And you should too, Mother.'

'Yes, yes, in a minute, dear,' Celia said, scarcely heeding her.

Lindsay was half asleep by the time she'd bathed and brushed her teeth. She was taking the carrier bags off her bed in preparation for falling into it herself when her mother's excited voice summoned her.

'Lindsay, Lindsay, come here!'

Startled into wakefulness, she hurried into the dining room. On the dining table the computer screen was glowing in emerald green, with the word 'Who?' in bright white capitals.

'Lindsay,' Celia asked, 'what's the answer to "Who?" '

'I've no idea.'

Celia made a sound of irritation. 'Lindsay! Say it! "Who?" '

Her daughter stood a moment letting the question hang in the air. Then she said: 'Who – me?'

'I think so! Normally, if it was voice-only, then only Tad's voice would work. But now I've altered all that. So let's try it.' She typed in: 'Me.'

The screen flickered, flared in little lights, then resolved itself into a menu.

'There you are,' Celia said in triumph. 'We're in!'

'That's wonderful, Mother. Now . . . can we find out what he's been doing?'

'Files,' muttered Celia, running the cursor down to that entry. She hit "Return" and the files were listed.

'Oh,' they said in unison. For one of the files was titled 'Dunforth'.

'That one,' Lindsay said, and scarcely knew whether she wanted to see what would be shown on screen. If he had downloaded personal information and then acted as if he were her friend, it meant that he was a despicable snooper.

The screen rearranged itself with the heading 'Dunforth p1'. The subheading was 'Selene'. And there, neatly displayed in columns, were the details of her bank account showing debits and credit for the current month. Page 2 was a precis of the negotiations for the purchase of her house. Page 3 was the plan for renovations with their costings. And so on, through all her financial affairs – insurance policies, investments, her mother's business book-keeping, the salaries for Eddie and Tracy Taylor and their Social Security records – everything to do with the Dunforth household.

Lindsay thought of how close she had been to the man who had perpetrated this act of intrusion. She had believed while they were in each other's arms that everything between them was open and honest. What a fool . . .

'Oh, Cecie, Cecie,' she whispered in total despair. 'What have I done?'

And in her head she heard the answer to that question. As the film title said, she had been sleeping with the enemy.

Chapter Seventeen

Her mother exited from the program on her computer and closed it down. She rose, stretching. 'I don't know about you,' she said, 'but I think that calls for a celebratory drink.'

'I think I'll just go to bed,' Lindsay responded. She was in no mood to celebrate.

'All right, goodnight, dear.'

'Goodnight, Mother.'

In her bedroom the bed, a moment age so enticing, held no attraction. She sat down in the chair by the dark wood bureau, her mind teeming with unwelcome thoughts.

And what should she do now? She had the proof she'd wanted, that Tad Tadiecski was involved in something dishonest. She should report it. But to whom? In times gone by she'd have gone to Peter Gruman with her problem but she no longer trusted Peter. Should she go to the bank's Chairman, Henry Wishaw? And say what? That she'd discovered Tad Tadiecski was hacking into the bank's computers. How, he would ask, did she learn this? By herself hacking into Tad's computer. The complexity of her explanation would be a drawback. And what would Wishaw do? Fire Tad. City companies rarely brought a case against employees caught misbehaving. It was bad publicity, bad for business.

So Tad would go, and would they ever find out if his activities were linked with the mysterious National Northern Concentral Inc and Global Soundfast? Probably not, because although the bank's lawyers would press for information, he would avoid disclosure. He would know they didn't want to prosecute and that he needn't reveal much – just enough to make it seem he was co-operating but leaving most things hidden.

So perhaps she should go straight to the Serious Fraud Office. Yet the publicity would be horrendous. Clients would leave the bank in droves. Some of her rich private clients were elderly, they relied on Oistrav's as if it were family. To find that this old friend had been hoodwinked, that its employees weren't to be trusted . . . Their dream of security in old age would be shattered. She must always remember, it wasn't only for herself that she must think; other people's dreams were important too.

There was a tap on the bedroom door. Her mother came in, bearing a little tray on which were two glasses of wine. 'Saw your light was still on,' she said, 'and you know I never like to drink alone. So come along, dear, and have a glass of Chardonnay.'

It was easier to accept than to argue. Lindsay took the glass.

'And now for heaven's sake, tell me what's the matter,' Celia commanded.

'What?'

'Your face when you saw those files! I thought you'd be delighted, but you looked ready to burst into tears. What's up, Lindsay?'

'It's too difficult to explain, Cecie –'

'No it isn't. Leave out the high finance, but tell me what it is about this man Tad Whatever that bothers you so much.'

'Who says he bothers me?'

'I do. Come on, darling, we've shared a lot of problems in the past. Is he the reason you broke up with Barry?'

'No no,' Lindsay said before she thought about it, 'the thing with Barry was over before Tad and I –' She broke off.

'Before Tad and you fell in love?'

'I never said that!'

'You didn't need to say it. It's in your face now. You're absolutely shattered because I showed you what he's been up to.'

'I can't bear to think that he . . . he . . .'

'He what? He broke into your files? But Lindsay – you're generally so clear-headed – *I've* broken into the bank's files and now into Tad's, but you're not calling *me* an outcast.'

'Well, that's different –'

'How's it different?'

'We're doing it because we're worried something bad is going on.'

'And what is Tad's reason?'

'Presumably it's something to do with National Northern Concentral Inc and so on –'

'Yes, I suppose it is.' Celia sighed. 'It's just that you're getting thinner and paler every day, and I can't bear it if you're getting in this state over a man who's not worth it. Do you really think he sent us that scary photograph of me and Alice? And made the fire in the wastebin?'

'Well, all of that only happened after he arrived on the scene.'

'Hm,' murmured Celia. 'Isn't that what they call something like "*post hoc ergo propter hoc*"? In other words, it happened after he appeared on the scene *therefore* he must be the culprit? It's not all that convincing –'

'But he got the job at Oistrav's under false pretences, I've proved that! His last employer was supposed to be a prestigious Wall Street firm so we took up references, of course, and it turns out his personnel file there is a fake. What's more, he said he'd come to London to be a bit nearer his father who lives in Provence, but his father died five years ago.'

'Oh dear.'

'Yes, oh dear.'

There was a pause while Celia thought it over. 'You've been worried about this man for a long time, then.'

'Yes.'

'Coming to it all at once, as I am, it seems to me you've made a lot of inquiries about him. Is there anyone else you've thought of?'

Her question gave Lindsay a slight jolt. After all, she knew – she *knew* – that she herself had done nothing to merit the threats that had come to her family. Try as she might, she couldn't picture Tad reacting in that way. But someone a bit paranoid might feel persecuted and, thinking that Lindsay was the persecutor, might have taken those strange actions.

Someone a bit paranoid . . . What had Tad said about Nan the other evening? 'She's unbalanced.' And hadn't Nan shown by her outburst how great a grudge she had against Lindsay?

Had Nan sent the photograph, set the fire, hacked into her private computer files? Had it been Nan who fled the dealing room when Lindsay startled her in the dark?

It had never occurred to her to make any inquiries about Nan. Nor about anyone else, it now struck her. From the first she'd been determined to suspect Tad Tadiecski. And why? Because from the first she'd been uneasy about him. Because he had lied at his interview – that was a fact, an undeniable fact. But did all the rest follow?

'Perhaps I've been unjust to him,' she said slowly.

'Well, then, talk to Peter Gruman about him –'

'Peter vouched for him!' she exclaimed, remembering it all too clearly. 'I don't trust Peter any more.'

Her mother said, almost crossly, 'Don't be silly, Lindsay. Peter Gruman is a lovely man and would never be involved with anything shady.'

'I thought the same, until I caught him out.'

'Exactly how, dear? I mean, what's Peter done?' Celia was unwilling to concede that Peter Gruman had done anything wrong. She'd met him on several occasions and if the truth were told, was rather in love with that handsome old man.

'Well, he pretended to ring up a man in New York to verify Tad's CV –'

'You mean he didn't really?'

'Well, he said Tad was okay. And Tad is very far from okay.'

'Hmm,' said her mother. 'I suppose you're right, dear, you usually are. I just find it hard to suspect Peter.'

They finished the wine. Celia said, 'Now let's get to bed. Try to get some sleep, Lindsay – you really look exhausted.'

Contrary to her expectations, Lindsay fell asleep at once. She woke next morning when the radio came on, then lay for a moment trying to think what day it was and what had happened the day before.

It all came back to her. And at first a wave of misery lapped over her. But she fought it off, dragged herself out of bed, and got ready for the day. Somewhere within her she had the feeling that today she would make a move, take a course of action: while she slept, her unconscious mind had been working at her problem.

She dressed in a familiar dark silk dress, one that Celia had brought from the house. Oddly enough it seemed to reinforce her sense that she was in control, made her more herself than she had been for the last few days.

Sudin greeted her as she got in the car. He had some little pieces of family news, then said, 'I am told your mother is going to my uncle's for the weekend. Do you go also?'

'Probably, Sudin, I'm dying to see Alice. Speaking to her on the phone isn't the same.'

'The weather is not so good now, she gets a little bored having to say indoors, I hear. No more picnics, eh?'

The weather was beginning to break up. The usual British summer: three fine days and a thunder storm. She thought of her housekeeper and her handyman, Tracy and Eddie Taylor, cooped up in a caravan in a muddy field. 'Poor things,' she said to Sudin, 'I ought to tell them they can come back – because nothing seems to be happening at the house, does it?'

'The security patrol is very reliable. I think no one could gain entrance, except perhaps an experienced burglar –'

'Well, I came to the conclusion that whoever was bothering us was a bit of an amateur,' Lindsay said with some lightness. 'I'll drop Tracy a line to say come home – they're not on the telephone there.'

At the bank she switched on her screen to see what the overseas markets were doing. The Hang Seng and the Nikkei were in a state of excitement but Wall Street had closed quietly.

Wall Street . . . Where Tad had come from . . . That at least was true, for he had a mass of background information that could only have been gained by working there. Even if his personnel file at Hurley Gounett were a fake, he had worked *somewhere* on Wall Street.

The firm for which he was supposed to have worked, Hurley Gounett . . . One of its Vice-Presidents had guaranteed his probity, according to Peter. Lindsay had thought that was some kind of trick.

Did she know that for sure? Her mother's outright condemnation of her doubts echoed in her mind: 'Peter Gruman is a lovely man and would never be involved with anything shady.' That had been her own instinctive judgement at first. Could she and her mother both be entirely mistaken in thinking well of him? Well, yes, because Celia was more than a little smitten, and she herself felt gratitude to him that made her desperately unhappy to think badly of him.

Was it fair to condemn him on a conclusion she'd drawn without ever verifying it? She *believed* he had tricked her. Oughtn't she to make sure?

How to do that . . . ? Well, Peter had said he would ring his old friend John Blebel and had seemed to have a conversation with him. Lindsay could ring John Blebel and find out if the conversation had actually taken place.

But not yet. Wall Street wouldn't come into action for another five or six hours. In the meantime she must get to work on what she was paid to do – look after her clients' investments.

At a leisure moment she wrote a note to Tracy Taylor at the

caravan address, asking her to return with Eddie to the house and get it aired out in preparation for their return. She didn't say precisely when they would be back, but to reassure the Taylors that all would be well she said she would keep on the security firm for a while longer.

The dealing room more or less emptied at lunch time. Should she make her call to the States on one of the office phones? Everything that went over those lines was recorded. Did that matter? Perhaps, perhaps not.

There were plenty of little shops offering cheap calls overseas. She went out, accepting the loan of an umbrella from Studley as another rain shower began. She hurried out of the courtyard into Pewter Lane and was lucky enough to flag down a taxi slowly making its way along that narrow thoroughfare. She asked to be taken to High Holborn and there, within minutes, she'd found a phonecall shop.

She had the number for Hurley Gounett on a scrap of paper. She was ushered to a booth and put through almost at once. She asked for John Blebel, identified herself as a member of Oistrav's Bank, and was connected.

'Mr Blebel?'

'Mrs Dunforth?'

'Good morning, Mr Blebel, sorry to call so early –'

'Not at all, not at all, we bankers keep early hours. What can I do for you?'

'I'm just ringing to verify a point about William Tadiecski.'

'Who?'

'William Tadiecski – he came to us from your firm –'

'Oh, Tadiecski! Yes, of course, William Tadiecski – how's he doing?'

'Very well, I'm happy to say. He's a great asset to Oistrav's.'

'I'm sure he is. Let's see, what did Peter say about him when he called? He was applying for the post of Research Analyst?'

Lindsay's heart gave a leap of pleasure. Peter had actually made the call! He and John Blebel had talked on the phone about Tad. She'd been wrong, utterly wrong, to mistrust Peter.

'Yes, he's our Analyst, and there's talk about merging the job with the Compliance Officer's, and what I'm asking is –'

'Whether I think Tadiecski would be up to that, eh?' Blebel said, accepting this invention without hesitation. 'Compliance Officer – it's a lot of work even for a merchant bank, making sure everyone complies with the ethics of trading. But . . . yes . . . yes . . . I'd have to check with Personnel about it because I don't know him all that well but I'd say . . . yes . . . Have you spoken to him about it?'

'Not yet, Mr Blebel –'

'Call me John. And you're –?'

'Lindsay – Lindsay Dunforth –'

'Of course, Peter's told me so much about you, Lindsay – it's a great pleasure to have this chat with you. Is there anything else you wanted to ask, because I've another call waiting –'

'No, thank you, Mr Blebel – John – That's all I wanted to know. Thank you very much.'

She replaced the receiver and turned her face up towards an unseen heaven in thanks for what she'd just heard. Peter Gruman had not misled her. He had rung John Blebel and John Blebel had given Tad Tadiecski a clean bill of health.

Not that he seemed to know very much about him. But that could be seen as understandable: the VP of a big Wall Street investment house was unlikely to know every staff member well. If someone faxed their Personnel Manager inquiring whether William Tadiecski was sober, honest and reliable, the Personnel Manager would call up the file on his computer. No matter that it seemed skimpy, as Buddy Tromberg had reported to Lindsay. It wouldn't occur to the Personnel Manager that Tadiecski had inserted that file himself into the computer, to be available when his reference was checked.

None of that concerned Peter Gruman. Peter had talked to John Blebel, there had been no pretence, John Blebel himself said so. Blebel probably summoned up the reference on his office intra-net while Peter was speaking to him, reading off what he saw, quite unaware he was being misled.

Now . . . thank heaven . . . she knew she could trust Peter.

She went to a busy cafe to have a snack lunch. Then in the taxi on her way back to Oistrav's, she called Peter on her mobile.

'Lindsay!' he cried when at length he answered. 'How lovely to hear from you! I've neither seen you nor heard from you since Derby Day.'

She was almost tongue-tied with embarrassment at the recollection of why she had been avoiding him. How could she ever have been so stupid as to suspect him?

'Can I come to see you this afternoon?'

'Of course, my dear, any time. You'll come for tea?'

'Yes, please,' she said, thinking that having to drink Earl Grey was insufficient punishment for her folly.

Everything seemed better for the rest of the day. Her team carried out the investment programme she'd set them on the intra-net, Millicent had good responses to phone calls and faxes, the clients who rang were in general happy with the statements of account which were now reaching them, and Tad Tadiecski was in a conference over a long analytical programme for the Venture Capital Department.

A little after four she arrived at Peter's penthouse in the Barbican. His man Darrow opened the door to her. 'Good afternoon, miss. Mr Gruman is waiting for you.'

'Thank you. Is he well?'

'A little extra touch of arthritis today so he's had to take extra painkillers, but don't mention it if you please.'

'No, of course not.' She went on into the living room, feeling guilty. While she was suspecting him of all kinds of iniquity, Peter was continuing his battle with his intractable disease . . .

'My dear!' he said, taking her hands and kissing them one after the other. 'I haven't seen you in an age! But I've been kept in touch, you know . . . People tell me things. So I know that Cupid has been causing trouble in the Investment Portfolio Department.'

'What?' And to her own dismay she felt herself go pink. Surely no one could know that she and Tad had become lovers?

'I hear you've broken up with your young man.'

'Oh,' she said, 'Barry. Well, perhaps it had to come.'

'Is it true, he was trying to detain you by force outside the entrance?'

'By force – well, he was holding on to my wrist –'

'Silly. If you can't hold a woman by strength of personality, physical force won't work. I always thought your Barry rather dull, you know, Lindsay.'

She shrugged. 'That's in the past, Peter.'

He went slowly into the kitchen in answer to the sound of the kettle switching itself off. Lindsay followed, and firmly forbade herself to offer to help.

'Something is worrying you,' he remarked as he painfully poured boiling water into the teapot. 'I watched what you did over that crisis with the grain forecast, you did well. You're not having difficulties otherwise with your portfolios?'

'Nothing out of the ordinary. It's something else.'

'What? That outburst by one of your team?'

'Oh, you heard about that too?'

'My spies are everywhere,' he said with a smile, and let her carry the tray of tea things into the living room. 'I gather it was a great drama.'

'A miserable business,' she remarked.

'Nan Compton, wasn't it?'

'Yes, strange though it seems. I always thought of her as being so steady, so reliable.'

'A second line player, I'm afraid. As you say, one thought her steady but she has no brilliance. I heard she attacked you?'

'Oh, no,' Lindsay protested, 'she only threw a cup of coffee over me.'

'Only!' said Peter. The armchairs faced windows speckled with rain. He lowered himself into one, nodded at her to pour the tea, and pushed a tray of Bahlsen chocolate biscuits towards her.

'What are you going to do about Nan?' he inquired, nibbling.

'Well, nothing.'

'Nothing?' He raised bushy grey eyebrows. 'You must do something, my dear.'

'But what? I can't reprimand her, she's clearly ill –'

'But people who have nervous breakdowns make bad money-managers.'

'That's true, of course. The Chairman was moaning about it to me – of course he's afraid she might bring a suit against the bank.'

'For putting her under so much pressure that she had a collapse. Do you think she will?'

'I don't know. I suppose I ought to talk to her about it.'

'You ought to fire her.'

'Peter!' She was shocked. Then she added, with irony, 'Then of course she *would* bring a suit.'

'Lindsay, she's handling other people's money – if she makes mistakes it could be disastrous –'

'I'll keep an eye.' She sipped her tea. 'What else do you hear on your grapevine?'

'I hear you reported an intruder to the night porter.'

'Yes,' she said, surprised. He really did keep in touch. 'Someone in the dealing room. He ran off when I went out of my office to speak to him.'

'Who was it?'

'I couldn't make out, you know how dark the room is –'

'You're sure it was a man?'

'Well – yes – I took it for granted –'

'Couldn't have been a woman in trousers?'

'What are you thinking, Peter?'

'Nan Compton, that's what I'm thinking. As I recall, most of the girls wear trousers now and again. Nan often wears what I regard as very regrettable trouser suits.'

'Yes, she does, but . . . Nan?'

'You don't want to believe it. But if she's been heading for a breakdown, who knows what she may have been up to?'

'You mean, something dishonest? Not Nan!'

'You're determined not to consider it. That speaks volumes for your loyalty, my dear girl, but is it good sense?'

'But you see, I feel sure it was someone else.'

'Who, for instance?'

'Tad Tadiecski.'

'Tadiecski.' Peter echoed the name, and looked thoughtful. 'Let me see, you came to me about him when he applied for the job. I rang Johnnie Blebel about him, didn't I?'

'You did. And –'

'I thought it odd that you seemed so set against him. Now you tell me you think it was him in the dealing room, though you couldn't see because it was so dark.'

'Well, it made sense because you see –'

'Are you sure you haven't got a bit of a bee in your bonnet about him, Lindsay? I hear you had quite an argument with him about something in the office –'

'Oh, really, you'd think people in the dealing room would have something better to do than talk scandal –'

'But I love talking scandal, my dear. I'm an old man living out his exile from the life he loved, and every scrap of gossip is more precious than gold.' Peter looked at her, then carefully set down his teacup. 'It seems from the look on your face that something more than gossip is involved here.'

'I came today on purpose to talk about Tad Tadiecski. I think he's up to something, and I know for a fact that what he told us about himself is a pack of lies –'

'Lies? That's a very serious accusation, Lindsay. What makes you say it?'

'I got Buddy Tromberg to check.'

Peter smiled. 'And you get indignant with me because I listen to gossip. What's Tromberg but a gossipmonger?'

'Oh,' she said, taken aback, 'there's more to it than that.'

'Let me hear it, then.'

'Don't you think it's strange Tadiecski should supply a family background that's all fiction?'

'Have you asked him about it?'

'No . . .'

'Some quite sensible people invent fantasies about themselves –'

'But Buddy told me –'

'What is it you want from me, Lindsay? Do you want me to take Mr Tadiecski to task on your behalf?'

'Of course not!' she cried, amazed he should think so. 'I wouldn't ask you to get mixed up in my problems, you know that.'

'Have you mentioned this to anyone else? To Wishaw? Or Cyril Bartram?'

She prevented herself from saying that Cyril Bartram, the Personnel Manager, was too lenient to be thought of as an adviser, and that Mr Wishaw didn't like to be bothered unless you could make a good case. 'I thought I'd ask your advice first.'

'Perhaps what you should do is speak to Mr Tadiecski yourself.'

'Confront him?'

'If that is the word. All you're going to do is ask him why he told a fairy tale about his father.'

If I confront Tad, that's not all I'm going to ask him, she thought to herself.

She was disappointed in Peter. She'd thought he would enter into her problem with more alacrity. But all he wanted to do was chat about personal matters: business seemed to bore him. Perhaps his arthritis was troubling him so much that he didn't have much energy to spare.

She stayed on until she had finished her cup of tea but was quite glad to get up and say goodbye. She found she was downcast. In times gone by Peter had always come to her aid.

She went for a swim at the Leisure Centre to help herself unwind. When she got home her mother came out of the dining room to greet her. 'Lindsay, I've done some more work on those files I downloaded last night.'

'Yes?'

'Your friend Tad has been a busy chap. He's been into a lot of the bank records, far more than I've managed to look at although of course he's been at it longer than I have –'

'How long?'

'Since early April.'

'That's almost as soon as he started to work at Oistrav's!'

'And he's got a lot of information from private files too. I didn't like to look too closely because . . . well, you know . . . it's somebody else's affairs . . . But you're not by any means the only one he's looked at. And what's more – there are sections of his menu I can't get into at all. There's another password needed, and I've no idea what it is.'

Lindsay shook her head. 'I think he's a very clever man,' she said.

'I agree. Cleverer than me, and where computers are concerned I'm no beginner.'

'Well,' sighed Lindsay, 'I talked to Peter. And Peter said I ought to have it out with Tad.'

'He didn't!'

'He did. Why d'you find that so surprising?'

'Because I just found this on my e-mail.' She handed her daughter a sheet of paper.

Celia's e-mail address was printed out at the top. Then came the words: 'Dear Whizzkid at this address: Please tell Lindsay it's now imperative that I speak to her. Since she avoids me at the bank and won't come to the phone, this is the only way to get a message to her. RSVP. Tad.' There followed his e-mail address.

Lindsay read it with amazement. 'How did he know how to reach you?'

'Good heavens, it would be child's play for him to find me.'

'What should I do?'

'Didn't you just say Peter recommended facing him with your accusations?'

'You think I should reply to this?'

'Well, I suppose you could ignore it.'

Lindsay put down the paper. 'I don't want to be rushed into anything.'

'Perhaps not.' Celia thought about it. 'The weekend's coming up. I'm going down to Exoproduce tomorrow and one of the nephews said he'd pick me up. You come too, and you can think things over.'

'Yes.' Lindsay said absently. She went into the dining room to look at the screen on the computer. 'Mother . . . Is Nan Compton's one of the files Tad's been looking at?'

'As a matter of fact, yes. What makes you ask?'

'Well, Nan's been a bit strange, and Peter suggested . . .'

'You want to look?' Celia asked, and sat down to move the mouse down the list of files. 'Compton', the screen announced, with the subheading 'Roulette'. Celia moved the arrow down the list of figures. 'He's awfully clever at getting passwords,' she muttered. 'How could he work out that one?'

'Easy. Nan's a gambler, remember?' She stood looking over her mother's shoulder at the screen. 'All the same, he only got mine because he found the book on Greek mythology.' She added with a shrug, 'That's what he was doing when he was snooping around! Looking for clues to passwords.'

'Was he snooping? You never mentioned that.' Celia shifted about uneasily. 'Do you want this screen up any more, dear? I hate having people's personal lives put on show like this.'

'Just leave it for a minute, Mother. I'd like to . . .'

Celia got up to let her take her place. 'I'll leave you to it,' she said as she escaped. 'But don't be long, we ought to go out for a meal.'

They went out about eight, but when they got back Lindsay went once more to the computer. She sat studying Nan Compton's files but could see nothing that would connect her with any fraud. True, according to her bank statements she was short of money but there was no sign of large unexplained sums being credited to her.

She exited from the file to call up those of Oistrav's Bank. Tad had pirated a large number. She worked her way through them until it was very late and the signs on the screen seemed to run together in a gigantic jumble.

Next morning she slept late because it was Saturday. She was still drinking coffee to make herself wake up when Modhi Goswami called from downstairs to say he was waiting.

'Oh, I'm not ready!' Lindsay cried.

'Get a move on then, Modhi's probably expected back to take out another load.'

'You go on, Cecie. I'll follow on later in the car –'

'No, no, I'll wait and we can both –'

'No, you go – I want to take some clothes to the cleaners, and I wouldn't mind having another look at those files –'

'Darling, it's Saturday, forget all that –'

'I'd really rather, Cecie, I don't feel like rushing to go with Modhi now and it's a shame to keep you hanging about. You just go, tell Alice I'll be there after lunch.'

'Well, if you're sure . . .' Celia kissed her goodbye then hurried out.

Lindsay drank another cup of coffee, had a shower and got dressed. She put silk frocks into a carrier. The cleaners usually called once a week, but that was at the house in Putney. If they had called to deliver the last lot of clothes they would have got no answer, so it was quite a good idea to go there, collect what was ready, and leave the new lot. She had to go to Chelsea to achieve all that, so it was getting on for midday when it was done. She would have liked some lunch but the chic little cafes in King's Road were already crowded. She ended up eating a meat pie at a coffee stall outside the car park.

Now she could go home to take a look at the files on the computer. But as she set off it occurred to her that she would be driving past Nan Compton's flat. She switched off the car radio so as not to be distracted. Ought she to go and see Nan? She'd told Peter Gruman she would. Peter's respsonse was, 'You ought to fire her' – but she couldn't do that.

Come on, she said to herself, don't be a coward. You've got to talk to her sometime. Do it now!

She turned off at Tower Bridge and, rather sooner than she wished, found herself in Little Wapping Lane. She found a place by the kerb, parked, took out the umbrella, and ran to the door through the rain.

Nan's flat was the ground floor of a Victorian house with bay windows. When she rang, there was no reply. Good, said the cowardly part of Lindsay, she's not at home. But she rang again, so that her conscience couldn't reproach her.

The Venetian blind at the nearside part of the bay window was parted. Nan looked out through the crack. Then the blinds dropped together again and nothing else happened.

Lindsay drew a deep sighing breath before she rang again. After a moment a voice said from inside, 'Go away!'

'Come on, Nan, open the door. We've got to talk.'

'I said all I had to say –'

'Don't be silly. You don't think all that rubbish counts as sensible conversation, surely!'

She heard Nan give an exasperated exclamation. Then the door opened. There stood Nan in a dressing-gown, her hair in a tangle, and a glass in her hand.

'Welcome to Round Two,' she said with an exaggerated bow. 'This is vodka – shall I throw it now or save it till later?'

Chapter Eighteen

Lindsay had been to the flat before, in the days – now seemingly so distant – when she and Nan had been friends. She walked without prompting through the dark hallway to the awkwardly made door leading to the ground floor flat. Inside, across a narrow passage, lay the living room and the bedroom. It was through the living room Venetian blinds that Nan had surveyed her.

It was a mess. The television was on with the sound turned down, and on its surface stood two or three tin containers from a take-away meal. A computer whose screen showed an Internet news site blinked alongside. Books, magazines and newspapers were scattered on the couch, mixed up with a blanket which dragged on the floor. On the blanket's end lay an overturned vodka bottle.

A film of dust clouded every surface. The blue hydrangea in an ornate pot was dying from lack of water. Unopened mail covered the coffee table. The telephone was off the hook.

'Home Sweet Home,' said Nan, throwing out a hand towards it. 'I wasn't going to ask you to sit down which is just as well 'cos there's nowhere to sit, is there.'

'What's been going on, love?' Lindsay said in a dismay prompted by memories of times past. 'This place looks –'

'What are you, a journalist from *House Beautiful*? Say what you've got to say and get out.'

'Did your doctor give you a prescription?' She looked about for a pill bottle.

'Yes, oh yes, little itty bitty capsules, very pretty, they're in the bedroom but what business is it of yours anyhow?'

'You're not taking care of yourself –'

'Ooh, how sweet. Has Mummy come to take care of her naughty little chum? Heart of gold, boys, heart of eighteen carat gold,' Nan announced to the world at large. She espied the vodka bottle. 'Ah, you startled me when you rang! Look what you made me do! It's all spilt.'

Just as well, Lindsay said inwardly. 'When did you eat last?' she demanded.

Nan looked at the containers on the TV set. 'Spring rolls and egg-fried noodles,' she said, waving a hand at them, 'but they tasted awful so I didn't finish 'em. You like Chinese food? You can have what's left if you like, old chum, old pal.'

By the look of it, it had been on the TV set for at least a day. 'Get dressed, Nan. We'll go out for a meal –'

Nan sat down on the couch. 'I don't wanna go out. It's pouring cats and dogs, and besides there's another bottle of vodka in the cupboard so what do I need to go out for?'

'Then I'll make you some tea and toast –'

'No toast. No bread.' She laughed. ' "When she got there, the cupboard was bare" – 'cept for the vodka. How's that, then, Old Mother Hubbard? You wanna have a likkle drinkie?'

'I came to talk, Nan, but I see it's no use –'

'No use. Nothing's any use.' Nan began to cry. 'If you're gonna fire me, get on with it! See if I care! I can go anywhere – *anywhere* – and be better off because I won't have to play second fiddle to you any more, Lindsay Light o' my Life!'

Lindsay sat down on the couch beside her. 'I'm not going to fire you –'

'You're not? Why not? Don't you think I deserve it? Or – no – I get it, it would spoil your image, wouldn't it? – chucks her oldest friend out on her ear – what *would* the neighbours say?'

'I'm not bothered about what people would say. It's quite clear you're not yourself –'

'Wish I wasn't!' sobbed Nan. 'Wish I were you, for instance. Then Tad would look at me the way he looks at you –'

'Tad?'

'Oh, go on, pretend you didn't know! He thinks you're the best thing since Compuserve! But he liked me best at first, I know he did –'

'Nan, this is silly –'

'He and I were doing fine until you went to the Derby in that stupid dress. The minute he saw that picture of you, he was gagged and bound hand and foot. "New York girls would die for that look" – his voice when he said it –'

'You're talking nonsense –'

'Sometimes,' Nan said, impatiently brushing tears from her

cheeks, 'I think what it would be like to be you. Ever so clever about money, and pretty with it, and then there's the lovable kiddi-winks too, all part of the image, career woman but perfect mother, and you had that ultra-cultured boyfriend, natter-natter-natter about Italian frescoes and Japanese netsuke. Why couldn't you have been content with that? Why did you have to break up with him and take Tad as well?'

'Honestly, you've got it all wrong –'

'But even in a perfect world like yours, things can go to pieces,' she surged on. 'I'll bring you down! Oistrav's will be glad to see the back of you by the time I've finished –'

'Nan,' Lindsay broke in, 'you haven't been doing anything stupid, have you?'

'Oh, everything I do is stupid, we all know that. Muck up the regroup after Bimondi Cruise and Leisure –'

'I didn't mean at the bank. I meant . . . have you been in my house?'

'In your house?'

'Or sent anyone there?

' "I sent a letter to your house, But on the way I dropped it" –' sang Nan.

'Nan! Did you send a letter? A photograph?'

' "A little girl, she picked it up, and in her shawl she popped it" –'

Lindsay took hold of her by the shoulders and almost shook her. 'Stop acting the fool, Nan! You're not as drunk as all that, talk sense! Did you send someone to damage my house?'

'Throw a brick at it,' suggested Nan. 'Knock it over with a bulldozer! Should I have done that, eh? Would that make you sit up and take notice?' She realized for the first time that Lindsay was holding her. 'Take your hands off me,' she said with a sudden fury that seemed to sober her. 'Don't you ever touch me! I hate you!'

Lindsay let go. The other woman sagged back among the soiled cushions of the couch. 'What are you doing here, Lindsay?' she demanded. 'Why did you come? To see what a mess I'm making of my life?'

'I came to ask you some questions –'

'Oh, I understand. "Why did you make a spectacle of yourself at the bank? How could you throw coffee at my fine new dress?" Let me tell you, it was easy. It all went beautifully. You looked such a *fool*! And losing my job is nothing compared with the pleasure it gave me.'

'You haven't lost your job –'

'Not yet, no, no. But you'll find a way to get rid of me by and by –'

'Nan, sort yourself out and get some therapy. You're in no danger of losing your job. Whatever you've done, we'll put it down to an emotional trauma –'

'Oh, you *forgive* me!' Nan cried in mock gratitude. 'I might have known you'd *forgive* me! Anything to make yourself look good –'

It was hopeless. Every word she said was twisted by her former friend into a slur, and as to getting information, it was like picking your way through Never-Never Land. Taking up her bag and umbrella, she made for the door. 'Goodbye, Nan. I hope to see you back at your desk soon.'

The drive home was made harder by the strong wind thrusting rain against the windshield. The depression promised by the forecasters had the whole of the south-east in its grip. The roads were awash with water, the cloud pressing almost on the rooftops cast a dark grey light over the City.

When she got back to Old Flag Wharf the first thing she did was make herself some hot tea. With a mug of it in her hand, she went to her mother's computer to call up the file she'd been looking at last night. '*Compton*,' said the screen. '*Roulette*. Page 1: Financial Affairs: Bank account, Cholmley's Bank Number 421144.' Columns of figures. Standing orders. Charges for foreign currency – that would be when she went abroad to some banking conference or seminar.

Lindsay dismissed the financial record to call up Nan's personal organiser. She tried to remember the dates on which the threatening messages had been delivered to the house, particularly the date on which the fire had been set.

The personal organizer was little help. It contained notes of when Nan's next dental appointment was due and what she had booked up for her vacation (a Club Med holiday). It wasn't a record in the sense of being a 'Dear Diary'.

How strange, Lindsay said to herself sadly. We've been friends for years yet I seem to know very little about her . . . And even now, after all that drunken nonsense, I can't feel she would really do anything bad.

She exited from Nan's file and called up those that Tad had downloaded from the bank. He had roamed widely through its computers, it was clear. There were records from Venture Capital, from Bond Trading, from her own department, Portfolio Investment.

That part of it was familiar and the rest of it was dull. Only when she came to the banking section did she feel a spurt of interest. She found to her surprise that Tad had been very thorough in his inspection of its work. He had found, as Celia had, that one of the clerks was working a small swindle by lopping off odd pence from many accounts and squirrelling them away in one of his own. The balance in that now stood at a few thousand pounds.

But in terms of the transactions at Oistrav's that was very small stuff.

Tad had singled out National Northern Concentral Inc, Global Soundfast, and two others – Mercier Delibes with a connection to what used to be the French Congo, and Powerlands Baker of Liechtenstein. He had highlighted these accounts by erecting a little graphic on the first page of data in each case. The graphic was an index finger, pointing like a gun.

Were these the accounts he had used for manipulation? Did he know whose money was being put through them? How much did his share come to?

She went back and forth through the pages, trying to fathom what was going on. She sensed that she should be able to read a message here, but it eluded her. She glanced at her watch.

Six o'clock! She'd meant to be on her way by now. But she was stiff and tired and ravenously hungry.

She went to the telephone. 'Cecie,' she said when she got her mother on the line at Exoproduce, 'I'm just surfacing after a session at the computer –'

'So that's what you've been up to! I was just going to ring you –'

'I'll set out in a bit –'

'Darling, did you do any shopping?'

'I took in the dry-cleaning –'

'Did you have lunch?'

'Yes, I had a snack –'

'And then you sat down to the computer? Good heavens, child, you'll reduce yourself to a matchstick! I know what it's like when you've been immersed in something, you forget to eat and drink and you get very wobbly – certainly you oughtn't to drive in weather like this until you've had a rest and a decent meal.'

Lindsay glanced at the windows. Rain was teeming down. 'Oh lord,' she groaned, 'it's still as bad as ever –'

'Perhaps it would be better to leave it till tomorrow, Lindsay. The light's so poor already –'

'Oh, but what about Alice –'

'She's here, you can talk to her.' The receiver was handed over for Alice to speak.

'Mummy, it's ever so wet here! There's been a puddle all day like a pond in the car park!'

'I know, love, it's the same here.'

'Granny said you were coming but now you're not?'

'Perhaps it's better to leave it till tomorrow –'

'If you leave it till tomorrow you can come with Sudin and Ambila in their minibus. Will you bring me a present?'

'What would you like, precious?'

'Can we have cards to play Mrs Bun the Baker's Wife? They haven't got them here and you can't go outside to play so there's nothing to do, Mummy, except the plants.'

'Of course, Alice, I'll get some on my way tomorrow.'

'Will there be shops that sell cards on Sundays?'

'Well, I'll get them this evening.'

'But it's all wet.'

'Never mind, I've got an umbrella.'

'Keep the cards under the umbrella so they don't get spoiled.'

'I will, sweetheart.'

Celia came on the line to say, 'So that's all right. See you tomorrow, then?'

'About ten o'clock, okay?'

'Right.'

She knew there was very little in the fridge: she ought to stock it up, and there were the Snap cards to buy for Alice. Besides, she would love a swim to get the kinks out of her shoulders.

She took the car. Traffic was fairly light in Docklands because the rain was keeping most people indoors. She did the shopping at a late-night supermarket, swam for an hour, had a substantial salad and a piece of fruit pie at the cafe in the leisure centre, and drove home. It was about eight-thirty, but almost as dark as nine. Time for bed, she told herself, yawning.

In the hall an envelope lay in the letter-cage on the inside of the door. It hadn't been there when she went out. Frowning in surprise she took it out to find out who it was for.

Her heart seemed to stop when she saw the familiar block letters of the address: LINDSAY DUNFORTH. It was hand-delivered, no postmark.

She tore open the envelope. Inside was a single sheet of folded paper.

'Thought you'd hidden her safely away, did you? ONE LAST CHANCE – CLOSE OUT YOUR INQUIRY.'

She threw it down and pulled her mobile phone from her handbag. Her fingers made mistakes on the tiny buttons at her first try but on her second she got it right – the number of the nursery garden.

An engaged signal. She thumbed down the connection then pushed the repeat button. Still engaged.

She ran out of the building and down the ramp to the garage. She almost dropped the keys in her haste to get into the car. In a moment she was driving up the ramp and onto the street. She swung round the corner into the main road. She barged her way through, causing other drivers to brake and sound their horns at her in rebuke.

She didn't care. She must get to her little girl before anybody could harm her.

Chapter Nineteen

The mobile phone was on the front passenger seat. She jabbed a finger at the repeat button. For a moment she had to concentrate as a group of motorbikes went by. She grabbed up the phone, put it to her ear. Engaged.

Driving conditions could hardly have been worse. As yet the July evening wasn't quite dark but the light was dreadfully bad. Water drummed down on the roof and poured off the windscreen at every sweep of the wipers. The strong wind buffeted the side of the car. She thanked her hire car firm that they'd supplied her with something so sturdy.

Again she tried the number. Still engaged. She must have dialled it wrong. At a traffic light she seized the opportunity to re-dial. The result was the same, the engaged signal.

She raged inwardly: what on earth were they doing? Good sense replied, They're taking orders for exotic vegetables. Or they're keeping up their strong family contacts.

Now she was leaving Greater London, heading out into Essex. Because there was less protection from buildings, the force of the wind increased. The car wanted to move to the left, she had a hard time keeping the steering wheel steady. When at last she came to a tree-sheltered stretch of road she tried the telephone again.

This time – thank God! she breathed – it was answered.

'Exoproduce, can I help you?' It was a girlish voice with a faint Indian lilt. At once Lindsay guessed the reason why the line had been engaged. This teenager had been talking to a friend – girlfriend or boyfriend. In the background she could hear a transistor or a Walkman playing, something by Oasis.

'This is Mrs Dunforth,' Lindsay said. 'May I speak to my mother?'

A momentary hesitation. 'I'm sorry, you have the wrong number, there's no one of that name here.' And the line disconnected.

Lindsay heard herself moan in frustration. She stabbed at the number again. When the young voice replied she said, 'Please may I speak to Mrs Celia Claydell.'

'Ah,' said the telephonist, 'that was you before? I'm sorry, I didn't realize. Mrs Claydell has gone out.'

'Gone *out*?' It was almost a shout.

'Yes . . .' Now her interlocutor sounded a little scared. 'She went out about half-past six.'

Lindsay took a hold on herself. She mustn't scare this child. 'Did Mrs Claydell take my little girl with her?'

'Your little girl?'

'Alice – she's about five years old – Mrs Claydell's granddaughter.'

'Oh, the little girl in the orange shorts?'

'Yes, yes, Alice, my daughter. Did Mrs Claydell take her?'

'I've no idea.'

'Will you please ask and let me know?'

'Well, as a matter of fact . . . there's almost nobody to ask. Most of them have gone to a wedding.'

'A wedding!'

'Well, actually, the wedding was this afternoon, but of course Babaji was busy and couldn't go, but they all set off for the party about half-past six –'

'Mr Goswami? Mrs Goswami? Tapti? Have they all gone?'

'Most of them, there's only a couple and they're in the glass-houses, picking for tomorrow's deliveries –'

Lindsay drew a deep breath to steady herself. Remember your man-management techniques, she said to herself. 'What's your name, dear?' she asked as gently as she could.

'Dalida.'

'Dalida, please go and see if my daughter is all right.'

'Why shouldn't she be all right, Mrs . . . er . . . Dunforth?'

'It's too difficult to explain. Would you please go and see if she's in bed and asleep?'

'But I couldn't leave the switchboard, Mrs Dunforth.'

'You must –'

'No, orders are coming in and Babaji said –'

'This is tremendously important, Dalida. You *must* go and see if Alice is all right.'

'I really can't –'

'Babaji would agree you have to go.'

'Would he?' The approval of the patriarch was clearly very important. Lindsay could picture her, pretty and dark and a little overwhelmed by the responsibility of her task.

'Yes, he would, he's fond of Alice, he'd want you to look after her.'

'Well . . . all right . . . I'll go . . .' A pause. 'Which room is she in?'

'She's upstairs in the main old building . . .'

'I don't know my way around very well, I only got here this morning from Bristol –'

'It's along the glassed-in passage to the house, then up the main staircase, and then there's a corridor to your right on the first floor –'

'Well, all right. I'll go.' A momentary hesitation. 'It may take a few minutes. I'll have to disconnect, I can't leave the line tied up in case a customer –'

'Yes, yes, I understand. Ring me back when you've checked.'

'Oh – yes –'

'Take my number.'

'Just a minute, Mrs Dunforth, I've lost the pencil – oh, here it is – yes?'

Lindsay dictated the number of her mobile. For safety's sake she got Dalida to read it back but she'd written it down correctly. 'Now, quickly, dear – go and look in on Alice.'

The line disconnected. She sat back. She was wet with perspiration. She moved into a convenient lay-by and switched on the air conditioning. For a minute or two she sat there, trying to steady herself, taking deep breaths as she counted: One, two, three, four, one, two, three, four . . .

Then she nosed out again into the road. A faint hiss from the phone made her look down. She herself had forgotten to disconnect. Dear God, she thought, I mustn't get careless – how could that child get through if the line were tied up!

She was eating up the miles – not fast enough for her wishes but she kept reminding herself to drive well. She could be no use to her daughter if she were to crash the car in these stormy conditions.

It seemed to her as if aeons had passed when the phone chirped. She seized it. 'Yes?'

'Mrs Dunforth? I had to go to the glasshouse to ask how to find the room, it's such a jumble here –'

'Yes, yes, of course but did you –'

'I went there and her bed's empty.'

'*What?*'

'It's been slept in,' Dalida said miserably, 'the covers are pushed back and rumpled. But she's not there.'

'Dalida!'

'What should I do now, Mrs Dunforth?'

'Call the police!'

'Call the police?'

'Yes, at once, tell them what's happened –'

'But I don't know that anything's happened, Mrs Dunforth –'

'Never mind that, call the local police, I'll explain to them when I get there.'

'When will that be?' asked the girl, clearly very upset at this drama that seemed to be closing in on her.

'I'm on my way now –'

'On your way? Oh, you're speaking on a mobile phone.'

'Yes, I'll be there in about half an hour. Please, Dalida, get things moving. I'm afraid for my little girl.'

She rang off. Now she concentrated on her driving, threw safety to the winds, the speed limit forgotten. She almost wished a police patrol would stop her so that she could tell the patrolman why she was raging down this country road in the dark and wet.

She turned off at Wickford. The road became more difficult, with bends and turns she had to respect. She was so focused on the task that she didn't notice the car a few hundred yards behind, a car that had stayed with her since she left Old Flag Wharf.

She stormed into the gates of Exoproduce. She didn't bother to drive round to the car park. She slammed on the brakes and leapt out.

A young girl in jeans and sweater was hovering in the doorway of the office. 'Mrs Dunforth?' she called.

'Have you found her?' Lindsay demanded.

'No, I –'

'When will the police be here?'

'I . . . er . . . I didn't call them –'

'You didn't call them?'

'I rang Babaji, at the party. I didn't want to do anything he might not like. He said he'd be back in a minute.'

'In a minute? Where is he?'

'Colchester.'

'*Colchester!* My God, it'll take him an hour in this weather –'

The phone in the office could be heard ringing. Dalida turned towards it, throwing up her hands in anxiety. 'I've got to answer it, Mrs Dunforth –'

'I'll come with you, I'm calling the police!'

With Dalida hard on her heels, she led the way to the office. Dalida snapped up the phone. 'Exoproduce, how can I help you?' she said in quavering politeness. And then, 'Mrs Dunforth? Yes, she's here. Yes.' She held out the receiver to Lindsay. 'It's for you,' she said in amazement.

Lindsay snatched it from her. 'Yes?'

'Lindsay! Thank heaven!' It was her mother. 'I'm at this party in Colchester, Lindsay. I only just got to hear what happened. Mr Goswami drove off about ten minutes ago. Lindsay, Alice is –'

'She's missing!' Lindsay wailed. 'She's not in her bed!'

'Lindsay, Lindsay, that's why I'm ringing. It may not be bad. For the last couple of nights she's been sneaking out of bed and going to sleep in the spare bed in Jamnu's room –'

'Jamnu!'

'He's leaving on Tuesday. Alice has been trying to stay close to him.'

'Which is Jamnu's room?' Lindsay said to Dalida, and then, realizing she was a poor source of information, turned back to the phone. 'Which room, Cecie?'

'It's in the extension on the back of the main building. Jamnu sleeps in the second room.'

'Right.' Lindsay thrust the receiver at Dalida. As she raced away she could hear the girl saying, 'Yes, Mrs Claydell. Yes, I understand. Thank you.'

Out of the office along the glass passage to the hall, across the hall to the door at the back. The corridor, the four doors. She opened the first one in her haste but realized it was wrong and backed out. The second door: it was ajar. She went in, found the light switch, snapped it on.

A muffled snort of half-wakened surprise. The little boy, in a sweatshirt that said: 'Hang on Snoopy', sat up in a narrow bed. He mumbled something in Gujarati.

In the next bed was a little light-brown head. Lindsay rushed to the bedside.

Her daughter lay there, fast asleep with her woolly rabbit clutched in her arms.

Lindsay's legs seemed to give way under her. She sank down on the bed. 'Oh, thank God, thank God,' she sobbed.

Jamnu rubbed his eyes. 'Whasamatter?'

'It's nothing, Jamnu, I'm sorry.'

He blinked his eyes to get rid of sleepy-dust. His gaze came to rest on Alice. 'Oh, not again,' he groaned.

'It's all right, I'll take her now, Jamnu. You go back to sleep.'

'Stupid kid,' growled the little boy, and lay down again.

Lindsay picked up her sleeping daughter. Alice made a little whimpering sound, put the ear of her rabbit in her mouth, and slumbered on. She was an almost dead weight in her mother's arms.

She went out, switching off the light. In the passage she found Dalida hovering. 'It's all right, Dalida, I've found her.'

'And she's all right?'

'Yes, perfectly. I'm sorry,' Lindsay said, suddenly hot with embarrassment. 'I was making a fuss about nothing, apparently.'

'Oh, that's all right – at least, Babaji is coming home –' The girl looked worried at the thought. One didn't summon the head of the family home from an important wedding without good cause.

'I'll explain to him,' Lindsay said. 'Tell him I'll ring him –'

'Ring him? Aren't you going to wait for him?'

'No, I'm going.'

'You'll put your little girl to bed in her own room first?'

'No, I'm taking her with me.' Because though she was safe now, how could she be sure nothing was going to happen? The threat on the paper she'd taken from the letter-cage had been very real. Alice couldn't be left here now the malefactor had found out where she was staying.

'But Mrs Dunforth,' Dalida protested, fluttering behind her as she walked towards the hall, 'I think Babaji would –'

'Get me a coat or a blanket to put round her,' Lindsay interrupted in the tone she used at the bank when things got difficult.

'Oh . . . yes . . . just a minute . . .' She plunged at the coat-rack in the hall, coming back with a chunky cardigan.

'Thank you. Now open the outside door for me.'

Dalida obeyed. Wind and rain rushed in. Alice stirred, moaned in protest, but stayed asleep. Lindsay, bending herself protectively round the child, went out to the car. She'd left the door unlocked and the keys in the ignition. She opened the back door, laid Alice on the back seat, tucked the cardigan round her, clipped the seat belt across her and got in the driver's seat.

Dalida, standing with the house door half closed for protection against the weather, watched in amazement as she wheeled the car round and out of the gates.

With perfect obedience to all the rules of good driving, Lindsay made her way out of the grounds of Exoproduce and into the muddy lane that led to it. She was almost at the end, getting ready to turn out on to the road, when a car came charging in and pulled up broadside on.

Lindsay braked hard. The Passat stalled.

She was stopped dead. Blocked in. On purpose.

Chapter Twenty

In the dark and with the rain lashing her windscreen, she could scarcely see what was happening. She made out the driver of the other car, getting out. She heard a shout – of triumph? Of menace?

Her brain was racing. She mustn't let herself be trapped. The front wheels of the Passat were entangled in the hedge. Her offside door was half-open with a hawthorn bush wedged into the hinge. She realized with a pang of terror that she hadn't locked the doors when she drove off. Impossible to lock herself in with Alice.

But she couldn't stay here either, for this dreadful man to reach them and do – whatever it was he wanted to do. She scrambled over into the back of the car, released the seat belt, dragged her daughter into her grasp, and got out of the back door – furthest from her antagonist. She had lost the protective layer of the cardigan around Alice, but flight was more important.

The rain seized her, the wind crashed against her. Alice woke up with a cry.

'It's all right, darling, Mummy's got you –'

'Mummy! What's wrong?'

'Nothing, nothing, there's a storm, that's all.'

'Did Granny leave the window open?'

Their attacker appeared on the other side of the car. He was mouthing words as he thrust himself through the far door towards her. Lindsay turned, saw the gap where the hawthorn had been forced to one side, and scrambled through it.

At once her feet sank into marshy ground. Mud came up to her ankles, dragging at the edge of her jeans. No, no, she thought, I won't let it trap me! But where was she? Of course, she was in the field they'd crossed a few days ago on their way to the jetty with the picnic food.

She felt a moment of small triumph. She knew where she was, the pursuer did not. She knew there was a hard path through this marshy ground, he did not.

The path, where was the path? She tried to picture herself on that hot sunny day, heading for the jetty. They'd walked up the lane, climbed over a stile on the far side, and the path had been underfoot there.

The stile must be about twenty yards back along the hedge. She crouched down so that it sheltered her. She began a heavy-footed progress in its shelter.

Her attacker was still trying to find out where she'd gone. He had come out of the far door straight into the hedge, which trapped him momentarily. Lindsay imagined this to herself as faint sounds reached her, curses and thrashing. Then they ceased, and she knew he'd fallen into the gap. He'd know that's where they'd gone.

But he couldn't know in which direction they were moving. Lindsay clutched at this hope – to have it destroyed immediately by a wail from her daughter.

'*Mummy!* It's all wet and cold!'

'Ssh, love, ssh. Never mind. Mummy's got you.'

'But *Mummy* –!'

Lindsay put her hand over Alice's mouth. 'Ssh, darling. Do what Mummy tells you. Be very, very quiet.' Alice jerked her head about, to get away from that restraining hand. 'Ssh,' warned Lindsay.

She heard a squelching sound behind them. He'd got their direction from Alice's cry.

She tried to hurry but in the boggy ground it was almost impossible. Then her foot struck a hard surface – the cinder-cover of the path to the jetty.

She hoisted Alice up in her arms. She began to run on the steady ground. In doing so she forgot to keep the little girl gagged with her hand.

'Flopsy!' shrieked Alice. 'I've dropped Flopsy!'

A shout of delight, only a few paces behind. He was there, almost within arm's length. Lindsay streaked ahead, no longer troubling to silence the little girl, who was sobbing with heart-break at the loss of her toy.

The man pursuing them was calling out: 'You won't get away! I'll get you! You'll learn your lesson!'

Right, she thought, waste your breath on threats!

She concentrated on running. She couldn't see where she was

going except that the darker patch ahead must be the trees bordering the river. And the sound footing told her she was still on the path.

A faint glint. The river. When she reached it . . . was there a footpath? She tried to recall. All her mind could conjure up was the jetty, and the two boys fishing. The lines dangling into the water. Rowing boats tethered to the legs of the pier.

Rowing boats! She would run to the end of the pier and while this madman was still trying to think where they'd gone, she'd untie the boat and push it away from the jetty. If he worked out where they'd gone, it would only be by the greatest good luck.

She summoned all her strength and tried to increase her speed. The dark shadows of the trees became bunchy outlines against the dark gleam of the water. The jetty – she couldn't make it out in the welter of rain and darkness.

Her foot struck wood. She was on it! She raced along it. To her dismay she heard the sound of her passage, thudding on the wood. He heard it too, and was coming. She heard the heavy thump of his feet.

She reached the end of the wooden jetty. She stopped to peer below at the water. Where were the boats?

Tapti had said . . . 'They use them at the weekends.' They weren't there . . . there were no boats tied up.

'Hah!' roared their pursuer. '*Gotcha!*'

Lindsay gathered her daughter close against her. 'Take a deep breath, baby,' she said into her ear. 'We're going for a swim.'

With Alice in her arms, she leapt into the water.

The shock as they hit was death-like. Cold and cruel, the water closed over them. They went down, down. It was deeper than Lindsay had expected.

It seemed she touched a riverbed of muddy silt. Her shoes slid into it. She kicked. Just as easily her feet slid free. She levered her shoes off as they rose towards the surface. Her heavy sweater, filled with water as she rose, bulked out and up.

They broke into the rainy air. Alice's head was buried in her mother's shoulder, the sweater swaddling about her ears. Lindsay dragged at it to get Alice's head free.

'It's all right, baby,' she croaked, muddy water lapping into her mouth. 'We're all right.'

'Mummy, Mummy –'

'We're going to *swim*, Alice –'

'Not in the dark, Mummy, I don't like it, I want to get out –'

'No, we can't, not for a minute –'

But even as she understood that they couldn't hope to pull themselves out at the jetty, the river was claiming them.

Lindsay had felt that strong suck of water many a time, when she was out with her scuba-diving husband Bob. A vigorous current was flowing, stronger than the river itself. The tide was going out towards the sea, and they were going with it.

She could hear shouting. It seemed a long way off already. The man on the pier – what was he shouting? Was he telling them to come back? Never, no chance of that! She and her little girl were borne along, and she knew better than to try to fight it. That way lay exhaustion and defeat.

The only course was to let the current take them. They must stay afloat, and Lindsay must try to edge her way towards the bank of the river. She must look out for some point of safety – a mooring line, a buoy, even a floating log.

She was holding Alice close to her. She said in her ear, 'I'm going to let you go, sweetie –'

'No!'

'Yes, just for a tiny minute, Alice. I've got to take off this sweater –'

'No!'

'I've got to, darling, it's dragging me down. I'll let you go and you'll tread water like in the pool –'

'But it's dark, Mummy, we never go in the pool in the dark –'

'Remember lifesaving? Remember we played at that?'

Alice threshed about with her arms, a little panicky. Lindsay held her as close as she could. 'Remember, we said we must never do that?' she protested, the water splashing into her face and over her. 'We had to be very quiet and still, floating on our backs. Can you do that now?'

'It's cold, Mummy.'

'I know, love, I know, but we'll float' – and conserve energy so we don't lose body heat even quicker, she thought – 'and we'll get into the bank and climb out. Ready?'

'We'll climb out? Soon?'

'Yes, in a minute. Ready? I'm going to let you go.' Before Alice could object she did so. One handed she held on to her, wriggling out of the sweater which seemed determined to drag her down to the very mud. One arm out, she held her daughter with that hand, and got the other arm out. The sweater gently swirled away, touching her and then vanishing.

She turned on her back. 'Mummy!' shrieked Alice as her hold totally ceased for a moment. Then she took her daughter's shoulders under the arms, kicked out with her legs, and they moved a little through the current, no longer entirely at its mercy.

'There, poppet,' Lindsay said, but the sound of the water rushing by drowned the words. She doubted Alice heard her.

But Alice could feel the steady pull of her mother's hands at her armpits. She was on her back, face upturned to the cold rain, but that was better than having the waves lap over her. She relaxed into the feeling of comparative safety that comes with doing something familiar: lifesaving, a game they'd played in the pool at home.

Lindsay was lying with her head directed upstream, trying not to let herself and her daughter be carried too fast down to the river mouth. But she had no notion of swimming against this current. Her main aim was to keep them afloat, to try to edge into the bank somewhere if the current would let her, and to find something to catch hold of.

It was very cold, though the calendar claimed it was the beginning of July. The wind was blowing from the north-west, the rain-spots felt like little spears of ice water.

We can't hold out long, Lindsay thought. Then she said to herself, We'll hold out, we have to.

She kicked now and then to try to direct their passage. What she needed to do was turn around, tread water, and try to see the bank. But to do that she had to let go of Alice, and she couldn't do that.

'Will we get out soon, Mummy?' asked a small voice.

'Yes, very soon, love.'

Time went by. Lindsay transferred her hands to her daughter's head, to ensure her mouth stayed above water. She was reaching a state where she could no longer feel the silky hair because her fingers were numb. Next she found her arms had lost the ability to move. She held on because that was the position in which her muscles had frozen.

Where were they? Were they closer to either of the banks? The river would be widening as it headed for the sea – were they in the midst of a great expanse of salt water?

Out of the corner of her eye she saw a gleam of light to one side. 'Help!' she cried. 'Help!'

The light slid by. It had probably been a house on the riverbank – too far off for her cry to penetrate above the noise of the wind.

Faintly there came a sound. At first Lindsay thought it was delirium, but no, the sound grew a little louder and closer.

New Orleans jazz?

A radio, a record player, a tape recorder – it meant a house, a boat, *something.*

'Help!' Lindsay cried. 'Help, can you hear me?'

Not above the united strains of the music and the howl of the wind. Desperately she kicked out in the direction of the music. The tide dragged at her, pulling her away, but she fought it. 'Kick out, Alice! We'll . . . get out . . . where the music is . . .'

Alice began to use her legs as if for back stroke. Together they struggled towards the sound.

Lindsay felt a tremendous jarring against her arm. It knocked her daughter out of her grasp. She went under, choking and spluttering. Terror went through her. She had lost hold of Alice! She struck up for the surface, to find her little girl paddling around nearby yelling, 'Mummy! Mummy!'

Lindsay grabbed her. They both trod water. What had she hit?

The music seemed louder. She glimpsed riding lights.

A voice called: 'What's that? Ahoy there?'

'Help!' shouted Lindsay. 'We're here, in the water.' She flailed about trying to find what it was she'd hit. Her hand hit metal. She realized it must have been a mooring chain.

'In the water?' exclaimed the voice.

A bright light came on. A beam was directed down at them.

'Good God!' someone cried.

Then friendly hands were lifting Alice from her frozen clasp, and next Lindsay herself was being helped aboard the *Blues Boy*.

'Thank you,' she gasped, 'thank you, I thought we were going to die . . .' The words faded away. She didn't even catch a glimpse of their saviour's face before she fainted.

She woke from terrible dreams – of drowning, of losing her daughter in a welter of waves. Before she even opened her eyes she threw out her hands. 'Alice?'

Someone took her hands in a warm clasp. 'It's all right, dear, Alice is quite safe.'

She opened her eyes. Her mother's face was above hers.

'Alice?' she gasped again.

'Look, Lindsay – sound asleep.' Celia raised her up, putting a pillow behind her so that she could see another bed in a corner. Her daughter's light-brown head lay there, cocooned in creamy blankets.

The nightmare receded. She saw she was in a white-painted room, vaguely clinical. 'Am I in hospital?' she croaked.

'This is the sick bay of the Estuary Yachting Club. You were brought here last night.'

She blinked. Watery sunlight was coming through the window. Her body ached as if from a beating. Her upper left arm was sore. She put up her other hand to feel it, and discovered she was clad in old-fashioned flannelette pyjamas striped in beige and cream. Under the sleeve she could feel a pad of gauze on her arm where it hurt.

'You've got a bad graze there,' her mother said, guiding her fingers away from it.

'Ye-es . . . That's where I hit the mooring chain.'

'It's been dressed and you've had anti-infection shots – so has Alice. The main anxiety was hypothermia.'

'What . . . time . . . ?' she asked waveringly.

'About five in the morning.'

She tried to put the recollections into a pattern she could recognize. 'I've been here . . . what . . . ? About six hours?'

'Mr Soames pulled the two of you out of the water, some time around eleven. He says he was letting the gale lull him to sleep while he listened to his radio. It seems he more or less lives aboard during the summer. Something hit the mooring line and made the boat sway. He put his head out the cabin door and heard you calling.'

'Thank heaven,' whispered Lindsay.

There was a rustle from behind her mother. 'Amen to that,' said a voice. 'We thought we'd lost you.'

And she saw that Tad was there.

Chapter Twenty-one

Lindsay's first feeling was intense pleasure at his presence. Then her brain began sending out warnings.

'What is he doing here?' she asked Celia in alarm.

'Lindsay,' her mother soothed, grasping her hands between her own. 'It's all right, really it is. Let me explain –'

'Are there other people here?'

'Of course, Dr Melbury and the skipper of the yacht club, not to mention the police who want to interview you –'

Lindsay relaxed. 'All right then, go on.'

'Darling, when I got here last night I was about half an hour behind Mr Goswami. I had to find someone who'd drive me back. Mr Goswami met me in a high old state. He found your car stalled in the lane with the doors open. He couldn't find you or Alice.'

'No . . . By that time . . .' Her body shuddered though she tried to control it. 'By that time we were drifting out to sea.'

'Lindsay, it's all right, you're safe now.' Her mother patted her hands. 'Babaji called the police, and while we waited for them I borrowed the computer and sent an e-mail to Tad's address –'

'But why?' she broke in.

'It was a ploy. I reckoned if he was here abducting Alice he couldn't be at home to answer. Instead he was on the telephone in ten minutes.'

'The message I got was "Re Lindsay, ring this number urgently," ' Tad added. 'Since I'd been trying to get in touch for more than a day, I grabbed the phone and when I heard what she had to say . . . well, I lit out of there like a bat out of hell!'

'By the time he got here Mr Soames had pulled you to safety and you were in bed asleep. The skipper of the yacht club told us he couldn't get any sense out of you – you were chilled through so that you could scarcely form any words, and exhausted too. Something about being chased into the river by a man?'

'He blocked me in the lane,' Lindsay recalled, the cogs

creaking into action in her brain. 'I got away over the fields – it was dreadful – dark, slippery with mud. He was almost at my elbow more than once –'

'But who the devil was it?' Tad's voice was rough with anger.

In her bed, Alice moaned and turned over.

'Ssh,' admonished Celia, 'we're waking the baby. And I think Lindsay needs to rest, Tad.'

'Yeah, it's too early in the morning for all this,' he agreed, trying for a cool tone.

Celia kissed her daughter and moved off. Tad took her place by the bed. 'You gave us all a scare,' he said. 'But you're here and in one piece so I guess we can't complain. See you later, Lindsay.'

'Yes,' she said, slipping away into a nest of warmth and comfort. 'See you later, Tad . . .'

When Celia came to collect them at lunch time on Sunday, Lindsay had been up for a couple of hours. Alice had roused her around ten o'clock, calling in a frightened voice, 'Mummy, where are you?'

She sat up to find her little girl staring around in bewilderment. 'Where are we? And why have I got these funny clothes on?'

She was wearing a nightdress belonging to the grand-daughter of Dr Melbury. Standing barefoot in a shaft of sunlight, she looked like an orphan. Lindsay jumped out of bed to take her in her arms. 'Sweetheart, we had *such* an adventure! We slept here last night and guess what this place is? It's a yacht club, and there are lots and lots of boats right outside the window.'

'Umm,' said Alice. 'I knew it wasn't Babaji's house. I'm ever so hungry, can we have breakfast?'

That was easy. The club had a kitchen, whose guardian gladly provided milk and cornflakes and toast in large quantities. The next problem was to find a substitute for the borrowed nightwear but club members rallied round. Alice was soon outfitted in a cotton skirt and sweater, Lindsay got a pair of jeans and a worn Guernsey. Shoes were more difficult and in fact weren't available until Celia arrived with a big carrier bag.

She found her daughter trying to explain away the worst part of the night before to her grand-daughter without frightening her.

'But did we really go swimming in the *dark*?' Alice was asking.

'Yes, we did, and very cold and horrid it was, so we won't do that again, will we?'

'No,' agreed Alice emphatically. After a moment she added in a quavering voice, 'I think I lost Flopsy . . .'

'No, no,' Celia told her, 'Flopsy's safe at Babaji's house.' Flopsy had been found on the edge of the cinder path and been put through the washing machine.

'Oh, well, then that's all right,' Alice said, with only a tinge of doubt.

They drove back to Exoproduce through a countryside gleaming in after-storm brightness. Lindsay opened the windows so that the warm breeze could flow through the car.

'In case you're wondering,' Celia said, 'Tad would have come but he's out with the police trying to track down the man who attacked you.'

'Track him down? The sergeant I talked to said there'd be no tracks after all that rain.'

'That's true, they only found faint impressions in the lane, the tyre marks had been almost washed away. All the same it's clear he was blocking the exit to the main road. And of course we found Flopsy so that told us you'd had to head for the jetty.' Celia hesitated, then glanced back at Alice, who was looking out of the window and singing to herself. Celia said in a low voice, 'And he pushed you into the river?'

'I jumped.'

'*Jumped!*'

'Ssh . . . There was nowhere else to go. The rowing boats were presumably on the other side of the river. Luckily Alice and I are good swimmers. The police sergeant said we might have been four miles out in the North Sea otherwise.'

'Oh, Lindsay . . .' murmured her mother, and gripped the steering wheel so tightly her knuckles shone white. Lindsay said no more. Even to speak of it caused a hollowness inside that had nothing to do with hunger. She was keenly aware of her own mortality as she sat in this comfortable car rushing through a tranquil green countryside.

The long midday meal was being served at the market garden when they got there. Alice headed at once for Jamnu to boast that she'd been for a midnight swim in the Crouch and had had jabs in her arm because of that. 'Look,' she swanked, showing the puncture marks. Lindsay was embraced by almost everyone, even members of the Goswami clan she didn't remember seeing before. Dalida was in tears of remorse. 'Oh,

Mrs Dunforth, if only I had done as you asked –!'

'Never mind, Dalida, it's all in the past.'

Food was urged on them. Jamnu, clearly impressed by Alice's story, even loaded a plate for her. But Alice had begun to look around her and saw Tad arriving. A new man! She made for him, ignoring her idol of yesterday.

For his part, Tad was concentrating on Lindsay. 'How are you? You're really pale, Lindsay.'

'I'm all right. A bit fragile.'

'Fragile – I love the way you Brits say that!'

Alice came to pull at her mother's sleeve. 'Who's *he*?' she whispered.

'Tad, let me introduce my daughter, Alice. Alice, this is my friend Tad.' She saw him arch his brows at the use of the word 'friend' and for the first time since she took the threatening note out of the envelope last night, she felt an inclination to smile.

'Are you a friend of Babaji's too?'

'I just met him but I think we're going to be buddies.'

'Buddies?'

'That means very close friends.' He squatted down to be on Alice's level. 'Like you and the bunny here.'

'This is Flopsy.'

'How d'you do, Flopsy,' he said, gently shaking the rabbit by one ear.

'Oh!' cried Alice. 'He shook hands with Flopsy!'

'All the best people shake hands when they're introduced,' Tad explained. 'Shall I shake hands with you? Or shall I shake one of your ears?'

'Oh, shake one of my ears! Oh, Mummy, he's going to shake my ear!' Alice was in gales of laughter. Tad was gently pushing back her soft hair in pretence of looking for a long ear. 'Here,' she said, putting a hand up to direct him, 'I've only got little ears.'

'How d'you do, Alice Little-ear – that's a Red Indian name, you know, like Laughing Water or Sitting Bull. Did you know your daughter was a Native American, Lindsay?'

'No, she never told me that.'

'I reckon it was a secret until I found it out. Well, since we belong to the same tribe I'll tell you my real name. I'm really Running Late, but you mustn't tell anyone.'

'But Mummy just heard you!'

'Mummy won't tell anyone – will you, Lindsay?'

'It's a dead secret.' Lindsay found herself smiling.

'That's better,' he observed. 'I was beginning to think you'd never relax. Shall I get you some food? What would you like, Alice?'

'I've got Alice's plate,' Jamnu interrupted, elbowing his way between this unexpected rival and Alice. 'Look, Alice, your favourite, nut pilau with cashews.'

'Lovely,' agreed Alice, and let herself be led away to make a start on it.

'Nice kid,' said Tad.

'I think so. Thank you for being so nice to her.'

'My pleasure. From the way she was laughing, I take it she's come to no great harm despite last night.'

Lindsay shivered. 'She seems to think it was some kind of dream. I accounted for it as best I could and she seems mostly puzzled. We'll have to see if it causes any problem.'

'You and I ought to talk, Lindsay, if you feel up to it.' He glanced at the people sitting round the table in the big dining-room. 'Is there anywhere a bit less public?'

She nodded. 'Let's get some food and take it along to the orchard,' she suggested. 'There are some chairs and tables there.' She led the way. The odd assortment of deck chairs and garden furniture was still drying off in the sunshine. Tad wiped off two chairs with paper napkins. They sat down.

'Your mother said this morning that I couldn't be here abducting Alice if I was at home answering that e-mail message. What did she mean? I asked her but she said it was better for you to explain.' His tone was serious, his expression grave.

'There's been someone sending threats to my family for months now –'

'Threats? What kind of threats?'

She pushed food around on her plate. 'Nothing you could pin down. The first thing was, he sent a picture of my mother collecting Alice from nursery school. On the back was written, "Back off." '

'Back off from what?'

'I had no idea.' She made a frustrated gesture. 'So of course I couldn't "back off". But I felt that it must have to do with Oistrav's, because that's the only thing that seemed to fit, and I packed my mother and Alice off to a safe place.' She nodded towards the buildings and glasshouses. 'No one would ever think of looking for them here.'

'True enough.'

'Then I got another warning. Someone set a fire in my house.'

'A *fire*!'

'Only a little one in a wastepaper bin. But it scared me, and I –'

'Moved out to that flat in Dockland. I see.'

'How did you find out about that?' she demanded.

'Easy. I tried to call you to apologize after that . . . little episode at my flat –' He paused, and they exchanged a glance in which recollection was mixed with a smiling embarrassment. 'I got an answering machine giving another number. It had a dialling code that implied Docklands, and when I told Peter –'

'Peter? Peter Gruman?'

'Yes, Peter Gruman. He told me it was the number for Oistrav's courtesy accommodation.'

'You and Peter are acquainted?'

'Yeah, but only since I got here. It was thanks to Peter that I got taken on at Oistrav's.'

'I know *that*,' she said, almost with irritation. 'It's because I felt Peter had connnived in some way that I began to suspect him.'

'You suspected Peter?'

'I certainly did.'

'And I suspected you.'

'Me?'

Tad laughed. 'Peter told me I was wrong but I couldn't afford to take anybody on trust –'

'So that's why you were hacking into my personal files –'

'Not just you – everybody that I could get at –'

'Oh, I know,' she said, and there was grudging admiration in her tone. 'Cecie followed your tracks – she said you'd been practically everywhere!'

'Your mother is *some* computer freak,' he commented. 'I could tell someone was on my tail but I couldn't find out who. Of course I thought it was you. And now that I understand what's been happening I can see why this guy last night got so scared. He thought someone was conducting an inquiry, and of course he was right – it was me. But he thought it was you, and that's why you got the threats.'

'He sent me a note last night,' Lindsay said. 'He said he'd found out where I was hiding Alice – so like a fool I set out immediately to take her to some other place –'

'With him right behind you, I guess.'

'I never saw him,' she confessed. 'I was thinking only of reaching my mother on the phone so as to warn her. But I couldn't get through for ages, and when I did the girl who answered the switchboard – Dalida –'

'Oh, yeah, Dalida – she was in tears when I arrived and she's been in tears off and on ever since –'

'It wasn't her fault. But when she said Alice's bed was empty it made things worse. I admit I wasn't thinking straight when I took her out to the car. I should just have stayed where I was with her and nothing bad would have happened.'

'Maybe,' Tad said. 'But then you'd still have been in a state of stress and anxiety . . . And still have been suspecting *me*.'

She studied him. 'I didn't trust you from the outset,' she told him. 'And as things began to get scary and mixed-up, I suspected you all the more. I thought Peter had got you into the bank for some underhand reason –'

'Peter as a participant in a fraud?'

'I know, it shows how unhinged I was. I rang John Blebel –'

'Oh yes, Johnnie Blebel – he called Peter to let him know you were getting inquisitive –'

'He called Peter?' she echoed.

'Oh yes, Johnnie B. and Peter cooked it up between them. A record of employment at Hurley Gounett, an affirmative response to any inquiries about me – I gather Johnnie fobbed you off pretty well and then warned Peter.'

'Who did the same,' she murmured, looking back at that conversation. 'I remember feeling perplexed at not getting more sympathy.'

'He was trying to keep the whole thing under wraps. But he called me to say that you were making waves and I'd better sort it out. The last thing we wanted was to have a big coming-out-of-the-closet. We've still a long way to go before we understand who's doing what.'

'So when you said you had to speak to me, it was to give me an explanation?'

'Right. And now I know what you'd been going through, I wish you'd told Peter about it at the outset.'

'I was trying to keep it quiet, Tad. My mother wanted me to go to the police but you know scandal is bad for a bank's reputation.'

'Tell me about it. But if we'd known you were being threatened it would have cast a new light on our investigation. We would have done something about it.'

'You and Peter, you mean.'

'No, me and the SEC.'

'The Securities and Exchange Commission?' she exclaimed, staggered.

'Yes ma'am. That's who I am, William Ignatius Tadiecski, representing the Securities and Exchange Commission of the United States.' He gave a mock bow.

She was shaking her head in amazed understanding. That was why he had been hacking into files, that was why he had a room full of ultra-advanced equipment at his flat, that was why he had had a false CV and a personnel file slipped into the computer at Hurley Gounett.

Bank fraud is very difficult to uncover. In modern financial circles money can be transferred almost with the speed of light. Large sums appear and disappear, difficult to trace, difficult to designate as involved in illegal transactions.

'The U.S. has been aware for a long time that illegal earnings from things such as drug trafficking are coming in,' Tad explained. 'I'm sure you know, Lindsay, that any cash deposit of more than ten thousand dollars has to be reported by any American bank that receives it. Cash made illegally can't be easily put into an American bank, and banks in many other countries have begun to look critically at large cash sums. But there are states where the authorities don't make inquiries, and so the owners of the cash take it there, and then they "wash" it through the computers of several banks until they get to a respectable layer of banking – for instance, Oistrav's of London.'

'And from there they transfer it to a company like Northern National Concentral Inc –'

'You know about that?' he said, startled.

'Oh yes. Celia found it, and Global Soundfast, and then she discovered you'd singled those out too, and a couple of others –'

'Yeah, and who knows what other companies they've set up. But I don't have to tell you, once the money transfers legally back into the United States, the crooks can get at it without trouble. In other words, they can enjoy the profits of their crimes.'

'I knew it had to be something like that,' Lindsay mused. 'But it meant of course that somebody at Oistrav's was helping them. Somebody had to open those accounts for them.'

'Right. Peter began to see disturbing signs months ago, while he was playing about with his computers in the early stages of his retirement. I guess you know, he sleeps badly, so he spends a lot of time going back and forth in the financial news sites of the Internet and kept records out of curiosity. That's where I came in – he alerted friends in Wall Street, among them John Blebel, and Blebel called in the SEC.'

'And you were sent with a phoney background to find out what was going on and who was behind it.'

'I'm not the only one. We try to handle it from different angles. This case has got a guy working it in the Dutch Antilles at this very moment, trying to get a fix on who's making the original cash deposits, and somebody else in Andorra, and so on. But it's not easy and we never intended anybody to be put at risk in the way you have been.'

Lindsay gave a rueful smile. 'I must have been a terrible nuisance.'

'Not at all. You've driven this guy to make a very stupid mistake – he's used actual physical force. The more he gets panicky, the better it is for us. If you'll agree, we'll put a tail on you from now on, to find out who's after you.'

'There's no need for that. I can tell you who it is,' Lindsay said matter-of-factly.

Chapter Twenty-two

Tad stared at her, putting down the forkful of rice he'd been about to eat.

'You saw his face? I thought it was pitch dark and a howling gale!'

'Yes, it was, but I didn't need to see him. It's a man at Oistrav's you've probably never even met. He's in the Banking Department –'

'Aha, the Banking Department!'

'He thinks he's God's gift to women and turns up at staff outings and Christmas parties ogling everything in a skirt. And what's outstanding about him is that he wears a dreadful after-shave –'

'Lindsay!' Tad cried, his lean face beginning to break into a grin.

'I could smell it last night, when he almost caught me by the elbow on the jetty. I only got my mind to remember it while I was watching Alice eat breakfast this morning. The girl making toast for her had some scented stuff on – hair spray or body lotion – and that was when it came to me. The man last night was wearing after-shave. Believe it or not,' and she shook her head, 'the stuff is called Paramor.'

'Never mind the after-shave – what's the *man* called?'

'Almost everybody at the bank's got a nickname. His is Scented Sel but he doesn't know that. His real name is Selford Whickes.' As Tad was about to rise she added, 'But he can't be the mastermind behind the fraud, whatever it is. He's a nobody, without enough iron in him to make a half-inch nail. He'd never take on the bank.'

Tad sank back into his seat. 'Even little wimps have big dreams, Lindsay. Perhaps his dream was to show how clever he is by tricking Oistrav's.'

'Perhaps. My feeling is that someone is directing him in what he does. I can't imagine the man I've met at staff picnics coming after me like that – not unless somebody sent him, somebody who could convince him he had to do it.'

Tad got up once more. 'Well, mastermind or not, I'm going to ask the Serious Fraud Office to bring him in for questioning. If you'll excuse me –?'

He strode away. Lindsay sat for a moment, watching the thin figure disappear among the orchard trees. He seemed so much in control of himself today, quite unlike the man with whom she'd shared that passionate encounter of a few nights ago.

And then her whole being seemed to come alive, and light seemed to flow through her. She understood that she no longer had to be wary where Tad was concerned. She could allow herself to think of that night without guilt and without regret. She could love Tad and not feel ashamed.

The warm July day enfolded her. A blackbird flew down from one of the old apple trees and began to prospect for a worm in the grass. She drew a deep, happy breath, and picking up her fork began to eat. At long last she had regained her appetite.

When Tad came back Alice was hanging on his arm. 'Tad says we can prob'ly go back to our house soon,' she announced. 'He says he'll come for swims in our pool but he says he doesn't swim well. Shall we teach him, Mummy?'

'I don't think he needs to be taught much,' Lindsay replied with a darted glance at him.

'Is that a compliment or am I what you Brits call a Clever Dick?'

'I thought you said your name was Running Late?'

He chose to ignore that. Surveying her empty plate, he inquired, 'Want some dessert? There's passion fruit ice-cream.'

'Passion fruit?' She laughed aloud. 'Are you serious?'

'Let's go and get some pashumfruit ice-cream, Mummy, it's lovely.'

'Oh, you know all about it, do you, Miss Dunforth?'

' 'Course I do, there's pashumfruit and mango and banana and everything. Me and Jamnu and everybody can have ice-cream every day because Babaji says it's good for us, full of vitamins.'

As they went back towards the farmhouse Tad said, 'She's been here a while, I gather?'

'Oh yes, ever since I got that first threat.'

'Gee, that must have been hard for you, parting with her.'

There was unforced sympathy in his voice. She nodded, taking his arm. He went on, 'The fraud boys will be picking up our friend Whickes any minute now. If he was the "threatener", seems to me it would be safe to go back home.'

'Oh, it would be nice,' she sighed. 'I'm so tired of living out of a suitcase. But we still have to remember Whickes isn't likely to be alone in this. Though he may have been the deliverer of the threats, someone else could have been in command.'

'Right, that's possible. But the "commander" never got close to you physically – you said the writing on those notes was always the same.'

'Yes, big black capitals written with a felt tip. Nothing recognizable. But if he left that last note and then followed me, I think that means he wrote them all.'

'So once he's been picked up, you could begin to think of getting back to normal. Your mother said she was going to ring . . . er . . . I think it was Stacey and Eddie?'

'Tracy – our housekeeper – yes, they may be back at the house now, which means they're accessible by telephone. I had to send them away, after that stupid fire in a waste-bin. I was afraid they might come to harm. But I sent them a note the other day saying they could go back, because the security firm hasn't reported any trouble –'

'You hired a security firm?' he broke in. It brought home to him how serious the threat had been, and how long it had governed her life. A stern glint appeared in his eye.

'It made sense, Tad. I didn't want the place to go up in flames. But I think Whickes soon realized we'd moved out and stopped being interested in it. I can't think how he found out that I was at the Docklands flat.'

'Your mother says she thinks it's her fault. She says she collected you from the bank in the Passat one afternoon?'

'Yes, she did.'

'Well, Whickes might have seen that –'

'It's quite likely.' She cast her mind back. 'I was leaving about five that day, which is when most of the banking staff clock off.'

'If that told him the Passat was the family car, he'd recognize it when later your mother drove it over to . . . what's the place where your house is?'

'Putney.'

'Yeah, Putney. If at that time he was still keeping an eye on the house, trying to find out where you'd got to, all he had to do was follow her back to Docklands. And there you were, the pair of you.'

'But not Alice. He never knew where she was till last night.'

'Well, that's not going to do him much good if he's in custody.'

They were in the dining room. A large carton of ice-cream was sitting in a bowl of ice. Alice made her way purposefully towards it. Tad watched her go. 'Pashumfruit,' he quoted. He looked at Lindsay. 'It's an omen,' he said.

And a bubble of joy rose up in Lindsay's heart.

She checked with her mother to see if she'd found Tracy and Eddie at the house. 'No, I got the answering machine, dear. Normally I'd say that means nothing, because Tracy ignores the phone when the machine's switched on. But I think she'd have answered if they'd just got back and were expecting instructions. So I think they haven't arrived yet.'

Lindsay sighed to herself. It would have been so nice to go home . . .

In the afternoon they went for a walk, Celia, Lindsay, Alice and Tad. Lindsay decided to take the path across the marshy meadow which led to the jetty, to see if it would arouse any bad memories with her little girl. But Alice was trying to monopolize Tad, a scheme which he succumbed to without much of a struggle. The two women could hear him naming the wading birds on the muddy estuary. 'That's a curlew, so-called maybe because it has a curly beak. That one with the orange legs is an oyster catcher but I've never seen one catch an oyster . . .'

'He's nice,' Celia observed.

'Yes.'

'He likes you. A lot.'

'I'm glad to hear it.'

'Alice is already his slave.'

'She was Jamnu's slave a minute ago.'

'Yes, but it all helps.'

'Helps with what, Cecie?'

'Well . . . you know . . . what might come in the future.'

Lindsay smiled and threw out her arms in a reviving stretch. 'Last night I thought the future was gone for ever,' she said. 'I'm just glad to have the present.'

'Darling, don't remind me! When I got to that sick bay and

saw you lying there so pale and quiet, I thought my heart was going to stop beating. But you know,' she ended, blinking back tears as she gave her daughter's arm a hug, 'a fright like that makes you appreciate what you've got. Tad was speaking to Peter Gruman on the phone last night . . .'

'Yes?'

'When he finished Peter asked him to put me on, and we had a long talk . . . And you know, it struck me that there he is, cooped up in that flat all by himself except for that taciturn manservant, and there am I cooped up on my own in Putney working away on computers . . .'

'And so?' Lindsay prompted, suppressing a smile.

'So I invited myself to see him one afternoon next week, and I'm thinking of ringing him and suggesting Wednesday.'

'Yes, why not.'

'That's what I say – why not.'

The day ran on. About six, when Lindsay was trying to persuade Alice that it was bedtime, Tad was called to the phone. He came back reporting that the Serious Fraud Office had Selford Whickes in custody.

'In a state of utter disintegration,' he said. 'They say that after a night in the cells he'll probably be singing like a canary.'

'That's great.'

'What do you want to do about tomorrow?' he asked.

'How do you mean?'

'You going to stay on here?'

She frowned at him in surprise. 'I can't stay on here. Tomorrow's Monday, I've got to be at the bank.'

'For Pete's sake, Lindsay, surely you can take a day off –'

'When Henry Wishaw will be wanting an explanation of what's been going on? When the SFO men might descend on the bank and scare everybody? I've got to be there.'

He gave her a glance of admiration. 'I suppose it's no use arguing?'

'Not much.'

'Okay, so where are you going to go? Back to your own house, or to Docklands?'

'I'd really like to go home.' There was wistfulness in her voice. 'But there was no reply when Cecie rang, and I hate to take her and Alice back to a place that's been empty for weeks.'

'They could stay on here a day or two.'

'You mean, go home on my own? It would seem so utterly *empty.*'

'Want me to come with you?'

She looked down at her hands. Had she been angling for that? Yes she had. 'I'd like that,' she replied.

When it was time to go, Celia elected to drive the Passat back to Old Flag Wharf. 'If we're going to move back home, I've got to start packing up my computers.'

'What about Alice?'

'Jamnu's leaving on Tuesday. I think she'd like to be here to wave him goodbye. I'll come back that morning to ferry her home afterwards – it'll take her mind off any sense of loss, don't you think?'

Lindsay set out in Tad's car, which proved to be an undistinguished Japanese runabout. 'The kind of work I do,' he explained, 'it's good to stay out of sight.'

The house in Edgefold Road was rosy with the glow of sunset clouds. Everything was tranquil. Lindsay let them in then hurried to key in the code that would silence the alarm system. Then they stood together in the big tiled hall, arm in arm, well aware that they had nine hours of delight ahead of them.

They were happy lovers, eager for each other and all the more so because of the drama of the day before. At one point Tad said, his mouth against her hair, 'To think that we might never have had this night . . .'

' "Gather ye rosebuds while ye may," ' she quoted.

'Is that what you are? My rosebud?'

She laughed quietly. 'I never thought of myself like that.'

'A whole bouquet of roses,' he suggested. 'Those longstemmed blooms all wrapped up with cellophane and ribbons . . .'

'That makes me sound unapproachable.'

'You were unapproachable. And how! But not any more, my love, not any more.'

So they turned to each other once again, ardent, joyous, grateful to life for giving them this magical time together.

It seemed strange to Lindsay in the morning to be sharing her early hours with anyone else. For so long now she'd been up before the rest of the world. To have a companion disorientated her a little, yet it added an edge to the brightness of the new day.

'I won't ask for a tour of the house,' he said as he poured the strong coffee he'd made. 'Some other time, huh?'

'Any time you care to drop by.' She was rushing about trying to do all the extra things called for by her return home: leave a note for Tracy on the kitchen table, close the windows she'd opened to air out the house, list the foodstuffs they needed.

Tad watched her. 'It's funny,' he said, 'the first time I saw you you were wearing that dress.'

She was back in the soft dark silks she habitually wore. She'd thought of putting on a short-sleeved summer frock but the bandage on her upper arm made her self-conscious. She'd put on the long-sleeved dress partly to hide it, and partly to bolster her morale for the busy day that lay ahead.

'The first time we saw each other,' she mused. 'That seems to have been in another world. Since then so much has happened . . .'

'But not all bad,' he prompted, 'not all bad.'

'No. Some of it very good.' And she leaned across the kitchen table to exchange a kiss.

As they were leaving he espied the blue plastic hairclips still lying on the table in the hall. 'What on earth are those?' he inquired with a lift of an eyebrow.

A shock of memory. Lindsay coloured up. 'They were a present for Alice, from someone who seemed important at the time.'

'The Big Bruiser?' he suggested.

'How did you guess?' She was really startled by his acumen.

'Lady, inspired guesses are part of my business. So he bought them?'

She nodded, escaping to set the alarm system.

'Don't tell me he ever went into a shop to buy those! I thought ancient art was his thing.'

'I think he sent the messenger boy,' she said over her shoulder. As she returned she picked them up. 'I'll drop them in a rubbish bin somewhere.'

'Good,' he agreed with perceptible pleasure. 'I'll pick one out for you.'

They drove off for the City. He remarked, 'You usually come by hired car –'

'How d'you know that?' she broke in.

'Sweetheart, I know all about you.' His grin told her that he was pleased at the advantage this gave him.

'I've got a lot of catching up to do, it seems.'

'Ask me anything.'

She hesitated. 'Are you married?'

'No.' He shook his head and sighed. 'A fairly long relationship is all, but she threw in her hand, said she was tired of not knowing what was going on. I couldn't tell her about my work, you see . . .' They negotiated Putney Bridge before he added, 'You are, of course. Married.'

'Yes. But Bob's been gone a long time.'

'So I heard. In fact, he's never even met Alice – is that true?'

'Yes.'

'Doesn't know what he's missing.'

He threaded his way through the empty streets of Fulham heading east. 'But the hire car – is it calling for you at Docklands now and waking your mother up?'

'Not a bit of it,' she told him, 'the Goswami grapevine let Sudin know that there was a change in the usual system. They keep in touch, you know.'

He nodded agreement. 'I'll drop you off at the bank then whizz home to change.' He glanced down at his Ralph Lauren slacks. 'Must look business-like for the Fraud Squad. Is that okay?'

'Whatever you say.' As she heard herself say the words, she smiled. It was a long time since she'd surrendered herself to anyone so completely.

The day at Oistrav's brought one surprise quite early on. Nan Compton appeared at her desk, a little determined in manner and with a certain defiance in her gaze. The rest of the dealing room eyed her askance but said nothing except, 'Good morning, how are you?'

Nan said she was quite well.

Lindsay wondered. Had she come back simply to demonstrate that she wasn't afraid, wasn't embarrassed at her own outburst? Or . . . was she expecting to hear from her accomplice? Had Selford Whickes been in touch on Saturday night or Sunday morning, with news of what he had done?

Yet there was little sign that Nan was waiting for anything special. She sat down, switched on her screens, busied herself tidying out the debris of some days ago from her drawer – sandwich wrappers, out-of-date info sheets. When they were called into Lindsay's office to hear the trading plan for the beginning of the week she came obediently, took notes, and returned to her place without apparent anxiety.

A little more than two hours went by. The first early morning rush of activity with the Far East was ended. Lindsay had already asked the Chairman's secretary to find a space for her in his diary, in preparation for the long explanations that must come. Dealers and brokers were sitting back a little, thinking about a cup of coffee, when two straight-backed men in sombre suits were shown in by the Compliance Officer.

Everyone stared because they were strangers: strangers didn't easily get into the bank's inner offices, even with an escort. But these two men walked across the room as if they owned it, steady-paced, unhurried.

They're going to arrest Nan, thought Lindsay.

They came alongside Nan's desk. Nan looked up at them.

But they walked by, and came to a stop at the desk of Ellaline Maitland.

Ellaline had been watching their progress, as had everyone. The elder of the men produced a card from his pocket which he showed to her. Ellaline's round face seemed to sag.

Lindsay came out of her office fast, but only just in time to hear him saying, '. . . accompany us to the station to answer a few questions.'

'No,' Ellaline said faintly.

'Come along now, miss,' said the detective. 'You don't want us to arrest you, now do you?'

'You've no grounds to arrest me!'

'According to your friend Selford Whickes we have plenty of grounds –'

'Selford!'

'We've had a long talk with him about fraudulent activities –'

'He's lying, I haven't done anything wrong!'

Most of the dealing room was on its feet now. Traders were standing thunderstruck, watching the interchange.

Lindsay came up to Ellaline's desk, to stare at her in disbelief. 'It was you?' she gasped. 'It was you who sent threats against my little girl and my mother?'

All at once the other woman seemed to straighten her spine. She stood up, to stare scornfully at Lindsay. 'Wasted my time, it seems,' she said. 'It wasn't you that was snooping in among the banking files, it was Tad.'

'How did you find that out?' asked Tad himself, appearing on the edge of the group that surrounded them. He had changed into a business suit but, unlike the other men in the dealing room, hadn't had time yet to shed his jacket and loosen his tie.

Shaking her head, Ellaline pressed her lips together in stubborn silence.

'Come on, Ellaline,' he said. 'It's all got to come out now.'

She leaned back against the edge of her desk, biting her thumb. Then she seemed to make up her mind. 'Sel drove to Burnham last night – he rang me to tell me what had happened and I told him to stay there, get information. That fool!' she groaned. 'He told me he had drowned you!'

'Not only me. My daughter Alice,' Lindsay said. 'You remember Alice? I brought her to the last Christmas party and you helped her open the present she got from Santa Claus.'

'I didn't mean her any harm!' Ellaline cried. 'I never meant that idiot to run you into the river!'

'And the fire in my house?'

'What fire?' And Ellaline looked truly mystified.

'He set a little fire in my living room, and left a note saying he could have burned down the house.'

'Oh, dear heavens,' lamented Ellaline. 'There was never any need for all that – I only wanted you scared off!'

'So Whickes hung around Burnham and found out Lindsay and Alice had been rescued –'

'And I told him to get out of there, go home, nobody knew who he was, he *told* me, it was dark and raining and she hadn't seen him properly –'

'As it turned out, she didn't need to see him,' Tad said, and exchanged a glance of amusement with the detectives.

They had remained passive while the exchange of information went on. Lindsay wondered if she ought, in duty bound, to remind Ellaline of her rights – but why should she protect the rights of a woman who had nearly cost the life of herself and her little girl?

Tad, on the contrary, was determined to get as much as he could out of her before British law prevented him.

'So Scented Sel thought he was free and clear,' he prompted. 'What did you intend to do now? You must have known that the police had to be involved after a near-drowning –'

'Yes, but only down there in the sticks,' she flashed, 'not *here*! It was only when he told me he'd seen *you* drive up to the place – yacht club, town hall, whatever – that I began to fit it together the right way. The prying into the files began after *you* appeared on the scene, Tad my darling. *You* were the one we should have been watching out for. We'd been on the wrong track all the time.'

'Trying to throw a scare into Lindsay –'

'My God, *she* threw a scare into me! When she walked out of her office that night –'

'That was you who ran off?' Lindsay said, remembering it.

Ellaline sighed in exasperation. 'I was going to trawl through the office intra-net, see if I could find out how much you'd uncovered about us – I'm not clever enough to get the intra-net on my home screen – and then you popped up and nearly gave me heart failure!'

'But why, Ellaline?' Lindsay begged. 'Why turn to fraud? You've been doing so well here –'

'Huh!' she grunted. 'You should try being married to a man who absolutely can't live without a high performance car, and needs to pick out his clothes in person on Rodeo Drive in Hollywood, and of course must have spending money to match.'

'You're going to blame it all on Tony?' Tad prompted. 'Well, it looks like he'll have to find someone else to support him.'

Lindsay felt she must at last remember the conventions. She looked at the detectives. 'Shouldn't you be reading her her rights?'

'No need for that, miss – she's just going to help us with our inquiries.' But the senior detectives got the message. Ellaline was incriminating herself with every word she spoke, and here were a roomful of intelligent people watching it happen. That kind of thing is not popular with the Crown Prosecution Service.

Ellaline was led away unprotesting. The audience broke into groups to chew over what had happened. Lindsay went back to her office to ring the Chairman's secretary. The Serious Fraud Office had of course had the Chairman's permission to come into the building for the interview with Ellaline, but now Lindsay must tell him how it had gone. Her heart sank at the prospect. She had wanted so much to protect the good name of Oistrav's, but it seemed that was now impossible.

Tad joined her while she waited to be called to the Chairman's office. She said, 'Tell me what you know. Mr Wishaw will want to hear it.'

'Scented Sel spilled the beans. Seems Ellaline met some entrepreneur when she was at a banking conference in Prague –'

'Oh, I remember that – summer of last year –'

'She was asked to set up accounts at Oistrav's to help launder dollars accumulated in the Ukraine –'

'The Ukraine!'

'Yes, this is money the Russian Mafia accumulated by selling arms to – well, to whoever wants them. The sums are enormous.'

'And Selford Whickes opened the accounts for her?'

'Right. In return for a rather close friendship with Ellaline and a percentage on every transaction that went through the accounts. Ellaline got an even larger cut, he says, and that makes sense. We've yet to find out where that pair have squirrelled their money but we'll find out – Whickes is willing to do almost anything rather than go to prison.'

'Has he been charged?'

'Not yet. According to British law I believe he can be held a bit longer without being charged. And I have to tell you that he's very worried about you and Alice. He sees of course that he might be charged with assault – even attempted murder. He's a very unhappy man.'

Lindsay dropped the pen she'd been doodling with. 'I hope he gets thrown in jail and stays there until he's ninety! Prowling around after us like a jackal –!'

'It seems, by the way, that he had no real idea where Alice was hidden. He followed Celia on Saturday morning – he'd been following Celia by car off and on for the last ten days when he could invent an excuse. Seems he had a lot of imaginary "clients" he had to confer with. He followed on Saturday when she went in a van to Exoproduce. But he lost her on the way.'

'Lost her!'

'He's no great brain, as you told me. He drove back to Old Flag Wharf to leave a note just to terrorize you, and had only just got into his Rover and was about to drive away when you arrived home, read the note, and rushed off in the Passat. So he followed you –'

'Oh no,' groaned Lindsay. 'You mean I led him there?'

'He was only able to keep up because he knew the first half of the journey,' Tad soothed. 'He claims, by the way, that when he shouted at you from the wharf, he was asking you to call out so he could find you and get you out.'

'Ha!' said Lindsay, unable to decide whether to believe it. She thought a moment then said, 'Is it over? Oistrav's part in this is at an end?'

'Well, not exactly, because we want to use Oistrav's to trace whoever hands in the cash in the first place – I mean ready for transfer at the offshore banks. If we can, that is. What remains here is a sort of long clearing-up operation.'

'So you won't be leaving London?'

'Not yet.' He pressed her hand, understanding her anxiety. 'I've got to go. I have to make a statement to the Serious Fraud boys. And then I've got to e-mail a lot of stuff through to the SEC.'

In full view of all those watching through the glass wall of her office, he gave her a kiss on the cheek before hurrying out.

And this time Lindsay didn't care what her colleagues thought.

Chapter Twenty-three

Mr Wishaw took the news badly. He kept Lindsay with him while he called the bank's solicitors. They arrived, two of the partners from a famous law firm, one elderly and one young. The young man was the 'interpreter' in matters concerning computers, which the senior partner had never yet come to grips with.

They heard Lindsay's story with a visible lack of enthusiasm.

'How much money has passed through the bank's system?'

'We won't know that until the criminals have given us full details. But . . . I think it may be in the neighbourhood of a hundred and ten millions . . . that we know of.'

'However,' Wishaw added, 'the bank has not in fact *lost* any money. No client of ours has suffered.'

'Ah,' said the solicitors, looking a little cheered.

'We have of course no option but to take them to court –' Lindsay began.

'Mrs Dunforth, that remains to be seen.'

'But the Serious Fraud Office –'

'Have as yet very little to go on, from what you tell us. And the money merely passed through Oistrav's computers. The main problem seems to lie in the United States, where these illegal gains are being invested in legitimate businesses. I gather,' said the solicitor with muted annoyance, 'that it was an American who called the Serious Frauds Office into what, after all, is a matter for Oistrav's Bank?'

'Yes. Mr Tadiecski. It seems that he is here,' complained the Chairman, 'with the blessing and even, if I may so call it, the *connivance* of the former Chairman, Mr Gruman. I knew nothing of it.'

'Dear me.'

The younger solicitor said, 'But you wouldn't have wished for a member of Oistrav's staff to continue laundering ill-gotten gains through your computers.'

'Of course not, of course not! One would have liked to be consulted, however.'

'Certainly,' said both solicitors in chorus.

Lindsay could feel irritation rising within her. She said very calmly, 'My daughter and I were attacked. We were fished out of the River Crouch. It became a matter for the police at that point – it had to come out.'

'My dear girl,' the Chairman said hastily, 'of course it had to come out . . . as regards the attack on yourself and your little girl . . . yes, yes, that had to be investigated . . . and really, it was Whickes? Extraordinary! That's to say, I can't quite call him to mind although of course I must have met him – at the Christmas party, for instance – yes, yes, to think that one of our staff could mean actual harm . . .'

'And was willing to take part in illegal transactions through your computer systems,' added the younger lawyer.

'But remember, Frank, the bank did not lose anything by it,' the elder lawyer reminded him.

'True,' agreed Oistrav's Chairman, brightening.

'But look here, Selford Whickes threatened me and my family over a period of months. He caused us great anxiety and nearly got us drowned on Saturday night –'

'That is definite, is it? Whickes *is* the perpetrator?'

'He's admitted it!' said Lindsay with some force, for she could see the Chairman and his advisers were doing their best to minimize the whole thing.

They went over and over the matter for nearly two hours. Lindsay was glad when at last the solicitors said they must contact the Serious Frauds Office to see what kind of case they were building against Ellaline Maitland and Selford Whickes. They could see that Lindsay intended to go on with the assault case against Whickes – and she had the feeling they wished she would just let it all die away.

Millicent had a pile of work for her in her office. She attended to the more urgent matters, then said, 'Look, Millicent, you know I wouldn't ask you to run errands for me if it wasn't absolutely necessary –'

'Of course not,' her secretary acknowledged. 'What is it you want me to do?'

'Well, now that things are going back to normal, I must say thanks to the people who've been so helpful to me in the last few weeks. So will you go out and do some shopping for me?' She'd decided to buy a portable CD player for Mr Soames, the owner of the *Blues Boy*, and with it a CD of the 'greats' of jazz. For the Goswami family she asked Millicent to order a huge cake with the words 'Thank you' written very large in coloured icing. The yacht club she felt would accept a cheque without feeling offended. She wanted to do this now, immediately after the events, so that they would see how truly grateful she felt.

It became evident as the next two days went by that Selford Whickes had a very good lawyer. After a conference with him he altered his original story. Yes, Whickes had followed Lindsay. Yes, he had gone after her when she left the car and took off on foot across the meadow.

But he had only wanted to speak to her.

And if the silly woman chose to jump into the water, was that his fault? He had shouted to her to come to the jetty and he would pull her out. But she had either not heard or had chosen to disregard him.

Lindsay heard all this from Tad, who had good contacts with the Serious Frauds Office. 'He says all he wanted was a friendly chat.'

'But the way he blocked my exit from the lane?' Lindsay countered, checking her first impulse to scream with frustration. 'He was broadside on to me, we nearly had a collision!'

'Bad driving conditions. He had a skid.'

'What you're saying,' she said, 'is that he's making the whole thing look as if I just got in a panic.'

'Yes, sweetheart, I'm afraid that's just what he's doing.'

'And the notes he wrote? I gave them to the detectives –'

'He says he didn't write them.'

'But if they did a handwriting test –'

'Maybe yes, maybe no. If that's all they take to court, he'll walk.'

'But the links with the fraud –'

'The fraud . . . Well, it may be a long time before we get the evidence together. Scented Sel has retracted all the facts about Ellaline being chatted up in Prague and asking him to open accounts to launder funny money. The story now is that it was all totally open and above board, he got an ordinary application – and he did – and expedited the opening of the accounts because he's so efficient. The money that went through came in legitimate transfers from other banks –'

'But Ellaline – she actually said –'

'If you cast your mind back,' he intervened, 'you'll realize she said very little except on a personal level. When the SFO boys set it down in black and white it sounds like a disagreement between two ambitious women –'

'Tad!'

'Don't be upset, Lindsay, Ellaline's got a good lawyer too and that's the line he seems to have recommended – that it's some sort of career thing. You of course remember how Nan went off the deep end about how you'd blighted her life – I think Ellaline got the idea from the way Nan behaved.'

'In other words we're just a pack of silly women!'

'It's a good way out for her, Lindsay. She specifically denies giving Whickes instructions to do anything illegal. And as to what he said at first, about receiving "special favours" from her, she says he's well known for having these ideas that women adore him.'

'That's only too true,' she sighed.

'So they're covering up for each other, and the police couldn't find enough to charge them, so they've had to let them go.'

'You can't mean they're going to get away with it!'

Tad gave her a weary smile. 'It looks like it, except of course they've lost their jobs and won't get another in the City –'

'Oistrav's isn't going to pursue it either?'

'Well, not officially. The auditors are going to go through everything with a microscope, naturally, but whether the SFO will be kept informed I can't say. They're not optimistic.'

'I can't believe it! You're telling me that Ellaline and Selford Whickes are going to walk away from this with the percentage they earned on those transactions –'

'Which probably runs into hundreds of thousands –'

'And a vast amount of money that went through Oistrav's books into American companies is not going to be impounded?'

'You *know* we get this a lot,' Tad said. 'If you think back, you'll realize that you yourself were trying to keep things under wraps – you didn't call the police when you got those first threats because you felt it might harm Oistrav's reputation.'

Lindsay stifled a groan. It was only too true.

'The financial system doesn't want to have spanners thrown

into the works unless it's unavoidable. What this pair have done isn't blatant – it's what's sometimes called "a victimless crime" – money's been moved about to benefit someone but nobody has actually lost by it.'

'The people who get killed by those illegally sold weapons – they lose by it!'

They were in the untended garden of the Putney house, sitting in the shade of an ash tree while Alice played at being a Red Indian chieftain. Tad had brought her a present, a handsome thing, a beaded headband graced by a single eagle feather. It was certainly not a toy and Lindsay couldn't help wondering if it had been sent by air from the States in response to a request on the Internet. Tad had erected a 'totem pole' for her when he arrived an hour ago, and now he let his eyes follow her dancing progress around it.

'I'm not saying it's a good result,' he acknowledged with a sigh. 'But arms deals abroad are beyond the remit of either the Serious Fraud Office or the Securities and Exchange Commission. All we can do is work with what we've got – and what we've got is a crime which is being whitewashed out of existence.'

'So Ellaline and Selford Whickes lose their jobs – and that's all that's going to happen?'

'That's all that's going to happen in *this* country.' He paused, perhaps to think about how much he could tell her. 'The SEC isn't going to let it drop. There's laundered money flooding into the States, and you can take a bet it isn't going to be used for any good purpose once the "owners" get their hands on it there. The State Department is putting pressure on the government of the Ukraine, I hear –'

'Ah,' said Lindsay. She herself had taken part in negotiations where government intervention had been called for. But those had been commercial cases, not criminal.

'Don't say "Ah" in that hopeful tone of voice,' he warned. 'The Ukrainians are officially quite eager to stop the trade because stolen weapons are being used in robberies in the Ukraine and elsewhere in the region. So if they really are taking steps to catch the ringleaders, I dare say there will be some dickering when they do –'

'Dickering? In what sense?'

'Well, it's anybody's guess who the ringleaders are. They may turn out to be influential officials or army commanders –'

'So the Ukrainian government can't just arrest them and throw them in jail . . .'

'I see you get the picture. But in the end a bargain may be struck – they get immunity or reduced sentences in exchange for information about how the scam worked –'

'What you seem to be saying, Tad, is that all you may get is the small fry.'

'I don't know, Lindsay. Politics in the former Soviets is complicated. I mean, look at it from the point of view of a colonel in charge of a Ukrainian arsenal – who's he going to hand over? Not his own friends. It's likely to be people like Whickes and Ellaline Maitland, people he only knows as names in a foreign country.'

'So then the Serious Frauds Office would be able to bring a case against them.'

'If they're still around by that time,' he replied with a cynical twist of the lips. 'If I were those two, I'd be off to the outback of Australia long before the Ukrainians started to talk. Oistrav's is going to be short of staff soon, I think, what with Nan finding herself a new job and the two money-changers being given the brush.'

'It's too depressing,' she said, and jumped to her feet to show she didn't want to talk about it any longer. 'I'm going to make some tea. This is a sunny afternoon in July and it's a rule that on a day like this you have to have a strawberry tea.'

'Ooh, strawberries!' shrieked the Red Indian chief, whose ears were attuned to any mention of goodies. She rushed after them as they went indoors.

At Lindsay's instruction Tracy had put the strawberries in a large bowl in a shaft of sunlight, to allow the full flavour to develop. Sugar was in a silver shaker, cream was in the fridge. Alice was allowed to carry the bowl of strawberries out to the shady spot under the ash tree. Lindsay bore the tea tray, Tracy followed with scones which she had freshly defrosted in the microwave, that being the limit of her abilities as a baker. Tad brought the folding table.

'Isn't your mother joining us?' he inquired when he saw Eddie Taylor bringing only one extra chair, for Alice.

'Mother's out for the rest of the day,' Lindsay said with a suppressed grin. 'Alice, don't grab at things, wait to have them passed to you.'

'What's amusing you about your mother?'

'She's spending the afternoon with Peter Gruman.'

'Is that right?' He too began to grin. 'Does it mean anything?'

'It seems to. He's asked her to go to Switzerland with him in August –'

'You don't say!'

'Purely platonic!' she insisted. 'He goes to the Alps every year, because he likes a cool climate and there's a clinic there that can do things for his arthritis. All the same, it's the first time he's ever asked anyone to go with him except his manservant Darrow.'

'Granny's going to send me a Swiss watch,' Alice told Tad. 'A special one that'll have my name on the dial –'

'That will look really sharp. What shall I send you from New York?'

Lindsay caught her breath. 'You're going back?'

'Pretty soon.'

'Could I have a pipe of peace? There's a picture in my story book, and it shows Red Indians smoking a pipe of peace.'

'But what would you smoke in it?' he teased. 'Your mom wouldn't let you have tobacco, so it wouldn't be much use.'

'When will you be back?' Lindsay asked.

'Who knows? We've got to do a verbal investigation of what's happened, what used to be called a debriefing. The idea is that they might shake something out of my memory that isn't in the report. And then we'll be conferencing to see what we can use out of what we've acquired. I expect I'll be reassigned since nothing much is going to happen here by the looks of it.'

'If I can't have a pipe of peace, could I have a tommyhawk?' Alice demanded.

'From peace to war in ten seconds?' he laughed. 'Look, if it's got to be Red Indian, how about a wampum necklace?'

'What's wampum?'

'Little shells, threaded in a pattern on a leather thong. How about that?'

'That sounds lovely! Mummy, I'm going to have a *wampum* necklace.' Scooping strawberries into her mouth, the little girl went into a dream of showing off her presents at nursery school.

Her mother too was forming a picture – of life without Tad. The sunlight on the garden seemed to grow dim, the sleepy murmur of bees among the neglected roses lost its note of contentment. She must come to terms with this thought: Tad's career was taking him away.

'I'll have some leave due to me,' Tad was saying. 'You haven't had your vacation yet –'

'No, you know I've been rather preoccupied.' She managed a smile.

'So what are you going to do?'

'Well, we generally all go to Scotland, we have a time-share flat in a Highland castle –'

'Ugh! It's always damp and misty in the Highlands! What do you say to a month on a beach in St Lucia?'

She looked at him in surprise, but her feeling of despondency began to lighten. 'I must say that sounds attractive . . .'

'Great. And maybe while we're there I can talk you into changing your name to Tadiecski.'

'Not a chance, not a chance!' Her spirits soared. She was teasing now. 'It's too difficult to pronounce.' Then, growing serious again, 'You haven't forgotten? I'm already married, to a man who's been gone for about five years.'

'It's time you did something about that, Lindsay.' He was smiling, but very much in earnest.

'You're right. But it can't be done in a minute, darling.'

'But we can start planning, can't we? We can sort it out while we laze on that beach watching Alice build sandcastles. Come on, Lindsay – when I first met you you gave me a lecture about respecting other people's dreams. Isn't it time we started to make something from our own? We belong together, we know that.'

She knew it was true. The last few months with their perplexities and dangers had shown her the man she needed in her life. At last, after mistakes and disappointments, she had found him, and to be parted from him was unthinkable.

Of course there were problems to solve. When were there not? Each had a career, each would have to make adjustments and changes. For her perhaps it would mean giving up this old house in which she'd invested so many dreams – but there were other dreams and other houses, perhaps in another country. She had to think of her little girl – but Alice was bright, intelligent, and already fond of Tad. Her daughter would adjust to a new life so long as she was surrounded, as she had always been, with love and care. Her mother, whom she would have hesitated to leave, might have found a new relationship, with Peter Gruman. Time would tell.

Lindsay and Tad would talk about it. Under the tropical sun and into the tropical night, they would talk it through, making plans for their future. Because they knew they couldn't live without each other, they would solve the problems.

Tad was watching her. 'What are you thinking?' he asked.

'I was thinking that when I first met you I distrusted you instinctively.'

He shook his head. 'How did you ever get to be a successful banker when your judgement is so bad?'

'Goodness knows.' She gave a little laugh, a mixture of nervousness and happiness. 'I know a lot about money but about men . . . that's a different tale.'

'It's the same for all of us, Lindsay,' he said. 'We're always being surprised by what other people do. But if we've any sense we learn as we go along. And what I've learned is that you and I were meant for each other.'

She knew it was true. Her life so far had been a preparation for this – that she and the man she loved should come together at last, a partnership all the stronger for the difficulties in which it had been forged.

'I think you're right,' she agreed. And meant it from her heart.